LEGACY FULFILLED

TAMAR SLOAN

JESS CONNORS
PUBLISHING

To anyone who has never given up...
It's totally worth it!
Oh, and Sean...

1

AVA

Some kisses you don't want to stop.
Some heartbeats you wish would never end.

Every moment with Hunter is like that.

But some moments more than others...

I push in closer, loving the familiarity that's joining the buzz of fitting my curves to his lean lines. I pull in tighter, reveling in the groan it wrenches from him. I'm inundated with images of the nights we've spent since we bonded.

Delving.

Discovering.

Dissolving.

Hunter pulls back, his copper eyes smoldering. "I thought you wanted to head out."

I breathe in the cool arctic air. "It's our last day. I definitely want to." Bringing my lips closer to his, I murmur, "But you're kinda moreish."

I didn't think it was possible, but his gaze heats even more. "We didn't think a week would be enough."

A week we've had to spend at Evelyn Island, even though the wolves and those from the captive breeding program have relocated to Jacksonville. Seven days of so much love and passion, I wouldn't have thought it possible if I hadn't lived it.

Finally giving in to the desire thrumming through my heated body, I slide my lips over his. "And it wasn't."

I feel when Hunter remembers. It's a hiccup in our connection, a pause in his moving hands. Darn it. I shouldn't have reminded him.

He strokes my hair back as he gazes down upon me. "Are you sure you're ready to go back?"

I roll my eyes. "I was ready the day after everything went down."

When I had to heal Hunter or would've lost him—oh, and those poachers were forever changed by whatever happened.

He arches a brow. "Not according to the doctor, you weren't."

Huffing, I step away so I can cross my arms. We've had this conversation more than once. "He didn't know what he was dealing with."

I may look human, but my Were and Fae blood are the invisible foundation of my powers.

"He saw what using all that energy did to you. You were out for a whole day, Ava. Then the dizziness didn't go away for a few days after that."

Narrowing my eyes at him, I pause as I let him know I mean business. "We're going back to Jacksonville tomorrow. I don't care what the doctor says this afternoon."

He casts me an unimpressed glance. "You've already booked the tickets."

I smile. "I know."

"But I want to see how you go on this run."

I smile wider. "I know that, too."

Hunter shakes his head as he pulls me in for a hard and fast kiss. "And then we'll get on that plane, anyway."

I laugh, knowing it's the deep connection I have with Hunter that means I can do that at a time like this. When we head back to Jacksonville, then the reality of everything that's waiting for us will be undeniable: the arctic wolves' future depending on a litter of three fragile pups. Humans wanting more and more wolf blood. Weres desperately trying to protect them. A virus we can't stop.

A faceless Helix we don't know how to find.

But here I am, laughter flowing as my heart sings. The enforced grounding has almost been a blessing. Following our unexpected—but always dreamed of—Bonding, we've had a precious gift of time to cement what was created over two years ago.

To realize how much stronger we are, now that we are one.

With a last quick peck, I release him. "Only because I'll prove to you that I'm perfectly fine."

The tundra around us has been swallowed by winter. It's layers of white on white, everything icebound and still. Even the air feels frozen, stinging my throat and lungs with each breath I take.

A few months ago, I would've been dreaming of being somewhere inside in front of a heater. But now that I'm a Were, I know it's cold, but it's not unpleasant. It's invigorating.

I stretch my arms out wide as I slowly spin. "I think this is just what I needed."

Hunter is smiling as he watches me. "You've become part of the fabric, Ava."

I pause, my breath condensing as I look at him. He's right. The tundra has become a part of me, and I a part of it. I smile right back. "This is home."

He looks around, probably cataloging all the parts he's going to miss. The quiet. The stillness one moment, the slow-moving changes the next. The raw power. "Yeah, it is."

"I'd like to come back here when this is all over."

Hunter's brows shoot up. "There are no big colleges on Evelyn Island."

"You know that's never been my dream." Although I haven't been able to figure out what career is going to fit my unique skills, desks and books were never one of them. "Mom and Dad will realize that." I angle my head. "You, on the other hand, could go to college here."

"Why does it not surprise me you've figured that out?"

I shrug, winking at him. "I hear the questions you ask Gareth." His father's best-friend, Gareth, is a park ranger on this island. Since moving beyond their stalemate over the captive breeding program, they've spent quite a bit of time together. "You'd love to do what he does, as a career."

Hunter nods, eyes somber. We haven't spoken about this, because it doesn't feel like that's a future we can spend time imagining. He gazes at the horizon. "First of all, we need to do whatever it is we're supposed to do."

I slip my arms around him, enjoying the strength I can feel beneath his layers. "But we'll come back? Once it's all over."

When he looks at me again, his eyes have their spark of warmth back. "Yes. We'll come back."

Which is going to be my ray of hope. No matter what's coming at us. "Good. That makes my heart happy."

There's nowhere else that could be my heaven—Hunter and the tundra.

With a pack of wolves holding the promise of a future we helped create.

Hunter grasps my hand. "Let's make this a run to remember then. A reminder of what we're going to come back to."

I grin. "You're on."

He shakes his head again, a smile dancing at the corner of his lips. "It wasn't meant as a challenge."

Rather than tell him it's too late for that, I show him.

Allowing myself to multiply from within, I let the shift wolf explode outward. It ripples across my skin; a release I didn't know I was craving. In the space of a blink, I shake out my fur, then I breathe in all the stories I never scent when I'm human. I love being a wolf.

Shifting isn't something I get to do often. Even way out here, all eyes have been on us, particularly since we Bonded. And as a golden wolf, my color isn't one that's easily missed.

I glance over my shoulder, catching a glimpse of the sculpted chest I've spent nights memorizing as Hunter shifts too. In a flash, he's a glorious white wolf.

My white wolf.

We both step in at the same time, foreheads touching as our gazes lock. There's something more about our touch when we're wolf, something...primal. The fact that it happens so infrequently makes it even more special.

Time to make it memorable.

Like the moments this all started, when we believed it was nothing but dreams, I brush him with my nose, smile the biggest smile I can, then run.

Tuning into the thread that's brought us out here, I head north. Extending my stride, I fill my lungs with arctic air as I try to fly over the snow. I'm under no illusion that I'm faster than Hunter, but I'm going to give him a run for his money.

Snow crunches beneath my paws as I shoot forward, glancing over my shoulder. It confirms what my ears have already registered—Hunter's a body-length behind me. His gaze is fierce with determination...and love.

The excited bark is involuntary as my heart gallops in my chest. He's giving me a head start, but not for long.

As the terrain slowly climbs, we take turns in being the chaser, neither wanting to be apart too long, both enjoying the act of getting caught far more than the challenge of evading.

As we go, the threads around us start to become a vivid, pulsing network of live wires. As I sense we're getting close to our destination, I slow, marveling at the golden web around us, wishing others could see this.

This knowledge that we're all connected is what people—human, Were and Fae—don't understand. Even as we head farther north than we ever have, as the terrain becomes harsher and the wind even colder, the threads are there.

I shift back to human, wishing I could somehow capture this moment.

Hunter shifts beside me and looks around, the snow a whirlwind around us. "We rarely come this far north because humans don't. I can see why he came here." He squints through the frigid air. "He's close, isn't he?"

I nod, excited at seeing Achak. His thread has become progressively more vibrant the closer we get. My excitement dials down a bit as I remember why we're here.

To say goodbye, having no idea how long before we'll be coming back.

Achak appears on the top of the nearby rise. Like always, he's a majestic sight. A grey wolf with shades of russet, he stares at us.

I want to move toward him, but I hold still. Despite our deep connection, so much has passed. He followed me here from Jacksonville, and then I put him in captivity. We were so sure he was the answer to a cure for Furious, then the weeks while he was caged, he did nothing but pace, hating his confinement. It was too painful to watch, so I released him, despite the dangers.

And now I'm leaving again.

He stands, surrounded by snow, proud and free. My chest tightens as I look at him. *It suits you, my friend.*

Hunter moves in to clasp my hand. I squeeze it tight, wondering if this is as close as I should get. Achak remains on the ridge of the hill, canine eyes calm as he regards us. He's come to greet me, but he's obviously not coming any closer. I rest my head on Hunter's shoulder. "He looks healthy."

"And happy."

With a sigh, I accept this will have to be enough of a goodbye.

For now.

Straightening, I'm glad I did this. It's the last thing I needed to do before we move onto the next chapter. The wind gusts a sheet of snow over Achak, obscuring him for a second. When it clears, I gasp. I figure I must be dreaming, maybe hallucinating, until I hear Hunter's intake of breath.

We glance at each other, the wind stinging our wide eyes.

We've just realized why Achak didn't want to leave.

2

AVA

As the gust of snow passes, the bodies fan out behind Achak.

Five of them.

All arctic wolves.

Hunter's shock is quickly dashed by delight, and it rings bright and true through our connection. We had no idea!

I blink several times, making sure it's not some illusion of snow and wind, but yes, five arctic wolves now surround Achak.

Hunter takes a tentative step forward. "We didn't think they'd go this far up."

Achak found a pack, far in the north of this island.

We watch, trying to process all of this, as one of the arctic wolves' steps forward. A female by the size, she moves in beside Achak. The two stand proud and tall, watching us.

"Son of a..." Hunter breathes.

No wonder Achak was desperate to leave Resolve. He had a mate!

And a pack...

I grasp Hunter's hand, just to make sure I'm not dreaming. "Hunter, there are more arctic wolves!"

I can feel his heartbeat thrumming through our connection, full of awe and excitement. "This is...amazing."

Achak stares at me, and I know what he's trying to tell us. *We're trusting you...*

I nod at him. "We'll keep you safe."

The wind whips my words away, but it's their essence that Achak would've understood. He spins around and lopes away, disappearing over the rise. His mate and the four others follow him. A gust of snow whips across the horizon where they were just standing, and they're gone.

I turn to Hunter. "Whoa."

He's still wide-eyed despite the biting wind. "Tell me about it. Sakari and the others aren't the last ones."

"What are we going to do about this?"

Hunter rubs his chin, staring at the place we just saw the impossible. "Like you said—keep them safe." He turns to me. "As to what that looks like..."

Leave them in the wild, vulnerable to poachers? Or captivity...

I step into his arms, appreciating the warmth even though I'm not cold. "You hated trapping and caging the wild wolves."

"But it was necessary."

Which is Hunter's strength as a leader and as the guy I love —his ability to shoulder tough decisions. "I think we leave them here."

The truth is, captivity is just as unsafe as leaving them in the wild.

Hunter's breath whooshes out. "I do, too."

I squeeze his lean waist. "I thought you would. The poachers believe there're no wolves left on the island. This is the safest place for them."

"But we'll need to monitor them."

"Good idea. We'll need to get some of the cameras."

Hunter looks around. "I say we leave a surveillance network leading up here."

I grasp his face, excitement buzzing through my body. "So we can keep an eye on our arctic wolves."

His grin begins at his mouth and ends somewhere outside of us. "So we can keep an eye on our arctic wolves."

We kiss, cold lips quickly become warm lips, our joy like a dancing heat. What unexpected news. What wonderful news!

With a last glance in the direction the wolves disappeared, Hunter grasps my hand and turns back the way we came. "You can head back while I get it done, if you like."

I stop, jerking us both to a halt. "What?"

Hunter nibbles his lip. "This is going to take a bit of time. It's cold, and there's quite a few cameras to install…"

I stop myself from frowning. "You think I should head back?"

Hunter stops, turning around to grasp my upper arms. "I think that's up to you. I do know that you take your responsibilities very seriously. You always put them first, Ava."

"Oh."

"And I'm quickly figuring out my job is to put you first." He smiles, his eyes serious. "Put us first. If you need a break, then that's okay."

My heart swells with the too-big emotions I feel for Hunter. "You know I love you, don't you?"

His lips twist in that adorable way of his. "You've mentioned it once or twice…today."

"And you know it's you who makes me strong, don't you?"

He rests his head on mine, breathing in deeply. "I learned the hard way, it's together we'll make a difference."

I clasp his face. "Exactly."

Hunter blinks. "I just walked into that, didn't I?"

I try to contain my smile, but I can't. "I wasn't trying to make a point, but it's interesting that's where we ended up."

"I know you're strong, Ava. I know that more than anyone and I love you for it. But—"

"I don't know when to stop. I know." I brush his lips with mine. "Thank you for looking out for me."

His breath puffs out, icing the air between us. "Always."

My Hunter. My protector. "I wouldn't have it any other way." I pull back, reaching down for his hand. "Now, let's go get these cameras up."

Hunter's shaking his head as we start walking away. "Good thing we have them with us."

Luckily for us, we collected the last of the cameras before we went on our run, or I may have had more of a fight on my hands. "Let's head back to the quad, then make our way back, installing them as we go."

I can't help the little skip in my step. "I can't wait to tell the others."

Hunter frowns. "I'll text KJ to let him know the cameras will be going back up."

"Has he answered any of the others yet?"

The frown deepens. "Only a few. He did say he'd be out of range a lot while he was out looking for that wolf."

KJ and Hunter are more like brothers than distant cousins. It's unusual for him not to be in contact, even if it's only been a week.

"It's probably a good thing we're heading back, then."

Hunter pulls in a deep breath, holding it for a second. "Yeah."

He doesn't say anymore, but I don't expect him to. "I'm feeling fine, Hunter. Honestly."

I want to reassure him, take one thing off his plate. We know that even with this wonderful news, when we arrive in Jacksonville, our responsibilities are going to come at us like a herd of bison. "We're together."

I can feel him scanning our connection, searching for the truth. When he sees I'm not lying, his lips settle in a firm line. "Which means we're as ready as we'll ever be."

Preparing to shift, I nod, recognizing the caveat in his words.

It's hard to be ready when you don't know what's coming at you.

HELIX

There are a myriad of things programmed into our genetics. Our intelligence. Our predisposition for laughter, or empathy or violence.

Our need for power.

And when any factor has a tangible basis, it means it can be isolated. Targeted.

Manipulated.

I remember watching this one for a while. Understanding his history. Mapping as I observed him closely. He was sad. He was unhappy with how things are.

And he was angry.

I don't blame him. Humans are degrading what sustains them. What sustains all of us. Weres are sitting by, allowing it to happen.

Cowards.

No one should accept that. I knew I never would.

Just like a gene, I isolated what I want. Targeted it.

Next came the best bit—manipulating it.

It's fortuitous that the variables all aligned. He was young. Desperate to make his mark. The world around him needed to be fixed. He was like a fleck of snow balanced on the tip of a mountain, waiting to become an avalanche, a chain reaction waiting to hit critical mass.

It just needed a catalyst.

He'd run his hand through his rusty red hair.

"It's hard to sit back and watch some days, isn't it?"

He glanced at me, either surprised that I'd spoken, or shocked that I'd read his mind. "That's why I'm here, isn't it? Because I'm not willing to sit back and watch."

He was right. I never would've had the chance to cross paths with him if he hadn't made all the right choices.

I'd shrugged as I'd left. "The most frustrating part is that we have everything we need to make it right."

That's all it needed. A seed of an idea.

And Mother Nature had worked her wonders.

First with Kurt.

Then with his son.

Of course, neither realized they were working within a flawed system. The fools put so much faith in their prophecy.

It's what will be their undoing.

HUNTER

About the only thing Jacksonville and Evelyn Island have in common right now is snow. And even that isn't particularly similar...

Here, the snow climbs up rather than out. Jacksonville is a patchwork of houses and pine trees and massive mountains, and the snow is lathered over all those layers. Evelyn Island, on the other hand, looks like Mother Nature played pat-a-cake. Flattened, with randomly jagged and protruding outcroppings, the snow is more of a blanket.

I miss it.

Standing outside Jacksonville's captive breeding program, I pull in a calming breath.

It doesn't work.

Inside is Sakari...and her three pups.

The ones who KJ who KJ altered their genetic makeup, using my DNA.

The week we've been back on the island, Ava's parents have sent us photos. In each and every one, they look like normal arctic wolf pups. White and fluffy, cute and curious. What's more, they're growing at the expected rate.

Ava nudges me with her shoulder, her smile peeking up at me. "This is how you were when we arrived at my parent's house."

She's right, I was just as nervous. "Ah, that's because we were moving in there." Into the same bedroom.

She rolls her eyes. "They lived with my grandparents when they first bonded, remember? They've totally been there, done that."

Which is also true. It doesn't mean Noah and Eden are going to be happy that their daughter is sharing her room with a guy... "They've been very welcoming."

Ava wraps her arms around mine, snuggling in. "You passed the first test on the first night."

That draws a chuckle out of me. "You guys certainly do a family dinner in a big way."

Everything in Jacksonville feels bigger, more intense. There're more Weres, more humans, more Fae, more wolves. It's exciting and daunting at the same time.

"Your grandmother's charcoal chicken is unforgettable." I don't think I've ever seen a drumstick that charred before.

Ava giggles. "They loved you, Hunter. Just like I knew they would."

Ava could just be telling the truth. Noah's handshake was warm and solid when we arrived, and Eden was quick to make sure I had some alternatives to the cauterized chicken at the family dinner last night.

Now, it's time to meet the pups.

I hold the door open for Ava and she's only taken a few steps when she's engulfed in a hug. "You're here!"

Dawn's excitement swallows us both and it makes me smile. She holds Ava tight for a few seconds, her eyes closed.

With a quick squeeze, Ava releases her. "It's good to be back. How is everyone?"

Dawn's green eyes twinkle. "Well, Shaman's pregnant."

"That's wonderful! We were worried she'd never find a mate."

"Well, Grey is one patient wolf, he knew the timing had to be right." Dawn turns to me. "Hunter, it's wonderful to see you."

I'm glad she doesn't hug me. Although Dawn and KJ developed a strong bond, I could never seem to do the same. I respect Dawn but have never felt close to her. "There's nowhere else I'd be."

She smiles, glancing at Ava. "I have no doubt."

"I don't suppose you've heard from KJ?"

Dawn's smile dissolves under the weight of a frown. "No. But he was pretty upset when he left, so it doesn't surprise me."

The muscles along my neck bunch with tension. "Upset? About what?"

Dawn's brows lift in surprise. "I thought he would've told you. I don't want to say too much, but he made a...friendship with a girl. I don't think it worked out."

Ava and I glance at each other. Why would KJ have kept that from me? "A human girl?"

"No. One of the Tate pack. Her name's Sayen and she's been helping us out in the lab."

I almost let out a low whistle. If she's Were, then it would've been complicated. I want to pull my cell out of my pocket again, checking if he's reached out. It must've been serious if he's totally dropped off the radar like this.

Ava frowns. "Sayen. My mom mentioned her; said she's been a real help."

Dawn nods. "Yes, she's quite the whiz in the lab."

Again, no wonder KJ was drawn to her. "Let us know if you hear from him?"

"Of course." She slaps her palms on her jeans, all business. "Were you two going to have a look around?"

Ava slips a little closer to me. "We're going to go meet the pups."

"Wonderful idea. They're coming in leaps and bounds, no pun intended. You're going to love them."

I study Dawn for an extra second, wondering if KJ told her what he'd done. She smiles back before turning away. "I'll be in the lab if you need me."

The walk down the hallway feels like a long one. Ava holds my hand tight, and I can feel her comforting presence through our connection. She exudes a gentle confidence, a faith that this is all going to be okay. It's just what my tense chest needs.

Ava opens a door and we're in a room similar to the ones back at Resolve. Square and bare, there's a few chairs facing away from us. Behind us is a one-way window so the keepers can check in without disturbing the animals. A large pen takes up the back wall, a big wooden kennel inside it. That would be Sakari's den. The pups would be in there with her...

I'm drawn toward it, despite the unease winding around my spine. There's a quiet scuffling from within—Sakari is coming out to see who's here. A few feet away, I pause.

Out of the shadowy doorway, her snow-colored muzzle materializes. Her nose twitches, then her head jerks up.

She recognizes our scent.

Before I can let out the breath I'd been holding, Sakari leaps out. She runs at the fence, only pulling herself up at the last second. I fall to my knees, ignoring the jarring of the concrete floor. Sakari's tail is lashing back and forth as she works on containing her joy. It pulls up a smile so wide, it feels like my heart is doing the same thing.

She presses herself against the wire and I push my fingers through, scratching her head. She rubs against it like a cat. I'd underestimated the bond I have with this wonderful wolf. I'm glad she's been tough enough to endure all the changes she's had to see.

"Hunter..."

Ava is looking past us toward the makeshift den. Sakari sits, clearing a line of sight to what Ava's seen.

There's movement deep in the kennel gloom, and every muscle in my body freezes. First one, then two, small bodies creep out. Their little noses cautiously sniff the air, small eyes blinking in the light.

They're a pale grey like many arctic pups are, all fuzzy fur and stocky bodies. My legs give out and I land on my butt. The third joins its siblings, obviously the cautious of the three. It comes to stand between the other two, looking around.

Sakari drops beside me, obviously content where she is. She watches her pups, and I guess that Ava would be picking up on her pride. Sakari's always been such a wonderful mother.

The pups look around, quickly finding their mother, then noticing the two strangers in the room. They pause, sniffing the air again. I haven't seen an animal afraid of Ava—she says it's the same for all Fae, but I suspect it's more than that. They're quite likely to fall in love with her on sight.

Except I'm Were and sitting beside their mother.

Ava steps forward, dropping down further, and level with the wire. "Hunter, they're so gorgeous."

They really are.

Maybe KJ got it right. Maybe they'll be the tough wolves they're going to need to be. Especially now that there's a second pack out on the tundra. They'll cross breed and only become stronger.

The pups look between us, then at their mother. Just like a human child, they'll take their cue on how to respond from her, and Sakari's obviously unworried by the humans in the room.

Sakari's tail thumps a few times on the floor, showing exactly how relaxed and happy she is.

The pups' little ears perk up, their eyes sparking with interest. One steps forward and another follows.

Ava slowly crouches, and the two pups who came out first take a few tentative steps, glancing at their mother. Sakari simply leans into me further, possibly enjoying a bit of a break from her triplets. They take two more steps, looking curiously at Ava.

There's no doubt they'll head toward my mate. Her gentle spirit draws animals to her. It's like all threads lead to Ava. I relax, looking forward to seeing them greet her.

The third, cautious pup joins its siblings and they take a few more steps, now a close-knit huddle of fur. They look from Ava to me and back again. Ava holds herself still, letting the pups make their decision in their own time.

I hold my breath, waiting for the moment they'll make a move. Will they be tentative, or will they throw caution to the wind and barrel at her?

In one simultaneous movement, their heads swing toward me. I freeze, hoping I haven't scared them.

Like a switch has been flipped, the puppies move. Bounding like their enthusiasm is bigger than their bodies, they run straight at me. One tumbles and rights itself, the one behind is obviously no longer wary because it bulldozes straight over its sibling. Within the space of a blink, they're on Sakari.

They must've decided to go to their mother.

Except they don't stop there. They clamber up, her ribs a convenient ladder, and start pawing at the fence containing them.

I raise my hand, every muscle slack with shock. As I press it against the wire, they yip and lick and scrabble over each other. I push my fingers through, stroking their excited, wiggly bodies.

The pups tumble over each other, their licking quickly becoming playful chewing. But even their sharp little teeth digging into my skin can't wipe the smile off my face.

"Hunter, they know you."

Because they share my DNA. I'm forever tied to these pups, and I have no idea what that's going to mean.

Sakari groans as the pups use her as their personal trampoline, and I grin at Ava. "Maybe I should move?"

Except the pups begin to settle, their initial excitement over, not that they leave their vantage point. One stretches his little jaws in a yawn and starts tucking himself right on top of his mom. The other two move in closer, still seeking a scratch.

Ava shuffles closer. "They don't want to leave you." She looks at me, wintergreen eyes glowing. "We need to name them."

There's a muffled clattering outside and Sakari sits upright in alarm. Two of the pups are instantly alert, but the tired pup tumbles off as he leaps to stand. With a glance back at me, Sakari lopes back to her man-made den, the pups following her.

I glance at Ava. "What was that?"

She shrugs, any answer cut off by the door opening behind us.

It's a girl I haven't seen before, but I quickly figure this beautiful Were is Sayen. Her face is nothing but frowns. "Dawn sent me. They're back."

HUNTER

S triding down the hallway, a calm determination sweeps through me. Noah and Eden have kept us up to date about the protestors. Their demonstrations have become a daily occurrence.

We've still got two more doors to get through, but the chanting reaches my Were hearing.

"Wolves kill! Wolves kill!"

I notice as we get closer that it sounds like their numbers have increased along with the frequency. I move in a little closer to Ava. Eden calls them passionate to their cause. Noah pointed out that they're not always peaceful...

We all have to stop the moment we exit the building. What was sun-bright snow when we entered has now been trampled by the twenty-odd people who are milling around. A few hold placards, someone else has tied a banner across the front of the building.

Wolves Kill.

There's a pause at our appearance, then an upsurge of energy. One man looks away like we don't exist, another woman waves her fist.

There's not many.

But there's enough.

Ava steps forward, holding her hands up. "Please, this noise is distressing and disruptive for the animals."

One woman sneers. "What? Worried they'll attack us?"

Another female, this one freckled and not much older than us, rattles her placard. "Or you?"

Ava shakes her head. "Wolves are no more dangerous than any other animal."

I glare at them. Or human... "They deserve our respect."

Sayen crosses her arms. "We've had these conversations."

My guess is they didn't listen...

Ava steps in closer and I can feel her distress. "It's because they don't understand, Hunter."

The man who pretended to ignore us suddenly steps forward. "We understand perfectly. There isn't a resident of this state who hasn't seen what they're capable of."

Which is probably true. Between the news and social media, only hermits living deep in the mountains wouldn't have heard about the family killed by a single wolf.

The sneering woman sneers even harder. "It's only animal lovers like you who are willing to risk lives," She scans us in disgust, "Just 'cause you think they look pretty."

They form their line again, a resolute barrier at the front of the center.

Sayen lets out a breath. "We've got a school group coming through today." She glances at Ava and me. "One of the last few. Most of them have cancelled."

Well, if the inflated news didn't do it, then these protestors would certainly put someone off. My hands clench. "We need people to see there's another side to these animals."

There's the crunching of gravel in the parking lot, and we all tense. More protestors.

A voice reaches around the corner before we can see anyone. A voice I recognize. "Live on site, viewers, we're going to see exactly how the majority of people feel about the animals no one should consider safe."

Alistair.

He rounds the edge of the brick building holding a microphone, his camera man in tow. The protestors conveniently get another burst of energy and start chanting loudly.

"Wolves kill! Wolves kill!"

Alistair throws out his arm like some hostess showing off a new car. "People fighting for what they believe in. For the truth we must face."

He turns to the people behind him, and they raise their placards in unison. "Wolves kill!"

You've got to be kidding me.

"Our reserves are no longer safe. And these centers breed more just to release them into the places we picnic with our families."

I'm striding forward, my mounting frustration starting to feel like a pressure cooker, when Sayen overtakes me. Her face is twisted with the anger I know so many Weres feel toward humans. The freckled woman's eyes widen a little as a couple of others square their shoulders—it seems they've seen the wrath of Sayen before.

As Sayen's anger grows, mine abates. This fire doesn't need any more heat. I grab her arm and she spins to glare at me. I almost step back at the passion powering her gaze. "I'm going to tell them—"

But I hold my ground. Passion is power, but it needs to be used in the right way. "We can't meet them with anger."

Sayen opens her mouth to retort but Ava joins me. "Although you're right, Sayen. We do need to talk to them."

Turning back to Alistair, Ava takes him in. "Would you like

to come in and meet them, Mr. Davenport?"

Alistair's face is slapped with the same surprise I'm feeling. "What?"

Ava's smile is a small one, but it's there, nonetheless. "Have you ever met a wolf, Alistair?"

Alistair is blinking rapidly, possibly trying to gain some equilibrium. "Well...ah...no." He straightens, finding his frown again. "But I don't—"

Respecting Ava for what she's doing, I uncross my arms. "You're welcome to bring your cameras."

Every wolf in the center is a product of captive breeding. Temperament wise, they're more like their dog cousins than their wild counterparts.

And none of them have Furious.

Alistair's hand comes up in a short, sharp movement and the camera man zooms the big black lens away from us. Alistair combs over his non-existent hair, obviously trying to regain some composure.

When his gaze returns to us, it's flinty and hard. He leans forward, keeping his voice a hoarse whisper. "I have no desire to be anywhere near those killing machines. Nor would it change my mind."

Then it's time I had the same conversation I've had with Alistair too many times. He and the protestors need to leave. I'm about to lean in, too, knowing full well that I can't get him to move on any more than the protestors, when another group of people walk around the side of the building.

My heart sinks as Alistair grows a smile. It's either more protestors, probably organized by Alistair, or a group of teachers realizing they're about to disappoint a bunch of kids.

Except at their head is a face I know. And behind him are two more humans I'm not likely to forget.

It's Mike and his two poacher friends, the ones forever

imprinted on my brain as Turkey and Fridge. Mike's glance at us is brief as he passes us, but it's loaded.

Now isn't the time to find out why, though.

Alistair's already striding toward them, waving his hand at his camera man urgently. "Get that camera rolling!"

Mike smiles at him as he comes to a stop, glancing at the camera pointed at him. "Alistair, I'm so glad you're here."

Alistair puffs out his chest. "Mike. As a long-time poacher, someone committed to keeping us safe, I shouldn't be surprised to see you here at this important protest."

Mike nods, his mouth holding in a smile in a way that doesn't make me comfortable. Mike is holding an ace card, and I have no idea what it is.

After their statement of commitment when they saw us at Resolve, Mike and his friends had returned to the mainland, promising to do what they could to help.

They promptly disappeared without another word.

And now here they are.

I count the people behind Mike. With five extra people in his posse.

Mike scans the protestors holding their formation beside the building. "I'm glad you're here to hear this, I have some exciting news. Some of you may recognize me," I glance at Ava, but she looks just as nonplussed...and concerned, as I am, "My name is Michael Hennessy, and I'm your Congressman for the district of Wyoming."

He's a federal representative?

Alistair is beaming so hard it makes my gut clench. Michael Hennessy has no doubt been a staunch supporter of hunting.

"What's been occurring in the media has been concerning me, and once I asked around, discovered it's concerning many people in our community."

The posse behind him nods like a bunch of bobble heads.

Mike glances back at Alistair, who nods encouragingly. Alistair even makes a point of smiling at the camera.

Ava tightens her hand on me. She can sense every cell in my body feels like a loaded gun. Knocking out the camera man isn't going to help this cause, that's something the rational part of my brain can recognize. But the anger that wants a voice is a whole lot louder and a whole lot stronger.

I don't know if it's Ava's gentle touch, or some thin thread of self-control, but I stay where I am. Ava touched these men when she healed me. *Please let that count for something.*

Mike lifts the folder he's holding, some fancy, leather-bound one. "I've introduced a Bill to the committee. They will vote in a week."

I should've taken out the camera man. It's too late now, whatever Mike's about to say is going to be heard by the thousands of followers Alistair has amassed since the wolf attack.

"The single-minded extermination of a species is not what humanity stands for. Not the death of a species. Not the death of an animal." He scans the crowd who are as open-mouthed as I'd like to be, his gaze coming to rest on Ava. "Not the end of wolves." He looks back at Alistair and his camera. "I have proposed a moratorium on any wolf culling. We will put an end to wolf deaths."

So many things happen at once. My breath disintegrates as Ava gasps, but our shock is the same. The people behind Mike cheer and punch the air. The protestors angrily shout their denials.

I keep my smile contained as Alistair furiously indicates for the camera man to stop filming.

I look back to celebrate with Sayen, only to find she's gone.

Mike and his supporters move around us, and I start to pay attention to who's here. It seems the three poachers were forever changed by what happened in the warehouse.

Mike is the first person I shake hands with. "Thank you." I say the words simply, hoping they capture the emotion that's welled in my chest.

Mike just nods, his face serious but proud, when Ava engulfs him in a hug.

"Yes, thank you, Mike. The wolves need every champion they can get."

Mike blinks, and I grin. Welcome to my world. He gently, a little awkwardly, pats her on the back.

Ava returns to my side. "Thank you all."

Turkey is doing some sort of little jig on the spot. "It was you who showed us, Ava."

My mate slides closer to me, her hand weaving through mine. I feel Ava's awe, her astonishment, her hope. And she wants to make sure I'm there with her.

Squeezing her hand, I breathe out one word, knowing she'll hear me. "Always."

Fridge rubs his hands together. "Now, we set up camp."

The protestors are all varying shades of frowns as they discover they now have company. Within minutes, Mike and his little pro-wolf clan have set up their own space, complete with a banner and placards of their own.

Looking around, I discover Alistair left without anyone noticing. I doubt we'll see his red-faced frown anytime soon. He's got damage control to do now that he's inadvertently filmed support for wolves.

I glance down at Ava to find her wintergreen eyes already on me. She smiles. "It's started."

An unknown wolf pack.

Three healthy, normal pups.

And humans fighting for a moratorium on wolf culling.

I let my smile show exactly how I'm feeling. "It really has."

KJ

T here aren't many escape points in a lab.
  Especially when it's built in a basement.

And believe me, I've tried.

Until I found the note. Tacked onto the microscope, like they knew this would be the first place I'd check out.

Escape and she dies.

Then all attempts had stopped.

Not that the accommodation is lacking. Whoever set up this lab decided it needed its own bathroom, and for some reason, the single bed tucked in the back corner feels like it was here before my kidnapping. There's even a fridge that was well-stocked for my arrival, and a microwave.

But it's been a week according to the computer sitting on one of the benches. Even if he's been fed a lie, Hunter knows this is unusual for me. He's bound to start looking soon, and he has enough on his plate.

Plus, there's Sakari's pups...

A week of being left alone in this place. With nothing but beakers and Bunsen burners to keep me company. The first day, I spent discovering I was in a vault. There's one door in, and it looks thicker than the brick walls around me. And I refused to be one of those pathetic hostages who bangs and slaps the door and demands to be let out. Sayen put me in here for a reason— she ain't letting me out just 'cause I've screamed and pleaded.

So, day two I started looking for other ways to get the hell out of here. The computer didn't have internet access. There were no corrosive acids on the shelves. The biggest tool I could find was a pipette.

That was when I discovered the samples.

They were clearly labeled: Sakari. Zephyr. Desna. Kayuh. Achak.

And one I hadn't heard of—Warrior.

Day three came and went. The samples had sat in their frozen home, calling to me, but I ignored them. Sayen, or whomever was keeping me here, had to come and check on me eventually.

Day four, I cracked. Those vials of blood were holding a wealth of information. It would be like putting Hunter in a coffee shop for three days and expecting him not to touch anything.

As I'd set up my first slide and slipped it under the microscope, I realized that's exactly what Sayen was betting on. But it didn't matter. Knowledge can be discovered...it doesn't have to be shared.

Not that I've discovered anything new...

I left Achak's sample till last. His blood was the most analyzed out of all of them as we desperately hoped we could find a cure for Furious. I doubt I'm going to find anything new, but it's not like I have anything else to do.

The drop of blood sits on the rectangle glass as I add the stain, figuring I must be pretty bored to be doing this. All I'm going to see is what I saw over and over back at Evelyn Island.

Red blood cells as pink little doughnuts, platelets as small blue granules. The same you'd see on any other wolf.

I'm upright the instant the door at the top of the steps rattles. I've had seven days of nothing but my own thoughts to keep me company. The only noise is the clinks or creaks I create myself.

But it seems that after seven days, someone is finally coming. Achak's over-tested blood can wait.

I head to the end of the bench, the closest point to the bottom of the stairs. Having to get the anger under control doesn't surprise me. It was always going to flare hot and fast.

But I don't bank on the feeling of betrayal that stabs me in the chest. For a second, the pain is so stark I wonder if it's left a puncture wound. As the door whooshes open, I grit my teeth and cross my arms. This isn't the time to dwell on what an idiot I've been. Getting out of here is the only priority.

My hastily built composure cracks for a split second when legs appear on the stairs. I know those legs.

I was really hoping I wouldn't be seeing those legs again.

Sayen stops at the bottom of the stairs. She's beautiful like she's always been. She's serious and unsmiling like she usually is.

She's the traitor I should've known she is.

My arms tighten—they're the only armor I have right now. "About time. I was getting low on OJ."

Sayen looks around like she's checking the place out, but I know she's buying time. There's no way they don't have a couple of cameras in here keeping an eye on me.

When her gaze returns to me, her eyes are shifting sands of emotion. I look away before I try to decipher whatever she's trying to tell me. Those days are gone.

She walks past me to the slide I'd just been setting up. "Not bad for a converted basement, is it?"

I turn around to face her but stay where I am. "The ideal place to keep a lab-lover hostage."

The wince I was hoping for doesn't give me the jolt of victory I was expecting, which is annoying. I channel that annoyance into a frown. First things first. "Why am I here, Sayen?"

Sayen steps away from the slide and over to the microscope, running her hand over it. "We discovered a lot of things in this lab."

Another smart-ass comment springs to my lips, but I don't give it breath. If Sayen wants to dance around the Mulberry bush, then I'm willing to step up. "Like the fact that Furious isn't contagious?"

Her gaze snaps to mine. "Yes."

"My guess is that when you mutated the rabies virus to have it travel through the bloodstream, you inadvertently disabled the main way it's transmitted."

I don't expect Sayen to smile, but she does. Nor do I expect my chest to lighten, like my heart just blossomed, but it bloody well does.

Freaking great.

Sayen takes a few steps toward me. "I could've used you when I spent all those months down here."

My breath whooshes out. "You created Furious?"

She shakes her head. "I was more the lab assistant. Doing all the mundane gene multiplication once the genes were identified and spliced."

I slice my hand through the air. "That's semantics and you know it. You may as well have pulled the trigger on that family, Sayen."

She rears back like I just slapped her, and I ignore the next stab in my chest. If I was stupid enough to fall for someone like Sayen, then I've only got myself to blame for becoming a pincushion.

Her face clouds with a frown. "And yet no one is held responsible for the countless wolf deaths that have occurred."

"They will be."

"No, they won't!" She shouts, then quickly reins herself in. "They won't be, KJ. That's why tough choices have to be made."

I'm shaking my head, not sure if I'm denying what she's saying, or whether I'm trying to sort out everything in my head. "Who told you this, Sayen?"

She snaps her head to the side, looking away. She's taken a few deep breaths before she turns back to me. "You know I hate Furious as much as you do."

"I doubt that."

Her dark gaze glints like obsidian. "When do we say 'enough,' KJ? When do we realize things are getting desperate and that you need someone with the guts to solve this? That there are some Weres willing to do what it takes?"

Sayen's questions have a jittery, jagged turmoil whirling in my head. It makes me uneasy, even a little nauseous. "I can already guess who those Weres are." My father had his supporters both within the Channons and the Tates—Sayen's pack. "And who is that person? This leader with all the answers?"

Someone who would go as far as creating Furious.

Sayen takes a step forward and alarm bells start to ring as she closes the distance between us. She stops in front of me, watching me with an intensity that quickens my pulse. "Why do you think we were drawn to each other, KJ?"

I keep my lips tightly shut, but the words blaze in my mind, anyway. Because you're beautiful. Because you're smart and complicated and I'm an idiot to have hoped...

"Because we recognized a kindred spirit in each other."

I step away. "No."

She covers the lost space. "Yes. You're someone who's willing to do what it takes to end this."

I hate myself because I look away. I loathe myself because what Sayen just said is true. I justified genetically engineering those pups because I couldn't see any other solution.

Because I believed I was someone who would do what it takes.

A muscle is ticking in my jaw when I look back at her. It's through gritted teeth that I ask the question I should've started with. "What do I need to do to get out of here?"

I quickly figured out I'm here for a reason, one that has to do with my genetic-loving brain.

And the heritage I've never been able to escape.

Sayen's gaze softens and warms. It somehow enhances her beauty and has me swallowing, trying to moisten my parched throat.

It tells me I'm not going to like the answer.

"Join us."

7

AVA

I don't think the common room at the center has ever been this full. My parents are here. Dawn and River, another Fae Elder, are here. John and Mary, the Alphas of the Tate pack even made the trip. Uncle Mitch and Aunt Tara, even Joshua and Riley are here. Mike is here with the other two ex-poachers, unaware they're the only humans.

Tara looks over and gives me a jaunty wave and I wave back. Josh and Riley join us, and I give my cousin and best friend a hug.

Josh squeezes me tight before moving around next to me. "Impressive, little cousin."

I nudge him with my elbow. "Don't pretend you haven't listened in on the Assembly meetings before."

Some of them even had more people than today.

Riley shoves in between Hunter and me. "He was talking about how much you've managed in such a short space of time."

"Yup." Josh nods slowly as he looks around. "Impressive."

Riley nods too, but with a whole lot more enthusiasm. "Who would've thought? Ex-poachers leading a movement to stop wolf culling. You wouldn't read about it."

I look around at the people milling and chatting. Weres. Fae. And now humans.

I catch Hunter's gaze. Is it possible? Could this be the start of solving the problem?

His shrug and lip twitch tell me exactly what he's thinking. Hasn't our motto been 'anything is possible?'

Josh chuckles. "Well Alistair certainly will be, along with anyone else who saw it all over social media. My guess is he fired his camera man after he streamed Alistair's reaction to the moratorium announcement."

There'd been a lot of spluttering and shouting of 'Cut! Stop filming!' but then, 'Start filming, you fool! Are you getting this?' as the protestors had shouted their denials. But it'd been too late. Mike's announcement had already aired.

And so, the sharing began. And the comments. And the dialogue.

The moratorium became the topic of every channel's current affairs discussion. The opposition had been swift and loud.

But so had been the support.

Mom and Dad walk over, both smiling. I slip out from under Josh's arm so I could hug them both, even though I only saw them this morning.

Dad looks at Hunter and me. "How do you guys want to run this?"

I feel Hunter's surprise as my own hikes up my brows. "We kinda assumed..."

Mom's eyes soften. "Ava, Hunter. This is your legacy, not ours."

Whoa. Having some sort of responsibility back on Evelyn Island had felt almost natural. But here, in Jacksonville? The expectations are staring at you through a roomful of Were eyes.

Looking at Hunter, I see him calm, and my heart rate does the same. He's getting his Alpha face on, which means I will, too.

Hunter nods. "Let's see what Mike and the others have to say. Then we have some news of our own."

Four curious faces look at us, but we simply stare back. It's nice to have good news for a change.

Hunter grasps my hand, looking like the leader he is, even as I feel his nervousness. "Ready?"

Not really. I nod once. "Let's do this."

Stepping forward simultaneously has a hush instantly falling over the room. Whoa, intimidating much?

Hunter clears his throat. "Thank you all for coming. As you've seen, we finally have a way forward. I'd like to thank Mike and his friends for that."

A round of applause circles the room,

Mike steps up. "With the Bill being debated in the Senate, we need to show the community wants a moratorium."

Dad nods, rubbing his lower lip. "We've already reached out to several animal welfare groups we have a connection with. They're excited that this is happening."

Dawn glances at River, who nods, too. She smiles as she takes in the support already in the room. "The Fae are involved in many environmental groups and companies. We'll be getting the word out."

John Tate raises his hand. "We're funding a flyer drop. There ain't no house in this state that won't know why we need a moratorium."

A bubbly sense of hope fills me, and I'm not sure if it's mine or Hunter's or the room.

Mike claps his hands together. "We have a week, people, before this Bill goes to the Senate floor."

Dad crosses his arms. "And culling certainly won't be as popular as this decision is being made."

"Exactly." Mike points at him. "So, it will give us time."

Riley puts up her hand, and when I feel Hunter's surprise, I know he's as clueless as I am as to what she's going to say.

"I'm going to try the celebrity angle. We all know what happens if someone like Ellen supports a cause."

Ellen?

But then I'm smiling. Riley is synonymous with tenacious. If anyone can do it, it's Hunter's bubbly, determined little sister.

Josh raises his hand and grasps Riley's in the air. "We're going to start small, though." He grins at the crowd. "Like with Ashton Kutcher or something."

There's a round of chuckles and smiles and grins. All of a sudden, more hands, all gripped tightly into fists, rise into the air.

There's a lightness in the room I haven't experienced since this all started. It makes what we have to say feel like a beautiful cherry on top of this happy little cake.

Hunter nods at me, knowing it's time to tell. I raise my hand and silence settles again, everyone looking at me expectantly. I'm so keen to tell them all, that I almost feel comfortable heading this meeting. "We have so much to celebrate. Hunter and I discovered something our last night on Evelyn Island." I scan the faces, loving that everyone doesn't have that shuttered look people have when they brace themselves for what they're about to hear. "We found Achak."

My mom's smile grows. She knows how deeply connected I am to that wolf.

"But we also discovered something else. We had to travel far north to find him, and he had friends."

Riley gasps, and Josh's eyes widen the biggest I've ever seen them.

"We found another arctic wolf pack."

Riley's squeal hurts every Weres' ears in the room, but no one loses their smile. She launches herself at us, both arms pulling us in close. Hunter's chuckling as I squeeze her right back.

"Best news ever, guys!"

The room erupts into chatter as everyone processes what this means. The handful of arctic wolves we have here aren't the last ones. There will be more pups. More packs.

Mike heads over, his face not as joyous as I would've expected. He waits for Riley to skip to the next person she wants to hug before speaking. "You'll be leaving them in the wild?" he asks quietly.

I try not to frown, unsure why he looks so worried. "Yes. They're safer there."

He lets out a sigh and his shoulders relax. "Good. The poachers have given up on Evelyn Island."

Hunter nods. "That's what we figured. They'll be safer out there."

"Yes, they will. From those who don't realize what they're losing by killing, but they also can't afford to get that sickness."

Hunter finds his voice before I do. "You know about the virus?"

Mike's brows shoot up. "I thought you realized."

We glance at each other, asking the same question. "Realize what?"

"That Helix paid Kyle to inject wolves with something. They reckon the compensation was even higher than a kill."

I rock back, shock making my mind go blank. Helix paid the poachers *and* is also behind Furious?

Mike frowns as he registers our surprise. "I figured that's what explained that wolf attack. In all my days as a poacher, I never saw a wolf kill like that."

Hunter is a rock of fury beside me. "Whoever Helix is, they're going to extremes to rid the world of wolves."

Mike nods. "Sure is." But then, incongruously, he smiles.

"But he didn't bank on opposition. We get this Bill through, and he'll become public enemy number one."

He's right.

I square my shoulders. "Once this moratorium becomes law, the world will see that wolves have a right to exist. They'll be protected."

Hunter's lips settle in a grim line. "And that bastard Helix will quickly lose supporters."

Mike shrugs. "And those who decide the money is too tempting, will face jail time."

Riley rushes back, her face sparkling with excitement. "I have another idea!" She turns to Mike, looking at him up and down. "Good. You've got a face for TV."

The surprise yanks us out of our somber mood. Mike chuckles and Hunter relaxes.

Helix doesn't know what he's up against.

8

AVA

"I thought I'd find you here." I startle as I look up at Dawn from where I'm sitting on the concrete floor. Sakari's pups went back into the den a good twenty minutes ago, but I can't bring myself to leave. Maybe I've gotten used to the quietness of the tundra, or maybe I'm just taking a break from all the expectations, but I feel drawn to Sakari's pen.

Maybe it's because there's a part of Hunter in those pups...

Sakari, who was sitting on the other side of the fence in companionable silence, rises and trots off to her pups. It's probably feeding time.

I smile. "I've always loved the pups."

Dawn pulls up a chair. "Yes, you always did." She glances at the dark entry where Sakari just disappeared. "These are special though, aren't they?"

I tense, wondering what Dawn's Fae senses have picked up, but when she simply smiles at me, I smile back. "We were so worried they were the last ones."

"It's wonderful news that there are more out in the wild. I suppose you'll have to capture them, too?"

I'm already shaking my head. "We're leaving them out there. Only a select few know they exist—they're much safer in the wild than in captivity."

I hold my breath as Dawn thinks this over. Her drive for the captive breeding programs inspired most of my childhood. But things are so much more complicated and grey. I'm not sure if there ever was any black and white, to be honest.

Poachers threatening the wild wolves.

Furious seeming to affect those in captivity.

Dawn nods, her gentle smile growing again. "That makes sense. You're really growing up, Ava."

I rest my head against the wall, letting her words sink in. "For a long time, I was worried that I wouldn't see a way forward."

That I wouldn't have what it takes. I don't look at Dawn, because the reality is, many others were wondering the same thing.

I smile, staring up at the ceiling. "But I met Hunter."

More than that, I fell in love with Hunter.

"And now Furious hasn't turned out to be the threat we thought it was."

Despite its violent potential.

"And now even the wolf culling is meeting with opposition."

From humans as well as Weres.

When I finally look back at Dawn, her Fae green eyes are serious. "I've never seen you so sure."

One of the pups must be curious at the new voice, because a small, furred nose peeks out of the den entrance. I wait, breath held, knowing if it scented Hunter, it would probably be out in a flash. Instead, it mustn't find anything worth leaving the warmth of its siblings and mother, because it disappears back into the gloom.

Dawn stands, now smiling again, but I can see the strain around the edges. "I doubt Helix knows what he's up against."

Helix.

The one who's paid for wolf deaths, counting the toll in pelts. And, as we recently discovered, created Furious.

"Helix is about to face a united front." I grin. "And as we all know, united we conquer."

Dawn doesn't laugh, but that doesn't surprise me. Faith takes time.

She steps over and brushes a kiss on my head like she did so many times when I was a child. "I couldn't have said it better myself."

She heads out and I rest my head against the wall. I should get up and head out, too. The pups have gone back to sleep, and I have responsibilities waiting. Instead, I wait another couple of heartbeats.

When the door opens again, my smile has already blossomed. I sensed Hunter was nearby a few minutes ago.

He creeps into the room as silently as possible, and it's almost comical watching a guy in the prime of his Were years tiptoeing toward me. He folds down beside me, and I fit into him, loving the sensation of our lines blending into each other.

He brushes a kiss on my head just like Dawn did only a few moments ago, but this time, the feeling fills me with sweet warmth. "Dawn looked tense."

"We were just talking about Helix. I think it makes everyone tense."

Hunter stares at the den, his unfocused eyes telling me he's not thinking of the pups. "He's going to react one of two ways to this moratorium. He'll either give up..."

"Or he'll up the ante."

Like they were waiting, coiled and ready for the sound of his voice, the three pups shoot out. Tumbling over their own feet, and then each other, they race over to us. Hunter shuffles forward as I stay where I am. It's not me they're here to see.

Leaping, their tongues lolling and licking, the pups fight to get at Hunter. He chuckles as he reaches his fingers through the wire, but then pauses. "You guys are really growing, aren't you?"

I lay my hand on his back, resting in the smooth hollow between his shoulder blades. "They're growing at just the right rate."

The tension beneath my palm dissolves. "So much could go wrong with these guys, Ava."

My hand curls in a little, fingers finding the strength in the muscles that bunch beneath. I wait, knowing I no longer have to convince Hunter of what's coming next.

One of the pups starts to chew on Hunter's pointer finger and he winces but doesn't pull away. "And yet so much has gone right." He looks up at me, copper eyes alive with determination. "Because people are beginning to understand."

That we're all connected. That hurting one life hurts many.

My smile feels too big for the room, but I let it stretch out anyway. "They sure do."

One of the pups come to curl up on the floor beside Hunter, his body resting against the wire, his pale fur poking through and pressing against Hunter's leg. The other two quickly join their sibling, one yawning, the other clambering over so it can get as close as it can, too.

"That's what we need to harness, Ava. That momentum."

I nod, having already thought of this. "We need to show people."

Hunter looks at me steadily, and for some reason, anticipation builds in my gut. "I think we need to go on the road. Talk to people. Help them understand."

I grin. "I've already started packing. It'll take a couple more days to organize everything we need, but then we can be off."

Excitement sparks in Hunter's eyes. "Helix won't stand a chance against the tide of goodwill this will build."

I grasp his chin as I kiss him fiercely. "We've got this."

One of the pup's yips and we pull apart, grinning. I glance at them, to find one pawing at the wire. It's the female. I giggle. "I think she's jealous."

Hunter shakes his head. "I think we should name them before we go."

I angle my head, studying my mate. "Got any suggestions?"

Hunter glances down at the pups, almost looking bashful. "I have some suggestions." I wait, heartwarming as I watch the lightest of blushes color his skin. "Ari, which means eagle. Asta, which means tree. And Akyla, which means intelligent."

I clap my hands. "I love it!" Turning my attention to the pups, I grin. "Well, she's obviously Asta." I point to the one who's already asleep. "That's Ari." My grin grows as I poke my finger through the wire to stroke the pup who made sure he was closest to Hunter. "And Akyla."

Hunter's arm snakes around my shoulder as he rests his head against mine. "It'll be hard to leave them."

I brush a kiss across his temple. "When we return, they'll have a world they can safely grow up in."

9

SAYEN

E ach step down the stairs, my heart thumps out a triple beat. For three days I've been visiting KJ. Every time I enter, I don't miss the glance over my shoulder at the door that just shut behind me.

But I also don't miss the flash of a glance at my lips. The way that look hitches something in my chest.

It's that second glance I cling to.

Everything in my being wants what that graze of hazel eyes promises.

"So, I'm packed and ready. What time is departure?"

I roll my eyes at him. There's always some variation on his 'get me out of here' statements. He's allergic to basements. A Tate ancestor visited him last night, inquiring about the logistics of possessing a body. He has a theory that vitamin D deficiency is deadly to Weres...

I haven't missed the urgency that grows with each day. I fire back my usual response. "So, you've decided?"

Although this time, the routine changes. Instead of walking away and throwing his arms in the air, KJ steps forward. My pulse skyrockets. KJ this close reminds me of what I thought I couldn't have.

But when Helix brought him here, all that changed.

KJ stares at me and stares hard. "Sayen. I need to get out of here. I'm no longer asking."

There's a pressing need to his words that has my breath stalling. "Why?" Does KJ have someone else out there?

He looks away. "I can't tell you." When his gaze returns, there's a touch of desperation in its depths. "But it's important."

My hands burn with the desire to move, to finally touch him again, but I hold them still. "I want you to trust me, KJ."

He swallows. "Why, Sayen?"

"Because we need you."

Something dims in KJ's face, and it's only then that I realize there was a light I was drawn to. A light that has nothing to do with Helix or our cause.

Thank goodness that light is what the others want, too.

He turns away, fingers spearing into his russet hair and gripping it tightly. He stalks over to the bench, only for the agitated energy to bring him back. "And who is we?"

"You already know. Mostly Tates. A few Channons who had the courage to stick by their beliefs. We won't be hiding for much longer."

KJ points an angry finger at me. "Well, when I start to talk to you, Sayen, and not the group mentality you've been brainwashed with, then we can start talking about trust."

I frown, the familiar anger I'd stopped feeling around KJ bubbling at the edge of my consciousness. "These people have the courage to fight for the peace wolves need."

"No matter the cost?"

My hands fist, mirroring the feeling in my chest. "The reality is, there was never going to be an easy road to solving this, KJ. What were you willing to do to save the wolves?"

KJ blinks, and it's the fact I hadn't expected that, that has me pausing. The building tension, so entrenched in hate, abates.

What has KJ done?

I reach a decision. KJ wants trust? I'll show him trust.

I step in again, almost like I need the comfort of his nearness. My heart hammers as the truth I've been wanting to share for a long time rises through my body. "I do trust you, KJ. It's why I was drawn to you right from the beginning."

KJ must see something in my face, because he goes a little wide-eyed. Then his lips flatline as he holds up his hand. "Don't give me your kindred spirits theory, Sayen. We both know all chemistry needs is a catalyst. For us, that was probably a lonely childhood created by this legacy. We were like poster children for the law of attraction—like attracts like."

I grasp his hand, wrapping my own around it and bringing it to my chest. "It's always been more than that, and you know it."

KJ falls silent, eyes heating even as his mind rebels.

"You're right. There is someone who coordinated all this, someone who has the determination to see it through."

KJ begins slowly shaking his head, his lips silently mouthing "no."

I nod. "It's Helix."

He yanks his hand free, shock, a thick vein of horror running through it, slaps across his face. "But Helix has been coordinating the wolf culling."

I nod again. This was always bigger than anyone realized.

KJ glances around the lab, eyes growing wider and wider, mouth working as he processes everything. He turns back to me, the horror now overtaking the shock. "Helix created Furious?"

I swallow. "At first, I couldn't understand how hurting wolves would help them. But then Helix explained that sacrifices have to be made."

Anger, no, raw rage, explodes across KJ's features. He strides toward me, gripping my arms with such ferocity, I can feel the hot emotion pouring from him. "You're working to kill off wolves?" His voice rises with each word. "You want them extinct?"

I've been around too much rage all my life for KJ to scare me. I shake my head slowly, trying to be an antithesis for the fury that KJ needs to redirect. It's not Weres who are responsible for this. It's not Weres who need to pay. "Never. Wolves are part of us, our stronger, more powerful half. It's time we honored that."

KJ pulls away, something about the way his hand retracts, making me feel like I'm somehow soiled. Something flashes across his face, and I can't help the wince deep in my heart. KJ almost looks...disgusted.

He retreats, hazel eyes never leaving me. "Helix told you that?"

I frown. "I know it."

"Who is Helix, Sayen? Is it one of the Channons? The Tates?"

I shake my head. "That's not for me to share. I've told you more than I was supposed to." I bite my lip. "Because I trust you, KJ."

Kurt Junior. Son of the Were who started it all.

KJ looks like something is tearing inside of him. I wish it was something I could fix, but I know from personal experience, this is something he has to go through. Realizing this, I suddenly feel buoyed. It's only a matter of time...

Stepping back, I head toward the steps. KJ has enough to think about at the moment. His words stop me as I reach the bottom of the stairs.

"Do you trust me enough to let me go, Sayen?"

I pause before I turn around. I need to know KJ won't leave me—this cause—before I can do that. I look at him: his handsome, intelligent face, his mussed red hair, his tortured eyes making me want to stay. "I can't let you go. Not without betraying everything we've been working toward."

KJ nods, like that's what he expected me to say. "Then whatever you're feeling, Sayen, it's not what you think it is." I stare at the ceiling as he lets out a sigh. "It's important that I see the pups."

Sakari's pups. The ones that seem so drawn to Hunter and Ava. Ava's attraction is understandable. It's her gentle compassion that's always been the weakness of her people. But Hunter? Watching the two of them through the one-way mirror had felt like voyeurism—the sickly-sweet love between the two drawing me in like a child to cotton candy—but then the pups had run toward him. Clambered at the wire. Wanted to be with him.

That hadn't made sense.

And now KJ wants to be with them, too.

I narrow my eyes. "Why?"

"Those pups are the last remaining litter of arctic wolves. Sakari had a difficult pregnancy; I need to make sure they're okay."

KJ wouldn't know about the wolf pack discovered in the north of Evelyn Island. It's not something I'm going to tell him right now—there's pieces missing in what KJ's saying. "They're in the best place they could be when it comes to post-natal care, KJ. They're well looked after."

Ava and Hunter have visited them every day as they prepare to leave. It's like they're leaving their own children behind.

KJ's jaw tenses. "I need to see them."

I wait for the space of breath before I ask again. "Why?"

When KJ's fingers spear into his hair again, I know this is more than just the regular concern someone would have for a litter they've been involved in. Even if they believe it's one of the last. My jaw slackens. "What have you done to those pups, KJ?"

His fingers tense, tugging at his hair. KJ's eyes are a cyclone of frustration, regret...and pleading.

I want to go to him, but I stay where I am. I can feel we're standing on a precipice. I just told KJ about Helix. "You can trust me. Those pups are important to me, too."

He looks away. "You need to keep an eye on their growth."

I wait again. "Why?" is hanging in the room like a ripe piece of fruit waiting to be picked.

KJ glances at the door behind me. His only way out is to overpower me, or to forcefully grab the card out of my pocket. Somehow, I know he won't do either.

Which leaves him trapped for as long as we can hold him. With this basement designed as somewhere to store food for months, the walls are two feet thick. KJ isn't leaving anytime soon...

His shoulders sag in a way that has me sucking in a breath. *You can trust me...*

"There was a genetic bottleneck. I made sure those pups had the best chance of survival they could have."

I whisper the next question. "How?"

He looks away. "By introducing Were genes." Staring at the microscope that would've been very similar to the one he used to splice and dice that DNA, he squeezes his eyes shut. "You need to keep an eye on their growth rate and their development."

Air ceases to exist for long moments, and it's not because of what KJ just told me. It's why he told me.

KJ is beginning to trust me.

As happiness glows in my chest, I grip the bannister. "I'll keep a close eye on them, KJ. You won't need to worry about them."

When he doesn't answer, doesn't look at me, I head back up

the stairs, practically floating. It was obvious that wasn't easy for him to do.

But it's just the step forward we need.

I've just shut the door behind me when my phone rings. Glancing around to make sure there isn't anyone near, I slip into a nearby bedroom. Mary gave me the run of the place when I arrived here as a child. It was she who convinced her Alpha mate, John, to build the lab in the basement for me.

Keeping my voice low, I answer, "Yes?"

"Well?"

The voice on the other end is sharp with command, and it has me involuntarily straightening. "He's coming around."

"You've said that the past two days, Sayen. I'm not seeing any proof."

"I wouldn't lie about this. It's only a matter of time before KJ is one of us."

"We don't have time for your heart to rule, girl."

I duck my head, flushing. I've shown Helix over and over where my heart lies. I've done things that will stay with me forever in the name of our cause. Any feelings for KJ are a pleasant bonus.

They're proof that KJ is one of us.

I wouldn't be attracted to him if he wasn't.

I glance at the door like KJ could hear me from here, the red in my cheeks blazing even hotter. "He told me something today."

There's a pause. "This had better be good. There's been enough bad news as it is."

Furious failing to spread.

Arctic wolves gaining numbers instead of decreasing.

Humans starting to support wolves.

So much work is being threatened. All the sacrifices would've been for nothing if we don't succeed.

I pull in a breath. I know we're reaching a turning point... and we can't afford to lose.

"KJ genetically modified the pups. To increase their genetic health." I let the air whoosh out. "He used Were genes."

There's a pause, and I can imagine the slow smile the news has sparked. "Clever, clever KJ."

"He's worried about them."

"I suppose Sakari's pregnancy would be an indication whether he should be concerned."

I frown. "Should he be?"

There's a rustle outside the door, and I know I need to hang up. The order has always been to hang up the second there's a chance of being overheard. Many of the Tates support us.

It's the ones who don't we need to be careful of.

Just as I'm about to press the button, a low chuckle trickles from my cell.

"Yes. He should be."

10

HUNTER

A va looks up at me, excitement sparkling in her wintergreen eyes. "Their first solid feed."

I put the plate of wolf premix in one hand as I push open the door with the other. "Didn't you say they don't always take to it straight away?"

Ava breaks into a smile when she sees the pups are already out. Just within a couple of days they've become so much more active, their limbs starting to take on a gangly look.

I push away the uneasy feeling that always comes before Ava notices it. The pups have been nothing but normal since the moment they were born. Just like Weres, although they develop faster in utero, their growth rate is that of a normal wolf once born.

There's no reason to think these guys are going to be anything but robust wolves.

The pups leap at the fence separating us as we approach. Within a day they were just as attached to Ava as they are to me.

Ava kneels at the fence. "Dawn did a quick health check this morning. She said they ticked every box."

"That's good."

We enter through the gate, and the pups get even more excited. It was decided on the day after we arrived that these pups wouldn't be returned to the wild. Born and raised in captivity with so much human contact from birth, it was inevitable they would be too tame to be released.

Their love of Ava and I had only cemented that decision.

It means we can now enter their enclosure, sitting on the floor as they climb all over us. Sakari would always use the opportunity to disappear into her makeshift den and have ten minutes of puppy-free time.

Asta immediately starts to chew on Ava's shoe, her usual greeting. Ava smiles down at her. "It's going to be hard to leave them."

I sigh. "It is."

We leave today, off to garner support for the moratorium. A week of just Ava and me, traveling around the state, educating others. Not being here to see these guys for a couple of weeks is going to be tough, but I don't think I've ever looked forward to anything more.

The pups start to sniff the air, obviously scenting the plate in my hands. Ari leaps, showing that naming him in honor of an eagle was fitting as he gets some serious airtime, and soon Asta and Akyla are following.

My eyebrows shoot up. "I get the feeling they make take to this just fine."

As I lower the plate, they crowd in, their excitement becoming frenetic. Akyla almost knocks the plate out of my hands as I rest it on the ground. The three of them dive into the moist pile of food, little jaws gulping and gobbling the food.

"Whoa," Ava gasps. "I've never seen a first feed like that!"

As we watch in awe, the pups finish the plate, tails wagging as they lick it clean.

I try not to frown. "They must've been hungry."

The plate now spotless, three noses start to sniff around, looking for any crumbs they may have missed. Ava reaches out to stroke Akyla's snowy back, he looks up at her briefly before returning to sniffing.

An uneasy feeling is sitting heavy in my gut. Even Ava looks at me, her green eyes a little muted.

They'd seemed normal...up until now...

Their chart hangs outside on the fence, so I head out to grab it. Flipping back the pages, I note that their growth is a slow, progressive diagonal line. "They seem to be growing as expected."

Ava's shoulders relax. "That's good. They must've been hungry."

I scan a second time just to make sure. Dawn weighed them this morning and they were just where they're supposed to be on the charts. I shake my head. "I don't think the worry will ever go away."

Ava leaves the plate for the wolf pups to polish and joins me on the other side of the fence. She rests her head on my shoulder as she slips an arm around my waist. "Worrying means you care. We've spent a lot of time focused on these little lives."

I nod, knowing what Ava's saying is true. We believed that the future of arctic wolves rested on their little shoulders. Discovering a second pack has taken some of that pressure off. I pull my mate in close to my side. "I think worrying is programmed into my genes."

She squeezes my waist. "That's what protectors do."

I pull her around, the flash of pleasure as we fit into each other's planes and curves just as thrilling as the first time. "And yet you always ground me."

She gives me an impish grin. "Someone's gotta look after the protector. It's why we're such a kick-ass duo."

Tucking a finger under her chin, I bring her lips to mine. I fill the kiss with everything my heart holds—gratitude, devotion, love.

Ava takes it all, like I'm filling some beautiful well, then quickly turns it into something more. She presses in, her body flush against me, her lips against mine, and the sensations sharpen. Deepen.

And explodes into desire.

The world and its responsibilities dissolve as my mind is consumed with everything that is Ava. Her scent. Her touch. Her heart. My hands find all the places I've learned will get me the response I'm looking for; my mouth can't get enough of her. My mind is flooded with all the memories we've created together each night.

And we're about to have two weeks of only us. No house to share with her parents. No eyes watching and waiting to see what we're going to do next.

Just a guy and his gal and their forever love and its infinite passion.

When three little voices start barking, we pull apart, smiling. Ari, Asta, and Akyla have obviously decided that the plate is definitely clean, because all their attention is on us. They yip in their high, puppy way as they run up and down against the wire.

I chuckle as I kneel down. "Yep, definitely going to miss you guys. You look after your mother, okay?"

Like Sakari knew I was talking about her, she pokes her head out of the den. The pups yip even louder as they run toward their mother, their full tummies not slowing them down. Sakari looks at us for a short moment, probably thanking us for the break, before disappearing into the darkness with her brood.

Ava's giggle subsides. "It reminds me of KJ getting on the speaker every time we kissed back at Resolve."

I grin as I think of my cousin, but then the feeling dims.

Despite the short replies by text, I'm worried. Girl or no girl, I'd feel a whole lot better if he'd answer one of my calls.

Ava, perceptive as always, brushes my arm. "If what Dawn said is true, he may be nursing a wounded ego."

I sigh. "I know. KJ wouldn't fall easily or lightly for someone."

Ava smiles. "Give him a little more time before deciding to hunt him down."

"I will." I press a swift kiss on her lips. "But if I have to go looking for him, when we have all this other stuff going on, I'm not going to be nice to his beanie when I find him."

She kisses me right back. "After you bear-hug him, that is." She steps back and heads to the door. "I'm going to talk to Dad to make sure we haven't missed any key places we need to go. You okay to do the last inventory check?"

I nod. "One tent. One sleeping bag."

Ava grins. "Damn straight."

She heads down the hall as I stand in the doorway, watching as she adds a sexy sway to her natural grace. Behind me, the sound of the pups grumbling at each other as they settle down to sleep reaches me. They'll probably fall into a coma after the meal they just had.

They just gave meaning to the term "wolfed it down." This is the sort of thing I'd talk over with KJ. Pressing the speed dial button, I wait tensely as it rings. The fact that it doesn't go straight to voicemail tells me he's obviously keeping it charged.

But despite the rhythmic rings, KJ doesn't pick up.

Pulling in a deep breath to settle the uneasy feeling that's creeping up my throat, I scent someone I'd forgotten about.

Sayen.

Was she watching us through the one-way window?

I follow the faint scent trail to the back of the building. Behind a heavy door, I find her in the same place KJ called the lab of his dreams. Like all of them, it's full of grey and glass. Sayen is leaning over a microscope at the back. KJ had a thing with this girl, the one who very clearly has some serious back-off vibes going on?

I lean against the bench on my right. "The pups took to their first meal well."

Sayen doesn't look up. "Yep."

Okay, now I'm seeing some similarities between the two of them.

Rather than talking about what just happened outside, though, I decide to get to the point of why I'm really here. "Have you heard from KJ?"

There's the subtlest tensing of Sayen's neck before she reaches forward to twist something on the microscope. "No, I haven't."

"Dawn said you guys had something going on between you."

Sayen finally looks up. "She said that?"

"Yep. She thinks it may have something to do with the reason he's gone MIA."

Sayen flips her dark hair back from her face. "Nothing happened. It was never going to work out with KJ and me."

Because she's Were.

Although, KJ even thinking of falling for a Were is impressive in itself. There must be something about Sayen.

"But he left just after you had that little conversation."

"He was determined to find the wolf with Furious."

The unease spreads through my entire chest. KJ wouldn't disappear like this if he wasn't hurting about something. "He would've liked to have seen the humans rallying behind wolves."

Sayen straightens, her gaze now focused on the door behind me. She marches past, her jaw set and tense. She stops only when she has her hand on the handle. "His father wouldn't have put much stock in it."

The heavy door thumps closed behind her. Holy crap. Sayen knows who KJ's father is!

Why would KJ share that with her?

Alone in the lab, I know I have stuff to do—as long as everything goes according to plan, we leave this afternoon. But staring at the cell in my hand, I have to admit the unease isn't going away. In fact, it has me agitated...edgy.

Am I being a pessimist? Am I lacking in faith?

Shaking my head, I head out the door. What Ava and I have was born of hope. I believe in it with my whole heart and soul.

I'll try one more time...

I press the speed-dial button I've tried repeatedly for a week. If KJ doesn't start answering soon, I'm going to hunt him down myself.

The cell phone rings. Then rings again. I try to ignore the sinking feeling that he's not going to answer, when a vibrating sound carries from the open door beside me. It's another lab, smaller than the others, one that I haven't seen used. It's what's on the bench across the room that grabs my attention. *Brrr-brrr.* Each shiver on the bench matches the ringing tone playing in my ear.

Letting the phone fall to my side, I walk over slowly, hoping this is some weird coincidence. KJ would never leave his phone behind. Or if he had some brain-glitch, he wouldn't go away for a week without it.

The cell is sitting on the bench, screen brightly lit, a name flashing across the front. As I try to process what this means, it stops, just as the faint ringing tone from my phone does. It goes black for a second before lighting up again.

15 missed calls from Hunter

11

HUNTER

Ava and I stop at the top of the hill we just marched up, looking around. The vista is magnificent, I'll give it that much. There are more angles here than the tundra, less white drowning out the world. Pine trees, some still conifer green, zigzag in every direction. In the distance, giant mountains hog the horizon.

I'd sat in shock in the lab after finding KJ's phone. I knew without a doubt that he wouldn't deliberately leave it behind.

Which means, someone who has access to the center had known it was there. Hiding in plain sight. And wanting to make sure I didn't know he was missing.

I know deep in my gut, that it's Helix.

I'd sat there long enough that Ava had come looking. She probably followed the uneasy feeling like a thread and found me in the lab. My guess is, my face didn't say good news.

I'd held up the cell and she'd frowned. "No reception?"

"It's not my cell."

She'd frowned deeper, knowing she wasn't going to like the answer to her question. "Whose is it?"

"KJ's."

There and then we'd formulated a plan. We couldn't tell anyone that KJ was missing yet. To be honest, most people didn't know KJ exists. We'd delay our trip by a few days as we looked for clues.

Try to figure out who Helix is, and why they'd want KJ.

It was logical to head to the last place we knew he'd been.

Now, we're trudging through soft snow trying to find some sign of him, and one thought keeps intruding...no matter how much I try to block it...

KJ could be anywhere.

I grab a drink from my canteen as Ava does the same, enjoying the cool moisture sliding down my throat. The further we walk, the more I realize we don't know the first place to find the needle in this pine-stack.

Ava rubs her arms even though she wouldn't be cold. "For the first time in my life, the pine forests of my childhood feel too big."

As I cap it again, I look around, not liking the desperate feeling building like a scream in my chest. "And you're sure you can't feel him?"

Ava closes her eyes, trying again. She says she brings everything she knows of KJ to mind. His smiling face, his beanied head, his determined heart, and reaches out.

And just like every other time, Ava's face doesn't change.

She shakes her head. "It doesn't make sense."

My chest darkens with grief. "Maybe—"

She grasps my face and kisses me before I can finish the sentence. "I would feel it if something serious had happened to him."

She's explained that, although she can't trace him, she knows KJ's life-force is still very much alive. She could feel if it had been severed.

I pull in a breath. "Okay. I trust you."

She holds me for a second longer, making sure I mean what I say. When I grasp her face, too, and plant a longer, slower kiss, I feel her melt just a little. I pull back. "I do trust you, Ava."

She meets my gaze with a soft smile. "I trust us."

Grabbing her hand, I look at the landscape around us, knowing I've just made a decision. "Me too. Which is why I think it's time to tell some others he's missing."

"Others?"

I sigh. "We're not going to find him out here, Ava. There's nothing to track, no hints as to which direction he took. We're gonna need some help."

"I think you're right. He's Were, which means filing a missing person's report gets complicated. But we don't want this to be public knowledge."

"Maybe some members of his family can help."

Ava visibly swallows. KJ's identity has been a secret I've kept from her, although never by choice. It wasn't my truth to tell.

But things are different now. KJ is missing.

"How far away are they?"

"Well, KJ's pack is right here in Jacksonville."

Ava freezes. "What?"

I study her for a second, knowing this is big. How will Ava respond knowing KJ is the son of Kurt Channon? "His name is Kurt Junior. KJ Channon."

Her eyes widen as her hand flies to her mouth. I watch, waiting for her to process this.

Her hand falls away, and I sense as her shock dissolves, changing into something else. "Poor KJ. No wonder he's so determined to fix this."

And went to the lengths he did.

The tension abates. I should've known Ava would respond with nothing but compassion. "He hates everything his father stood for. And he hated that the Channons was synonymous with a drive for power."

"Gosh, Tara, the Channons. They looked for him for the longest time."

I shrug. "It seems when KJ decides he doesn't want to be found..."

Ava grasps my hand. "But now he *needs* to be."

I take her other one. "Damn straight."

BACK AT THE CENTER, the first person we look for is Sayen. After that, we've decided to call Tara and Mitch in, along with Ava's parents, Noah and Eden—the only people we know we can trust right now. Who knows how Tara's going to feel when she discovers her little brother is alive...and now missing? What's worse, I don't want to predict how KJ is going to feel when he discovers I told them.

Although, I'd be willing to have even that uncomfortable conversation right now if it meant he was here.

Sayen is where we'd thought she'd be—in the lab. She's leaning over something on the bench, pipette in hand. She doesn't bother to look up when we enter, but then again, her Were senses would've told her who's here.

Ava closes her eyes for the briefest of seconds, and I know she's tapping into the thread she shares with Sayen. As I lean against the bench, stopping myself from crossing my arms, I wonder what she senses...and how it ties in with our theory.

Ava moves in closer to me. "Hey, Sayen. Have you got a minute?"

Sayen looks up, brushing her hair out of her face in the process. "Sure."

I wonder if KJ ever managed to get her to smile. "We're wondering where things are at with the vaccine for Furious?"

Ava smiles. "For when we head out on the road. It would be great to add to our list of good news."

Sayen frowns. "We haven't learned anything new at this stage."

I rub my chin. "You've been working on this a long time."

Ava nods. "It would have to be so frustrating." She angles her head. "It was so important for John and Mary to do their bit."

After some members of their pack betrayed us.

Sayen shrugs. "They knew it was important to move forward after everything that happened."

I resist glancing at Ava. That's what we're here to find out.

Ava's smile grows. "And despite Mary's cooking, you're still lean, trim, and terrific. Now, that's impressive."

Sayen's lips twitch. "Luckily, it was tradition to do a walk around the ranch each morning."

Which means, Sayen would've spent a lot of time with John and Mary.

As painful as it is to acknowledge, odds are, Helix is a Were. Sure, there are humans at the center, although only a few who would have access to KJ's phone. But the majority of people here are my own kind.

First, we discover who Helix is.

Then we find KJ.

Then we discover why someone is so determined to exterminate the very animals we're connected to.

I glance around the lab. From what I've heard, they set something up like this for Sayen back at their ranch. "They sound like pretty cool people."

Sayen shrugs again. "Well, you'll probably meet them today. They said they wanted to come and see me, but I'm pretty sure they're just here to see the pups."

That has Ava and I glancing at each other. The Tates are here?

Ava quickly finds her smile again. "That's wonderful. I haven't seen them in years."

According to Ava, Mary is sweet and nurturing, while John is the strong, quiet type. Two people who dedicated their lives and money to helping wolves. Neither of which you'd expect to mastermind wolf culling, but then again, wouldn't that be the ultimate alibi?

And Sayen is a Tate.

I cock my head, suddenly curious. "How are you related to them, Sayen?"

I'd always assumed she was a granddaughter or niece considering they took her in when she was orphaned.

Sayen's shoulders tense, a response I didn't expect. "My father was a Tate."

Ava looks like she's calculating, probably sifting through the Tates she knows, trying to figure out who that would be. "He must've been close to them, too."

Which is a logical assumption seeing as John and Mary took Sayen in themselves.

Sayen glances at the door behind us and my senses go on high alert. For some reason, this line of questioning is significant. I'm about to take a few casual steps to the left to block an easy exit when a phone rings.

Sayen shrugs an apology, then pulls her cell out of her pocket. She frowns as she registers the name on the screen. "Hey, Mary."

Mary's voice trickles out, our sensitive Were hearing able to make out the words. "Hi, lovely. Just letting you know we're here."

"Great." Although Sayen's voice says anything but that.

Mary's either used to it, or doesn't seem to mind, because she continues, "We were just looking for you when we came across the pups. They're adorable!"

Sayen almost smiles as she hunches over the phone. "I know. They're growing so fast."

"Tell me about it! I could've sworn they were a few months old, not a few weeks. What are you people feeding them here?"

I stop. Ava freezes. They look a few months old?

Sayen glances at us. "Just the usual. Are they doing okay?"

"We must've caught them when they were tired. They were rather lethargic. Dawn said you'd be in the lab. We're just heading over now."

Ava and I are out the door and down the hall before Sayen responds.

My heart feels like a bass drum as I shove open the door and stumble into the room housing the pups. Ava grasps my shirt as she stops beside me.

The room is dim as the light mimics the evening outside. The pups are nowhere to be seen—obviously back in their den.

We enter the pen, and I note that unlike every other time we've visited, the pups haven't come out yet.

They always come out the moment they hear or scent us...

Squatting, I whisper their names, "Ari, Asta, Akyla." I hold out my hand, hating that it's trembling. Beside me, Ava is holding her breath. I can feel her heartbeat, thrumming as loudly and as quickly as mine.

Please let this be my worry becoming contagious.

There's a shuffle in the makeshift den, then the sound of a tiny, puppy yawn. I relax a little. They sound like they always do.

But when a nose pokes out from the darkness, it comes out higher than I expected. When the body attached to that nose follows, it's not the size it was yesterday.

My legs give out. My butt hits hard concrete.

The pups have more than doubled in size.

12

HELIX

S cience involves following a recipe.

Your ingredients are your variables.

You combine those ingredients to make a product.

There's comfort in the predictability of it. Just like knowing your sponge is going to wow the neighbors, it's satisfying to repeat a test, and getting the same outcome.

Then you experiment. You change an ingredient. Try a different variable.

It's the waiting to see what the new product will look like that's the most exciting.

The room is quiet and dark, just like I expected it to be. It's during the dark that the most interesting things happen.

Sakari is fast asleep, just as expected. Wolf plus sedative means no objections. I don't need a protective mother getting in the way.

I draw them out, one by one. Pups are harder to inject than others.

They wriggle. Their veins are far smaller and more fragile.

But the human growth hormone has made these ones placid

and sleepy as their bodies consume energy to grow. Each one barely moves as I fill their veins with liquid.

Unexpected variable—genetically engineered wolf pups. New ingredient—human growth hormone.

The result was better than I hoped—exponential growth.

Now to add the piece de resistance. As the last drop empties into the young body, my heart is thrumming.

They thought they'd win.

But war is as essential as it is inevitable. Unity can never be achieved when there are so many millions of pieces, so many not even wanting to be part of the picture. There will be nothing left of this Earth by the time someone realizes that puzzle is impossible to solve.

The solution isn't easy, but it's always been simple. So simple I thought Sayen would figure it out, but the poor soul was so desperate for a cause that she never questioned it too deeply.

It just needed someone willing to sacrifice.

The pups start to twitch, and it's nice to see at least that part is predictable. Next, will be a need to pace and move.

There's a small door that leads to the outside pen.

That pen has a gate.

It won't take long for this new variable to take effect.

Then, I sit back and wait.

13

AVA

The following morning, I curl into Hunter as we lay in bed, not sure if I'm seeking comfort or giving it. The pups yesterday...their growth had been undeniable.

And to anyone who doesn't know about the genetic engineering, it's inexplicable.

Hunter's arms tighten around me and I breathe in the scent of his skin. It's becoming so familiar, yet it has my pulse jumping every time I do it. If only we could stay in bed and enjoy this fascinating exploration we've discovered. Just like the dreams; it's something you recognize deep in your soul, and just like real life, so full of intricacies you need to experience to believe.

Hunter's chest rises with a sigh. "We'd better get up. Go see how the pups are doing."

My hand curls in, right above his heart. "Are you angry at KJ for starting this?"

I feel Hunter startle. "No. He wanted to save the arctic wolves, and we were running out of options."

I wait, letting his words sink in. If he can't be angry at KJ for doing this, then he needs to extend himself that same compassion. "This isn't your fault, Hunter."

Hunter stares at the ceiling as I listen to his heartbeat. Slow, steady, steadfast. It's like my foundation. The pulse that keeps pushing me forward. I'm not sure how I'll be if Hunter loses faith again.

His hand comes up to stroke my hair, and I doubt he's even aware he's doing it. "It certainly isn't anyone else's fault," he murmurs and my breath sucks in and stays there. "But playing the blame game isn't going to help anyone. We need to stay focused."

The air in my lungs releases as I smile, tucking my head in a little closer to the hot skin I can't get enough of. "I love you, Hunter."

His arm tightens further, its mate wrapping around me, too. "I'll always be here for you, Ava. You're my heart."

Our kiss is slow and sweet and full of sensation. When we pull back, we're both smiling, both a little raw. Our love is solid, but our future is unknown.

Downstairs, Mom and Dad are already at the table having breakfast. We join them like we have every morning, but for the first time, things are subdued. There's no chatting about what to pack, who is talking to who about the moratorium, or how Gareth is going back on Evelyn Island as he keeps an eye on the northern pack.

Instead the dominant sounds are the crunch of toast being buttered or the tinkling of spoons hitting cereal bowls.

Mom is the first to speak. "We thought we might come into the center with you this morning."

"I figured you might." Mom's a vet, and the pup's growth needs to be monitored a whole lot more closely now. "We're heading in first thing."

Dad is rubbing his lower lip. "The pups grew fast in utero, too. We're concerned."

I nod, but Hunter speaks before I get a chance.

"The truth is, Noah, these pups were altered to increase their genetic fitness." Hunter looks between my parents, and as my chest tightens at what he's about to say, I also grasp his hand, proud of my courageous mate. "The most effective way to do that was introduce Were genes."

Mom sits back, eyebrows high. "They have Were genes?"

I nod. "KJ thought he isolated our wolf DNA. The fast growth didn't seem an issue after Sakari gave birth..."

Until yesterday.

Hunter leans forward. "It was my decision to go ahead. KJ wouldn't have done it without me giving the green light."

Mom and Dad sit and blink. We wait, hands held tightly, knowing this is a lot to take in. It's strange, feeling almost protective of Hunter as we sit across from the two people who have supported me unconditionally. Surely Mom and Dad understand why KJ and Hunter made the decision they did?

Dad looks at Hunter, blue eyes calm. "So, what's this going to mean?"

Hunter holds my father's gaze. "We're not sure. These pups are important, but they're also an unknown. We'll do what needs to be done."

Mom glances at me. "Will you?"

Hunter's hand tightens around mine. I know what Mom is trying to get at. "They aren't dangerous. I can feel it."

Hunter is a part of them. They could never be dangerous.

Mom pulls in a breath as she leans back, looking over at Dad. His lips are tense, his brows low. They'd be sensing everything the other is feeling, just like Hunter and I do. I'm just too wound up to be able to tell what that is.

Dad nods, like they've reached some sort of agreement. He reaches out to grasp Mom's hand as he turns back to the two of us. "All we can do is watch and wait."

RUNNING into John and Mary Tate in the foyer of the captive breeding center isn't what we needed right now. Their smiling faces and warm hugs are a reminder that things haven't been what they seemed.

Mary pulls back to hold me at arm's length. "Look at you, Ava. So grown up now."

John and Hunter shake hands, and although Hunter is smiling, I can feel his tension.

Is one of them Helix?

Are they both?

The fact that I'm considering that these two, warm devoted Weres could be capable of such deception and cruelty, shows me how unstable the world around me has become. A few months ago, I would've trusted these people with my life.

I pull up a smile before my thoughts can show on my face. "Looking wonderful yourself, Mary. It's great to have you at the center."

"Well, that Sayen of ours barely came up from the lab back on the ranch. We figured if we didn't stop by, she'd turn thirty before we saw her again."

Mary laughs at her own joke as John shakes his head.

Hunter nods. "She's very dedicated, this granddaughter of yours."

John's chest fills with pride. "She's not our granddaughter, but she certainly is amazing. Her mother would be proud."

Hunter's brows shoot up in surprise, his acting flawless. "Oh, I'm sorry. I assumed..."

Mary flaps her hand at Hunter. "There's nothing to apologize for. Most people jump to the same conclusion, and Sayen is most certainly a Tate."

I frown just like I did when we were in the lab with Sayen yesterday, feeling like a terrible actor. "Then who's her—"

John straightens. "It sounds like someone else is on their way in."

What? I turn, Were hearing tuning into the sounds on the other side of the door. He's right. Someone else is coming up the path.

Hunter's frustration flashes through our connection. I wish I don't notice the fleeting glance between John and Mary, but I do. It was one of relief.

My heart sinks as I realize they have something they're hiding.

But there's no time to discover what they were side stepping because Mike strides through the door, coming to an abrupt halt when he finds four people before him.

He breaks into a grin, but it quickly washes away. "I thought you two were leaving yesterday."

Which is today's decision.

Do we head out, leaving the pups and their sudden growth spurt for others to look after?

Or do we stay, failing to lend our support to the moratorium?

And what about KJ? Alive...but missing.

Hunter reaches out to shake Mike's hand. "Something came up. We're looking into it today."

Mike's brow furrows. "But you're still going, aren't you? This is important, you know."

I reach out to brush his arm. "We know, Mike. We just need to check on the pups."

"If we don't get this moratorium in place, those pups won't stand a chance."

Mike's right. This moratorium is the only way we can guarantee a world that is safe for them to grow up in.

Hunter and I look at each other, sensing our thoughts

through our connection. I feel when Hunter reaches a conclusion, and I know it's the same one I just did.

"It's not cancelled, just delayed," I say with a smile. "I'd say we'll head off this afternoon."

My parents have everything they need to look after the pups. Telling them this morning was the right thing to do.

Hunter nods. "We're just making sure everything is in order."

Mary steps forward. "We'll help any way we can." She looks back at her mate for confirmation.

John crosses his arms. "Of course. The Tates have always been a part of moving forward."

Hunter tenses ever so slightly, but I doubt anyone else would have noticed.

Mike nods, obviously relieved. "I just wanted to talk to Riley, if she's about. I think we may have a lead on a local celebrity."

I smile. Riley's bubbly personality is what Mike is trying to tap into. No one can say no to that girl. "I'd say she's in one of the outer enclosures. She likes to help with the morning rounds."

Mike salutes us as he heads out the side door.

With Mike gone, Mary and John start to look like they're off too—Mary hoists her handbag, while John straightens and stretches.

I grab Hunter's hand, happy to do the same. The opportunity to talk about Sayen is gone. We're going to have to leave that for another time.

"Bye, guys. We'll have to catch up later."

Mary's round face lifts in a smile. "That would be lovely. Now you two head out and do whatever it is you need to get done. You need to say goodbye to those adorable pups."

Mary and John head to the lab and we watch them leave. If we stay, we could try and figure out who Helix is...

Hunter sighs. "We need to go."

My heart aches. Hunter must be feeling like he's leaving KJ

behind. "I know."

I suppose this is what carrying this legacy means, though—making choices that will benefit the most lives in the long-term.

The wolves need this moratorium to survive.

And if it fails, Weres aren't going to sit by and watch them go extinct.

It just sucks that it hurts so much.

We stop at the one-way mirror that looks into Sakari's enclosure, but as I expected, there's no wolves to be seen. They'd be curled up in their warm, comfortable den.

I feel Hunter's frown rather than see it. He leans in, looking more closely. "I didn't think they'd be going outside yet."

"That doesn't happen for another few days."

Then I see what Hunter sees. The sliding door, just high enough for a full-grown wolf to pass through, is open. Sunlight streams through in beckoning beams.

I try not to feel alarmed as we rush in. Maybe someone made the call because the pups are bigger, and they needed more space.

We don't bother to check the den. There's no way a wolf will choose to be indoors after being cooped up for so long.

Hunter's out the door first.

This outside pen isn't very big. It's designed to let pregnant wolves have some time outside to exercise, but also to keep them within sight.

Except there's no wolves to be seen.

I gasp, frantic as I scan again.

The relief at finding Sakari, curled in the snow beside the door is overwhelming.

And short-lived.

She doesn't look up as we stand there. Her head is resting on her paws, staring at the opposite end of the pen.

Where the gate stands open.

14

AVA

D ad hoists his backpack as he pushes up from a squat. He rubs the wet soil between his fingertips as he stares into the forest. "They've stayed together."

Discovering the pups missing had been a wrecking ball to the chest.

Knowing someone had released them on purpose completed the demolition.

But there was no time to ask questions. The pups had to be found.

Hunter is scanning the trees, hoping like all of us that they decided to frolic in the snow nearby. "They can't have gone far."

They left sometime during the night, and it's still morning. I'd immediately called my parents, knowing we need to find those pups. And quickly.

I close my eyes, pulling in a lungful of cold air. "I'll be able to find them."

Drawing deep into myself, I pull up the image of Ari, Asta, and Akyla. Their precious white bodies, their puppy enthusiasm, their deep love for Sakari. Hunter's energy is there too, but so is the energy that lives in every sentient being. That's the energy that draws out from me, a gossamer thread, and arches into the forest.

"They've gone—"

"East." My dad finishes for me.

We look at each other and smile. His tracking skills, and my gift, both coming up with the same conclusion.

Mom shakes her head. "You two…"

We'd play a game sometimes when we were out in the reserve, when we were out searching for wolves. Dad would track, I'd seek out the threads. We always found the wolves quicker than anyone else could.

Now it's time to use those skills again.

Within an hour, we're deep in the snow-covered forest. The zigzagging line in the snow they left early on has petered out, either crisscrossed by other wild animals, but mostly covered by a new blanket of snow.

Not that it slowed us down. Dad would crouch periodically, bend over to inspect the odd print, the finest of twigs that's been snapped. For me, the threads were always there, braiding through the trees, leading us straight to them.

No one talks the whole time. We're all focused. All worried. The day is drawing on and we haven't caught up to them.

Hunter scans the brown trunks around us. "They've certainly made some ground."

I can feel his tension mirroring mine. We never thought they'd get this far or that we'd be trekking this long.

Mom rests her hands on Dad's arm. "Noah, they're just pups. They should've had to rest by now."

"I know. But I haven't seen any sign of that."

Hunter and I exchange a look. The pups are growing rapidly. Who knows what else is changing for them?

I hoist my backpack a little higher. "Then we can't stop, either."

Dad nods, the movement short and sharp. "Let's get our bearings and keep going."

I don't need to close my eyes anymore to connect with the threads, the golden line of energy is so vivid I don't know how anyone else can't see them. "They've angled to the north."

Hunter grasps my hand as we all start walking again. "They'll have to tire sooner rather than later."

We've only been trekking for about ten minutes when Dad stops, staring down. We've come close to a river, the icy water gurgling over rocks and between trees. He crouches, fingers touching the soil between his feet. "Eden."

I stop, frowning. "What?"

Mom leans over, her hand resting on Dad's shoulder. "The tracks." She looks up at me, the green eyes I inherited framed with tension. "We've been following the wrong wolves."

Hunter strides forward. "What do you mean?"

Dad stands as Mom points at the depression in the wet soil by his feet. "The prints are too big. These belong to an adolescent wolf. The pups are growing fast, but they're not on steroids."

I stay where I am. Could I have tapped into the threads of some wild wolves out here? Maybe ones who were released from the center, meaning I have a pre-existing connection with them?

But I'm already shaking my head, rejecting the question I never voiced. I know these pups. I know their energy.

And I know Hunter's energy. It's a force of spirit that I'll always be able to find.

"It's the right wolves, Dad. I haven't got it wrong."

Everyone stills, but it's Hunter that I tap into. If I'm saying that we've got the right wolves, then I'm saying that they've grown even more. And in a very short period of time.

Ari, Asta, and Akyla no longer look like pups nor are they behaving like pups.

Hunter's copper gaze traps my own. "You're sure?"

I nod, my throat tight.

Hunter looks at Mom and Dad. "Then we need to find them. We can't afford to keep going at this pace."

He's talking about shifting. I step up beside my mate. "He's right. We'll reach them faster."

Dad looks around and I know he's assessing how deep we are in the woods. The pups have been heading deeper and deeper into the reserve, and we haven't seen a human the whole time we've been trekking.

"Eyes and ears open, okay?" He looks at all three of us. "We can't afford to be sighted with the moratorium going to the senate."

A Were sighting would be the death knell for Mike's campaign. No one would believe a giant wolf could be safe at the moment. The fear frenzy that we narrowly avoided would be inevitable.

The metallic scent that heralds our shift has adrenalin spiking through my system. I let the change sweep through me, feeling parts explode on an exhale, others implode as I inhale. The transformation is quick, so natural, it feels like I've been doing it for years.

When I open my eyes a second later, I'm faced with two massive bodies. Both white, both tall and proud, but both so different.

Dad is an ivory pearl, the wisdom that raised me. Hunter is a frosted diamond, the strength that is my future.

Mom leaps onto her mate's back as Hunter and I take the lead. Our connection, so powerful even before we met, has been nothing but magic since we bonded. We move like a heartbeat—automatically synchronizing, unconsciously in rhythm.

Through the pines, hugging the edges of any clearings, I follow the thread, Hunter beside me. I can feel as we get close, and I amplify the burst of excitement so Hunter can feel it as well. Not long now and the wolf triplets will be in sight.

Hunter senses it first, because I feel his alarm. A blink later, and he shoots in front of me.

Then I smell it, too.

It's the unmistakable, unforgettable scent of blood.

Like we just hit a wall, we all come to a stop. The coppery bouquet gets stronger, the tang hitting the back of your throat. It's not only blood, but a lot of blood.

The trembling starts deep in my marrow as Hunter contracts in closer to me. My mother and father are on my other side in an instant.

Up ahead, the trees are slowly dispersing, the sunlight getting stronger. There's a clearing. And something has died in it.

Without saying a word, we all shift back to human. My throat works as I remember all the deaths we've seen thanks to poachers.

Please don't let it be the pups. Please...

Hunter's hand is a band around mine, and I doubt he realizes how much he's helping me hold it together. I don't want to see what's in the clearing. Severed threads always feel like they've been sliced from my own spirit.

Hunter tightens his hold and I know what he's suggesting, and for the first time, I'm grateful for it. He's not offering for me to sit this out because he thinks I can't handle it. He's offering because he knows how much it takes from me.

Which gives me the strength to do it.

The walk toward the clearing is punctuated with pauses as we listen and scan. The poachers could still be here. If it's wolves they've shot, then their pelts are what they're after.

But there's no sound beyond the natural rhythm of the forest, no scent diluting the sickening tang of blood.

I brace every muscle in my body as we reach the last line of trees. As much as I wish I hadn't, I've smelled wolf blood enough times to be able to recognize it. The sharpening scent of red in the air strikes me. It's different.

There are dead bodies ahead, but they aren't the bodies of wolves.

It's a big clearing, easily the size of a sports oval, and the snow had piled up high over much of it. What's been left behind has altered the landscape. Fear has trampled it. Violence has churned it up.

The puff of white is a testament to my gasp. Hunter grabs me as split second before my knees give out.

Mom's hand is on her mouth, only slightly muffling the cry that escapes.

The clearing is littered with the bodies of elk. At least thirty. Blood has melted the snow, leaving a gruesome patchwork of virgin white and flattened red.

Dad puts up his hand, telling us to stay put, as he walks cautiously into the clearing. His back is tight with grief as he kneels beside the closest elk.

Mom's arms are curled around her. "Noah?"

Dad's head falls back, his closed eyes staring at the sky. "They were slaughtered." His hands fist. "By wolves."

Hunter tenses, and I'm glad he doesn't walk over, even though I can feel he wants to. Right now, I need a set of legs to hold me up. "Wolves don't kill indiscriminately."

Dad's eyes finally open, and they're a deep blue filled with pain. "Wolves have been doing a lot of stuff they wouldn't normally do recently." He looks at the carnage around him. "More than one animal did this, and it was certainly a predator."

Very few animals at the top of the pecking order around here work as packs. Bears don't, other apex predators are highly reclusive. It's what's given wolves a natural advantage, made them more prolific, and therefore more of a threat to humans.

It also means it's undeniable that a pack of wolves are at the heart of this bloodbath.

Mom bites her lip. "Which leaves us with three options. One, a pack of wolves has gone rogue. Two, several wolves are now affected by Furious." Her eyes develop a sheen as she looks at Hunter and me. "Or the pups did this."

Because they've been genetically altered.

I lock my knees as the words slam through me. I want to shout a denial. There can't be any more wolf deaths. Furious can't be back.

Ari, Asta, and Akyla aren't violent or aggressive.

But the scent of red, the thick, coagulated maroon, the garish claret, can't be escaped. Even when you close your eyes and turn your head away.

I feel Hunter reach the decision I didn't want him to have to even consider. If the triplet pups show signs of being anything apart from wolf, they can't exist. They'd have to be destroyed.

And Hunter's had to make enough tough choices as it is. He carries the responsibility of every wolf he's known and cared for and lost, whether it's justified or not. I can't bear the thought of him having to live with the decision to end the three precious lives he's fought so hard for.

But he makes it anyway. I can feel it in the way his angles harden, in the way his soul aches.

He brushes a kiss on my hair before releasing me. "We're going to have to go back and get some help. We need to find the wolves who did this...before anything else can happen."

Mom's eyes soften with compassion as she nods. She knows what Hunter is saying. Dad walks over so he can grasp Hunter's shoulder. I know that look he's holding; I've seen it many times before.

Except this time, he's not looking at me with pride. His chest fills with it. "With a heart like that, Hunter, I can see why she chose you."

Hunter blinks and a glimmer of smile sparks in my chest.

With a squeeze to emphasize his words, Dad drops his hand. He looks over at Mom. "You're right. With these two, anything is possible."

All business, he strides back toward the trees. "The highway isn't far from here. I'll call Mitch, and he can meet us there."

Hunter looks down at me, trying to get the bemusement under control. His lips twitch. "I can see where you get your optimism from."

My smile gains life. "I've never been able to tell if it was nature or nurture."

Mom walks past, her hand brushing my arm. "We learned the hard way so you wouldn't have to."

The walk to the highway is due west and we hike at a determined pace. The urgency of what this means, the swathes of snow don't slow us down, and the beauty of Mother Nature goes unnoticed. We need to find those wolves before humans do.

When we finally come across the highway, we start heading toward Jacksonville.

When I first hear a car, I stop and turn, glad Uncle Mitch has found us quickly. He told Dad he'd bring a search team, those familiar with tracking wolves, but also those that can be trusted.

Dad made sure Mitch brought a vet pack. Those black bags contain the tranquilizer guns.

But also, the medication used to euthanize animals...

Except the car coming at us isn't a familiar truck, and it's barreling down the road like it's trying to break a land-speed record.

The blue sedan peaks on a rise, then bottoms out on the other side. Despite the jarring landing, the car only accelerates as it heads down the straight. Great. Rev-heads out in the reserve isn't what we need right now.

We all step back, giving the highway a wide berth. Once these people with a death wish zoom by, we'll get back on and take a break from trudging through the snow.

As the car approaches, it suddenly brakes. My guess is the driver's seen us. We all pull in a little closer, contracting like a muscle. We don't have time for anyone wanting to make trouble.

The driver must brake hard, because the car screeches and fishtails to a halt only feet away. Hunter steps in front of me, his tense body my armor. Before I can blink, Dad is beside him, Mom right next to me.

The front doors are thrown open as two men jump out and race toward us.

The eldest of the two reach us first, his eyes wide with panic. He gestures at us frantically to come to him. "You need to get in the car. Right now!"

What is going on? I can feel their alarm, see it in the trembling of the younger man's hands. I glance over Hunter's shoulder, but there's no one behind them.

Hunter and Dad cross their arms simultaneously, their shoulders a wall before me.

Dad frowns. "Let's settle down here."

"And explain what's going on," Hunter adds.

The young man steps forward, his hands out pleading. "No, you don't understand. Your lives depend on it."

I quietly step around, coming up beside Hunter. These people are scared. Really scared.

Everyone else must sense it, too, because their alarm quickly morphs to concern. I look at them a little more closely, trying to see if they're hurt. "Are you okay? Is there anything else we can do?"

The older man throws his hands up in the air. "You can get

in the bloody car, people! I ain't risking my son's life another second if you don't."

Dad steps forward. "Who's after you? Maybe we can help."

Both men spin around like Dad's words can conjure whatever it is they're so frightened of. Mom steps up beside me, her brow furrowed with concern.

The younger man takes a step backward. "It ain't a who. And if you guys have a death wish, then it ain't no skin off our nose."

Hunter reaches out a hand. "Wait! Our car isn't far away, we'll be fine. But what are you running away from?"

The men glance at each other, then over their shoulders again. The younger one speaks first. "We were bird-watching in the reserve when we were attacked."

My breath freezes in my chest. Attacked?

The older man nods. "Luckily they came upon us as we were heading back to the car. We almost didn't make it."

Mom frowns. "They?"

"Weren't too happy that we locked ourselves in, either. Freaking things went at the car, they did."

I'm about to repeat Mom's question when Hunter strides forward, heading straight to the car. The men's eyes widen at the sudden movement, but they quickly follow him.

Hunter is scanning the car as he walks around it. When he comes to the driver's side, he stops. My heart feels like it's jammed itself in the back of my throat as I watch his face.

He holds still for long seconds before reaching out to trace something on the side of the car. "It can't be..."

I walk over, my parents right behind me, knowing I don't want to see whatever it is. The sight hits me before I reach Hunter and I have to stifle my gasp. Sweet saints...

Three long gashes have been etched into the side of the car. The blue paint is gone, exposing a thin line of metal beneath.

The contrast of blue to silver is striking: three horizontal gashes that look like Godzilla took a swipe at the door.

"What animal did this?" Dad's voice is full of dread.

The younger man jams his fingers through his hair. "They were wolves."

"But bloody big wolves. Three of them."

Hunter swallows. "What color were they?"

The men seem to realize the question is significant because they glance at each other. The older man scratches his head. "Couldn't miss 'em. I reckon it's the only thing that saved us. They were white."

15

KJ

T he moment I retested Achak's blood was the moment I knew everything changed.

There hadn't seemed much point considering how many times we ran it through the testing gauntlet back on Evelyn Island. But when you've been locked away in a basement, lab or no lab, things get boring. I'd tested every other sample, all more than once, looking at basic metabolic status, done blood cultures, even ascertained mean hemoglobin levels just for fun.

And found nothing.

All of a sudden, the thought of retesting blood you've already analyzed more times than the Channon name has been dragged through the mud doesn't seem like a bad idea.

The instant I'd adjusted the focus and the cells came into sharp relief, I knew.

The pieces had fallen into position one by one, clicking into place.

I know who Helix is.

So as Sayen comes down those stairs for our daily chat, I know what I need to do. My world has shifted on its axis, and it's time to right it again.

I've come to look forward to her smile as she reaches the bottom of the stairs. It's never big, barely lasts a second, but is always transfixing. There's a flash of joy, a slice of sassy, a hint of vulnerability. It's been so hard to hide the effect it has on me.

It's nice to know I no longer have to.

When it sparks, glows, then dies, I step forward, rather than hanging back, pretending microscopes are my meagre defense. Sayen's eyes widen just a tad. She's noticed the change in routine.

I hold out my hand. "I want to know more about what you're trying to do."

Sayen stills like I just turned her to stone. Another step and I'm right in front of her. "I think I'm beginning to understand."

Suspicion flits across her face, just as I expected it would. She wouldn't be my Sayen if it hadn't.

It shows she's smart.

She glances around the lab, like maybe I've planted a booby trap. "Why the change?"

I head back to the microscope, the slide that showed me the light still resting there. "I didn't say I'm heading to the dark side, just that I'm curious about it."

Sayen heads to her usual stool, the one on the other side of the bench, and sits. She clasps her hands and I realize why— they're trembling. "What did you want to know?"

I pull up the stool across from her, excitement bubbling in my belly. Answers are what I've been looking for...for a very long time. "Why?"

Sayen arches a brow. "Of all the questions, Kurt Junior Channon...I had a feeling you'd go straight to the heart of it."

I grit my teeth at the use of my full name but then relax, recognizing it as the reflexive action it is. It's time to start facing my past. "It's every scientist's reason for breathing, isn't it?"

Sayen seems to soften, her shoulders loosening up. "It's your fearlessness that first drew me to you, KJ. If you had a question, you were willing to find a solution."

It's my turn to arch a brow. "You're stalling, gorgeous girl."

I must admit, I like the subtle blush that blooms across Sayen's cheeks at my endearment. It reminds me why I'm doing this.

"It's hard to know where to start, okay?" She glances around the room, and I can see the wheels-of-Sayen churning as she chews her lip. "When your father failed, we learned some important lessons."

Didn't we all.

"Those of us who could see we were turning our backs on everything that Weres stand for knew we needed to think this through." She makes sure she's caught my gaze. "To decide how far we were willing to go."

I nod. This much I've already figured out. "You knew that there were bigger sacrifices to be made."

Sayen pulls in a breath, something kindling in her eyes. "Your father failed because he was thinking of himself. Power for the sake of power."

I nod. What she's saying is true.

"My father, too."

Daniel Tate. Kurt's right-hand man, probably more of a lackey. He died just like my father did when their entire plan to dominate humans fell apart. But Sayen's confession surprises me. I thought she was doing this so they could give that plan another red-hot go.

She leans forward. "It's more than just wolves dying, KJ. It's much bigger than that."

Bigger?

Her hands reach out and grasp mine. They're warm and soft and sure. "What if we could make sure all wolves would be safe? That all living things would be protected?"

Sayen's touch is flooding my circuits. I can feel myself getting pulled along by her momentum. I try to blink it away. "Sounds like utopia to me. One you'll find in a book along with unicorns waltzing along rainbows."

"And when did we stop shooting for the stars, huh? What we were doing, if you can call it 'doing,' wasn't working. I saw it on the reserve with my mother. I saw it at the ranch. Humans wanting, taking, killing." Her hands tense around mine. "And no one was stopping them."

I try to pull in a breath only to find a band around my chest. Is it there because of the enormity of what Sayen's suggesting? Or is it there because I can relate to everything she just said?

Sayen's either noticed the crack in my armor, or she's getting caught up in her own passion, because her eyes blaze again. "We were running around putting Care Bear band-aids on wounds that are the size of this continent."

I've learned that passion is always based on a foundation of truth. My drive to save the arctic wolves, and to go as far as modifying their genetic makeup, was based on the truth that they're slowly, irreversibly going extinct.

Sayen's drive is based on the truth that a lot is going wrong in our world.

And Weres need to be part of the solution.

I frown, confused at the turn my thoughts have just taken. "So, we've covered the 'why.' What about the 'how'?"

Sayen pulls back, her hands retreating across the bench. As they cross again, I get the sense that's not an answer I'll be getting today. Not ready to give up, I stand. Sayen's eyes widen as she watches me walk around the bench and come to sit beside her. It's nice to give in to the constant urge to be close to her.

"Why pay to cull wolves?"

Sayen stares at me but doesn't answer. I'm missing something.

Sayen's been talking of sacrificing a few for the many. But how does culling wolves help anyone?

Lightning streaks down my spine as the answer hits me. "You want to show what humans will do for greed."

She nods, her eyes solemn.

Sweet Weres above. "Helix has done it all. The culling." I blink, almost wishing I could wipe away the knowledge that just became a part of me. "Furious."

"We needed to show what humans will do when they're scared."

My lungs feel like they've halved in capacity. "You want to make Weres angry."

Sayen's eyes flash with anger. "And finally trigger action."

I finally collapse, all this becoming too much. Sayen is talking about sparking a war.

A war that started with my father.

A war that Weres will inevitably win.

For some reason, Sayen's gaze slips away as she stares at her hands, now a tight ball in her lap.

I reach out, tipping up her chin. Her skin is smooth and pale, her pulse like a hummingbird just beneath it. "Sayen?"

When her gaze reaches mine, my own heart rate spikes and stabilizes somewhere in the stratosphere. Sayen's eyes are a mesmerizing vortex of confusion. She believes what she's saying, but it frightens her. She wants me closer, but...she's scared.

Giving in to what my heart's been longing for, I lean in. This has scared me from the minute I met Sayen, but it hasn't stopped me yet.

When she pushes forward and presses her lips against mine, I discover it ain't stopping her, either.

After that, all thinking stops.

Heat. Hunger. Hope. They all start and end with Sayen. I

stand and pull her to me, starved for more. Soft meets hard. Desire meets its mate.

Her arms wrapping around me tell me one last thing.

I'm home.

I pull back, shocked at the revelation.

Sayen smiles, her lips marked by our kiss.

The shock evaporates. I know it's true.

And it only reinforces that the choice I've made is right.

I relax my arms but don't let go. There's one thing more I need to know. Something I should've asked myself before I started messing around with wolf DNA. "How far is too far?"

Sayen slips her arms from my shoulders and pulls away. She heads for the stairs, and I wonder if I went too far.

She pauses, her hand on the bannister as she looks back at me. "How many deaths are too many lives lost, KJ?"

Her words slot into the space between us, and I know it's my last chance to make a different choice.

But Sayen's words, whether they're hers or Helix's, are true. The death toll needs to stop.

I take a step, then stop. I've made my decision. "I want to help. I can create a vaccine for Furious." I swallow. "For those who need to be protected."

Sayen's smile is like a star being born. It's all cosmic light and pure fusion. It tugs a grin right out of me.

Sayen heads up the stairs, looking like I just gave her a precious gift. I feel like I just received one myself, to be honest.

I rush to the stairs as one last question hits me. There's a last piece of the puzzle I haven't figured out. "You're close to Helix, aren't you?"

Sayen stops at the top of the stairs, her hand on the door. She looks like she's weighing on her answer. When her smile returns, so does my heartbeat. I can freely admit seeing Sayens' smiles are something I'll never get tired of.

She pulls open the door and I figure she's not going to answer me. Maybe she wants to leave on a note of mystery or something.

But just as she steps through, she speaks, the words staying behind long after she's shut the door.

"Of course I am. Helix raised me."

16

HUNTER

T he others arrived not long after the two men drove away. They didn't believe we were perfectly capable of looking after ourselves, but they weren't willing to wait around and convince us otherwise. Their fear stayed behind far longer than the smell of burnt rubber after they peeled away.

Even though it was only a few minutes between one vehicle leaving and another arriving, it felt like a long time. Too long.

I needed a distraction from the thoughts hammering to be acknowledged. They were more like battering rams trying to crush my skull. Instead, I channel my inner KJ and count the endless trunks as we continue striding down the highway. I can't afford guilt to cloud my judgment right now.

There'll be plenty of time for that later.

I need to feel like I'm doing something to fix this before someone gets hurt.

When Mitch and Tara arrive, they've brought backup. Mike and his two friends, Turkey and Brick, climb out of the Channon truck. I want to frown, wondering why having humans here seemed like a good idea, but I school my face. My guess is their hunting skills have made them expert trackers, too.

The greetings are short and brusque. Everyone knows we need to get moving.

Mike crosses his arms. "So, what's the plan?"

Noah glances at me, but I simply nod back. As a local cop, search and rescue is far more his forte than mine.

Noah's eyes narrow in acknowledgment before turning back to the others. "We have three arctic wolves who need to be returned to the center." There's a round of shuffles, but I know there's more to tell. If Noah doesn't, I will. "Two birdwatchers are saying they were attacked, so we don't know what we're dealing with here." He takes extra time looking at Mike and the other two. "Extreme caution is necessary."

I clear my throat. "As are all measures necessary to neutralize any potential threat."

I feel Ava's gasp even though she doesn't move, and it's like a dart in my chest. Ava's belief that these pups are good is looking flimsier and flimsier. Noah realizes, just as Eden would. We're dealing with never-seen-before genetically modified wolves. Who knows, maybe it's my DNA that's making them this way.

As that last thought slinks into my consciousness, Ava's hand wraps around mine. I feel her love through our connection, clear and true, and I tenderly return the message. It reminds me that so much of this puzzle is held together by the most impossible, amazing connection I've ever experienced.

Ava frowns as her eyes become unfocused. It only takes a second, because she blinks, looking back at me. "They've changed direction." Ava spins around, looking back down the highway in the direction the others arrived. "They're heading south."

That galvanizes everyone into action. The wolves are heading back.

Noah points at the truck. "Mike, you take Tom and Jimmy,"

Huh, they have names, "And head back to the center. We need you to patrol the perimeter."

Tara's hands look like small balls of iron. "We won't let them get that close, but we need a safety net."

Mike does his salute and they head back to the truck. "Keep us posted if they breach the line."

He means if they get past us. We all turn and head for the trees.

That won't be happening.

The truck roars away as we blend into the shadowy pines. We all turn to Ava, waiting to see where we head next.

She closes her eyes to get her bearings and I can tell when she finds them. There's a softening as she connects with them, but also a slight furrow of concern. Ava loves these wolves, but they're also worrying her.

Well, they're more than worrying me.

Suddenly, a frown blooms across Ava's beautiful face and her eyes fly open. She grasps my hand. "There's someone else here, not far away."

For Ava to recognize them, they'd have to be someone she knows. "Not Mike and the others?"

She shakes her head. "This person is in the woods." Her eyes widen, and her gaze shoots to the trees. "It's Alistair."

Shit. "And I doubt he's alone." Alistair has always had the buffer of others.

Eden gasps as her hand flies to her mouth. It's a sound that has a vice clamping around my chest. Her hand drops, her eyes wide with worry. "The protestors. They said they were going to Elkhorn Flat, to build a memorial for the family."

Noah's face hardens. "Elkhorn Flats are due south of the wolves."

Which means, we now have two locations they could be heading to. Two places we need to protect.

"We find the humans," I growl. "Two of us stay behind to provide protection," I glance at Tara and Mitch who nod in agreement, "then the rest of us head to the center."

The center is the place they're most likely to head—home.

We shift and run as wolves for as long as we can, pounding through the forest, layering speed onto speed. But returning to human comes all too soon, even though we're still some distance from Elkhorn. We can't afford to be seen, especially if Alistair is in the area.

The moment we change back to human, Ava turns to me. "The triplets. They're not far away."

Just as Ava finishes, the sound of human chatter wafts over our sensitive Were hearing. Dread wraps around my throat. It's almost like the wolves are heading straight for these people.

We run, six bodies ducking branches, flying over logs. I know that this is probably an overreaction, that the worst that's probably going to happen is Alistair being deeply unimpressed with the company of people from the center, but I don't slow down.

The risk is small, but if the pups find these humans, the ones who want their kind dead, then the impact is going to be significant.

Ava and I were supposed to be supporting this moratorium, not undermining it.

Alistair's voice reaches me, telling me we're almost there. "That's it, guys, just hold it there."

They don't see us when we first breach the trees. The area where the family was massacred by a wolf with Furious is open and clear. The police tape is long gone, as is the media frenzy.

Which is exactly why Alistair is here.

We stand in a line, chests heaving as we try to get our breathing under control. There's only a handful of protestors, all people I recognize from the center. They're standing around as one of them digs a hole. Beside them, is a large potted plant.

Eden narrows her eyes as she peers at it. "Is that an olive tree?"

Alistair is standing back, his phone pointed at the hole being dug. "An olive tree, people. A symbol of peace. That's what was shattered when a wolf attacked the Williams family, and it's what we will restore again when wolves are exterminated."

Noah snorts. "By planting a non-native species in a reserve."

Mitch scans the trees, then looks to his mate. "Tara, I say we head around the other side and keep low."

Tara smiles at him. "Not just a pretty face, huh? We'll take the vet pack."

With a quick wink, he grabs her hand and they disappear into the gloom. It's a smart idea. No sense in freaking Alistair out if the pups are just cruising past.

Ava frowns as she stills. I can sense her disbelief as her gaze lifts to mine. "The pups aren't far away."

I want to tell her to stay back. I want to tell her it's probably going to be nothing. "We need to be careful."

Ava starts walking toward the protestors digging their hole, her face resolute. I'm instantly by her side, her parents flanking us.

Alistair looks up with a smile on his face, obviously expecting more recruits, swinging his phone around to capture this happy moment. When he registers who we are, his smile flops like a dead fish. "Interesting, folks. Those who would oppose this statement of support for those who lost their lives have just arrived."

Ava and I stop, and even though I want to cross my arms, I don't. Ava shakes her head. "Any loss of life is tragic."

Noah and Eden head right, moving to stand behind the

protestors just as Alistair turns the camera back to his friends, who are now standing still, looking unsure.

Alistair frowns. "Looks like a boycott to me."

I grind my teeth. Alistair has no idea a line of defense is being set up around him. "Only someone who's looking for trouble would jump to that conclusion."

His shoulders stiffen. My guess is that recording is live, and Alistair would be aware that everything is being streamed. It's in his best interest to not look antagonistic. He glances above his phone at the people who are supposed to be planting that darned olive tree. "Okay, guys, let's show our tens of thousands of followers around the world what peace is going to mean."

The protestors glance at each other, but then pick up where they left off. The hole seems to be excavated, because two of them turn to the potted olive tree. Hopefully this means they'll be finishing soon and heading off.

The freckle-faced woman has just pulled the tree out of its plastic pot when Ava stiffens. Instantly, I'm on high alert.

She reaches out to grab my hand as her head angles to the trees across from us. "They're here," she breathes, just as three hulking bodies burst from the army of tree trunks on the other side of the clearing.

It takes a second for me to register what I'm seeing. I knew the pups would've grown, but I can no longer call them pups.

Three adult wolves stand yards away, and if it wasn't for their snow-white fur, I wouldn't believe they were the fragile little lives we were playing with only days ago.

They've grown so fast...

Although I don't take my eyes off them, it's obvious when the humans register them, too. There're one or two gasps, even a short cry. It's when Alistair squeaks that I know this isn't going to be good.

"Sweet lord, there're wolves here!"

Ari, Asta, and Akyla haven't moved, their chests heaving from their run, their tails high. There's no menace in their stance, but they're not relaxed, either. Their canine eyes scan the people before them, then stop when they come to Ava and me. They hold there, one by one, their heads coming up.

This is our chance.

Ava's always talking about the power of connection—this is how we prove its strength.

We step forward simultaneously, an unspoken agreement already reached. We'll calm these wolves; we'll lead them away. The greatest irony is that Alistair's phone will show the world these animals aren't dangerous.

The triplet's ears perk forward as they see us approach. I'm hyper-alert for any sign of how they're feeling. A tail wag of welcome.

The slightest snarl telling us to back off.

The wolves don't move, and I can feel Ava reaching out to them. It's like a conduit that thickens by the second. It feels like if you give it enough time, we'd all become part of this thread.

Except there's no time. Akyla steps forward, the eldest and the biggest, but then stops.

"He's not sure," Ava whispers.

Not sure of what?

I crouch down, making my presence less of a threat. "Hey, guys, we've been looking everywhere for you."

Asta cocks her head, her bright eyes pinned on me. Something seems to be trembling through her body.

"That's it, girl," I murmur. "We just don't want to freak these humans out, that's all."

There's a shuffle of movement behind us. "Viewers, could these be the same wolves who attacked the Williams family? Have we just risked our lives fighting for the very peace they make impossible?"

Alistair's voice is laced with fear.

Anger flashes like a lit match and I grit my teeth. These wolves have done nothing to give him that impression.

I hear Noah behind me. "Everyone stay still. This is all under control."

Alistair's scoff is loud and sharp, and the wolves startle. "Don't tell us we're safe, fool." His voice rises, driven by panic, but full of fury. "These animals are killers!"

Alistair's final word is like the trigger on a gun. Three white bodies shoot forward, bullets of speed that sweep straight past us.

"No!" Ava's cry is so full of anguish, it tears at my heart.

None of the wolves stop. Their heads low between their shoulders, I don't know if they can hear her over their growls. The rumbles pouring from these animals are full of nothing but rage.

The humans scatter, screams reaching up to the trees, as they frantically look for safety. One heads for the trees. The freckle-faced woman streaks for the path that leads back to the parking lot. Alistair, eye's wide with panic, runs to a nearby picnic table and clambers underneath.

The three wolves divide, two streaming out to the side as Akyla powers forward. I reach out as he races past me, having no idea what I'm trying to achieve, only to jerk back when a shiny set of teeth snap at my fingers. Akyla glares at me, eyes wild and feral, never breaking his gait.

He's coursing with anger.

He's heading to the humans.

Surely not...

Shit.

Ava races to my side. "I can stop them."

Simultaneously, we're running, just like Noah and Eden are. They move in on Ari, Asta is closest to us, but it's Akyla that has size on his side. There's a click from the pines, and I see Tara and Mitch standing at the tree line. The vet pack is open, the tranquilizer gun being loaded.

I point to Akyla. "Take him out first," I shout.

A nod from Tara is all I need before we focus back on Asta.

I have two goals: Stop the wolves. Keep Ava safe.

Asta has gone right, following the freckle-faced lady as she runs toward the path. She trips once, scrabbles as she refuses to lose momentum, and then rights herself. I streak across, aiming to cut Asta off. There're only a few seconds of running with my heart in my throat before I crash into her.

My shoulder screams as we collide midair. Asta yelps as she's propelled to the side, my body following hers. We hit the ground and I never see the snapping jaws coming.

I curl in, tucking my arms around my head, as we jolt and jar across the ground. Growling with rage, Asta tears at my shirt, narrowly missing my chest. I never expected her to attack me.

We slide to a stop and I'm on my feet in an instant, spinning around to face her. Asta is already upright, head low, teeth bared.

Ava dashes in front of me. "Asta, it's okay."

Chest heaving, shirt torn, and shoulder aching, I move up beside her. There's no way Ava is standing between me and this rabid animal.

Rabid...

It's then that I see it. The fine sheen of foam slicked across Asta's teeth.

Ava steps forward and my heart rate skyrockets. She puts her hand out. "You would never hurt Hunter."

I feel the belief in Ava's words, but the slash of cold across my chest tells me otherwise. I balance on the balls of my feet, unsure what to do. Do I trust Ava, or do I do what's going to break my heart, and that's end Asta's future?

Ava's hand comes up behind her, telling me to stop. She keeps her gaze on the wolf with violence in her eyes. "She just needs a little time."

I already know the answer. My role has always been to protect Ava. To be the armor for her soft, compassionate soul. To make the unforgivable decisions so she won't have to.

"Help!" The high-pitched scream seems to pierce my eardrums. "Help!"

Alistair's voice is full of hysteria, powered by the conviction he's about to die. I turn, only planning on glancing for a second, discovering that he's probably right.

Alistair is cowering beneath the picnic table, arms raised in protection, that darned phone still in his hand. Akyla, who was prowling like the predator he is a second ago, shoots forward and snaps at him. Alistair jerks backward, dropping the phone, trembling violently. "He's trying to kill me!"

Too much is happening at once. Noah and Eden stand before a growling Ari, who's staring single-mindedly at the protestors behind them. Asta has yet to show any sign of releasing the tension coiled through her body.

Akyla snaps at Alistair again, and it's then that I see the two feathered tranquilizer bullets in his side. There's a ping and a whistle through the air, as another lodges in Asta's side. Tara and Mitch need to reload, and Ari will be next.

The sound of a car screeching away tells us the freckle-faced woman has escaped.

Ava makes the decision for me. Her hand flutters over my arm. "We need to help him."

Alistair's screams become the background music as we race over.

I watch in horror as Akyla rears on his hind legs. What can only be described as terror engulfs my body as he stays there.

Looking like he was born to walk on two feet, Akyla spews out a roar, his open mouth a crisscross of saliva.

This time when he drops, he lunges at Alistair, head reaching in further than before. He snaps over and over as Alistair screeches in fear, tucking himself into the furthest corner, then scrabbling to get out.

Akyla sees his opportunity, and lurches forward. His powerful jaws snap at Alistair's leg. The screams change, morphing from a frantic voice of fear to a high-pitched shriek of pain.

Running, I don't give myself time to think. I yank Alistair out from beneath the table and shove him behind me. He stumbles, blood seeping down his leg, but rights himself. Akyla roars in anger, leaping onto the table, spiking into the air again, and landing right in front of us.

I retreat a few steps, shuffling Alistair behind my back.

Akyla pushes himself up slowly, eyes blazing as he watches us. His muzzle serrates on a growl, a fine line of froth lining his lips. Saliva drips onto the snow beneath him, and his tongue laps over his exposed teeth. His head drops as he takes a menacing step forward.

"Sweet lord, sweet lord, sweet lord," is a litany behind me.

I'm just weighing my options—shifting would be suicide for Weres, but right now we're staring death down a muzzle—when Ava materializes by my side. Adrenaline jackknifes through every muscle, knowing I'm now getting ready to do whatever it takes.

Ping. Another dart impales itself in Akyla, this time in his neck. *Ping.* And another. Tara and Mitch are standing side by side, each with a tranquilizer gun pointed at the wolf.

Akyla stumbles, shaking his head with a bellow. Sedatives never work that fast, but these darts are the second wave of tranquilizers in his body. He leaps, determined to see this attack through, but all I have to do is grab Ava and move us back a few feet.

The wolf lands, his front legs crumpling as his jaw hits the ground with a thud. He never gets a chance to right himself before he loses consciousness.

I don't let myself consider calming my racing heart until I've surveyed the clearing. Ari and Asta both lay on the ground, darts protruding from their lifeless bodies. They're each guarded by an Alpha pair. The humans have collapsed onto each other, some looking shocked and pale, another two crying uncontrollably.

I turn around to look at Alistair, just as his legs give out. He lands on his butt in the melted snow, his wispy hair is sticking up like he's just been electrocuted. He lifts trembling hands to his leg but doesn't touch the angry red gash. He doesn't seem to know what to do with the wound...what he just saw.

It's only a matter of time before he will.

Ava is my last port of call. In part, because I can already sense how she's feeling, but mostly because I know she's going to be my anchor after the storm we just went through. A storm that's going to look like a drizzle compared to what's coming.

Her wintergreen eyes are luminous with anguish at what happened, alongside the gratitude that no one was seriously hurt. Her lower lip trembles as her body sags, the adrenalin washing away. As I pull her into my arms, my whole body enveloping her, my face sinks into her gossamer hair.

I don't know what's coming next, but there's one thing I do know.

There will be no moratorium.

17

HUNTER

Evacuating the humans didn't take long—none of them wanted to hang around. The moment Alistair got his bearings, he'd limped over to retrieve his phone. Noah had checked his wound immediately after, and although he'd pointed out it was a shallow scratch that wouldn't need stitches, Alistair had insisted that he was going to call an ambulance the moment they were near the highway.

It was when he mentioned the rabies shot he'd have to receive that I'd walked back over to the pups...not that I could call them that anymore.

We'd dragged their adult-sized bodies into the center of the clearing, where they now lie in a row. Akyla, Ari, and Asta are now full-grown wolves.

They've grown so fast. In such a short period of time.

I have no idea how I'm supposed to feel about that.

Eden's been monitoring their breathing as we keep them sedated. Mitch is on is way with cages to pick them up. It's only a matter of time before they're back at the center, behind a fence.

Ava crouches beside Asta, stroking her alabaster fur. You can see the love in every brush down Asta's head, and I can feel the anguish each time her hand draws back.

For the first time since she healed me, we Bonded, then arrived here, I can feel us diverging. Ava's compassion sees the good in these wolves.

The world I've experienced has shown me things aren't always that simple.

She looks up, her eyes coming straight to mine. Across the feet between us something pure and elementary restores my equilibrium—love. I know I have to believe that's enough.

I walk over, crouching beside her as I wrap an arm around her shoulders. "They've changed, Ava."

Ava's hand maintains the rhythmic stroking. "I know. I can feel it." She looks up at me, wintergreen eyes almost translucent. "But they're still our pups."

I brush her hair with my lips. "They always will be."

That's what makes this so hard.

There's a rumbling in the distance that has everyone's ears perking up. Mitch and Tara aren't far-off.

Akyla's foot twitches which has me straightening. Eden must see it, too, because she moves closer, eyes narrowed as she watches. "I'm glad Mitch isn't far away. I don't want to keep pumping them full of sedatives."

Ava nods. "You've given them so much."

Eden frowns. "They needed that much."

I move in close to Akyla, not sure whether the heavy lump in my gut is because these gorgeous wolves are stretched out in the wet snow, unconscious, or because they've needed more sedative than they should've...

The sound of the truck gets closer, quickly becoming a noise that echoes around the clearing. Noah paces to the path leading to the parking lot. "There's enough room. Mitch can bring the truck right up in here."

I don't know if it's the sound of the engine, or Noahs' voice, but Akyla twitches again, this time his whole body jerking like a hiccup.

I still as I stare at him. "Is that normal, Eden?"

The second I speak, Akyla's front paw kicks as if he's reaching out to me.

Eden's already reaching for the vet pack. "It means he's regaining consciousness." She shuffles through the contents, then shuffles some more. When she finally turns to me, every muscle in her face is tense. "And we're out of tranquilizer."

They've probably never had to use this much in one outing.

Ava shuffles over, her hand now stroking Akyla. "That's fine. I'll keep him calm."

I blink. I open my mouth but then change my mind. Akyla will probably respond to the sound of my voice again.

Actually, it's probably a good thing. I need to stay mute—I can't think of anything to say right now.

Eden's tension doesn't abate. She's as comfortable with her daughter doing this as I am. I look to where Noah's standing, seeing the truck slowly coming up the walking track.

Good. We don't have much time.

I move back to stand beside Ava and Akyla, tension keeping me upright. I won't be able to relax until these wolves are in those cages.

The truck pulls up, the back loaded with three metal crates. I'm not sure why I'm surprised when the Tates, including Sayen, climb out behind Mitch and Tara, but I am. I don't have time to think about it though. We need to get these wolves contained.

We all assemble around the wolves. Eden pushes up from her crouch, dusting her hands on her jeans. "They're still sedated, but it's wearing off. We need to get them in carefully," She looks around at each Were, "but quickly."

I nod. She's preaching to the converted.

"A few of us need to move them one at a time. That way they're supported, and their airways remain open."

Noah moves around to stand beside his mate. "Exactly what I was thinking."

I don't move away from Akyla, even though he hasn't twitched again. "This one first."

All we have to do is lift, carry them a few yards, slide them in, and shut the gates behind them.

It's simple and straightforward until you pick up an unconscious wolf. Akyla is like a giant, loose sack of potatoes, limbs and skin moving in different directions. I take the top half, as Noah and Mitch take the bottom half. As we shuffle toward the truck, the weight is a stark reminder of how much he's grown. Ava stays at the head, keeping it elevated.

Akyla's eyes flutter once but that's it. Apart from that, there's no sign of awareness...or the threat of danger.

Still, I don't let myself breathe again until he's in the cage, the gate firmly closed.

Asta's next, and I find Sayen sitting beside her. She's leaning over, peering at Asta's mouth. At the fine line of white froth that coats the wolf's lips.

Mary must notice, too, because she shuffles over, wringing her hands. "Is it Furious?"

Sayen leans back, the movement quick enough to be considered a startle. "I doubt it. Furious hasn't been seen for weeks."

Mary frowns. "Then how did they grow so quick?"

I stride forward, not liking where this is heading. "There's a lot we don't understand. Right now, our priority is to get them in those cages."

John slips his arm around his mate's shoulders, urging her to step back. I find myself wondering again why they even came.

But Mary doesn't budge. "You okay, Sayen?"

Sayen's face softens so much that it makes you realize how

much tension it must've been holding. "I'm okay, Mary. You know I hate seeing this happen."

Mary reaches out, resting her hand on Sayen's shoulder. "I know. It's why we're here."

I squat beside Asta before I can think too much about those three. There're secrets strained taught between them. But there's also love.

Asta is loaded up as quickly as Akyla. The belt of tension strapped around my chest loosens another notch.

Two down, one to go.

Ava is already crouched by Ari's side by the time we return for the final lift. She strokes him in time to his slow, regular breaths. The tenderness in her actions have me pausing. She's probably wondering what's going to happen to these guys when we get them back.

I wish I knew...

We take the same places we did before and lift Ari. For some reason, he's a little easier to juggle as we try to keep him level without losing our hold. It's a relief that he's not quite as floppy.

Until I realize what that could mean...

My stomach bottoms out when I feel something move in my palm. The slightest flutter, but a flutter, nonetheless. My arms lose their strength for the briefest of seconds, and I have to jerk Ari's head up to make up for the slip. Noah and Mitch glance at me, frowning.

I falter for a second, unsure whether I should stop or get this wolf the heck in that cage.

Ari makes the decision for me.

His eyes snap open, his lips twitch across my fingers. I feel saliva slide across them.

"We need to move!" Noah shouts.

But it's too late.

Ari twists. Falls.

And lands on his feet.

Instantly, we step back and fan out as the others run in. Moving to stand beside Ava is a given. Before Ari can blink, we've made a crude circle around him.

He shakes himself, probably clearing the last of the sedative's cobwebs, then scans his Were prison. Turning slowly, he registers he's surrounded.

No wolf is okay with being trapped.

And Ari is no normal wolf...

The effects of the tranquilizer are gone, so gone that you wouldn't believe he was under only a minute ago. His eyes glow in his white face, his teeth gleam...circled by froth.

Sayen, who's ended up on my left, gasps. "It has to be Furious..."

At the sound of her voice, Ari whips around, his gaze lasered on her. Every one of my muscles is on high alert as I shift slightly closer to her. She just put a great big target on herself.

Ari seems to contract in on himself, and my heart is a battering ram in my chest as I wait for him to leap. When he throws his head back on a roar, I know it's only a matter of time.

Except his body keeps going. He rears back, slowly, inexorably, drawing himself up onto his hind legs.

Just like Akyla as he readied to attack Alistair.

Sayen whimpers, and Tate or no Tate, a connection to Helix or not, I know I won't allow her to be hurt. John, on her other side, steps in closer, ready to protect his ward.

Ari roars again, sweeping his head as if he's broadcasting his intent. I expect him to fall back onto all fours, except he doesn't. He holds himself there, chest heaving, mouth coated in foam.

His posture, his bearing...looks human.

My entire body slams with shock when Ava steps up beside me, then past me. Calmly and smoothly, she slots herself in front of Sayen.

She looks up at the ferocious wolf holding himself upright. "Ari..."

I contract around her like armor, every protective instinct on red alert. I can see the alarm and shock in the faces around me, but her family, not even her parents, can move or they create a gap in the circle.

Although the minute Ari attacks, they'll have no choice. And then all hell is going to break loose, and blood staining the snow will be inevitable.

Sayen's trembling as she steps back, mouth working around words that don't make sense. "Why would she do this..."

Ava doesn't let any of this break her focus. She's watching Ari, face calm, almost smiling.

So full of faith.

"Please, Ari. We're not here to hurt you."

Ari's gaze flickers like a flame being pushed in a new direction, only to settle again on Sayen. She's his target.

Then others will be next.

Ava takes a step forward just as my heart screams for her to stay put. "We can help you. I can feel this consuming you."

Something seems to touch Ari. If I wasn't watching him with hyper-vigilant focus, I wouldn't see the flare of his nostrils or the pause in his breath.

Ava must see it, too, because she lifts her hand. "There's a part of you that doesn't want to do this."

Ari swallows, so human-like it shocks me out of my preparedness to fight. And the moment I shift my mindset, I see it.

Not it, them.

Like the threads of a spiderweb, the fibers flowing between Ari and Ava are fragile...but strong. Golden energy flows between them, some exchange I don't understand, but can't deny.

Ava is reaching Ari in a way no one else can see.

This is the foundation for her faith and her power.

Ari drops to all fours, still pulsing with aggression, but downgrading his threat. Ava closes her eyes, her focus turning within, and the threads flare as they thicken. As she breathes out, they braid together, forming a precious rope that connects them both.

Ari shakes his head and I can see him fighting it, but Ava doesn't falter. She's the calm in this storm, determined to beat it.

Hope has just kindled in my chest when the outcry starts. A blast of roars echoes through the clearing. Not from Ari, but from the back of the truck.

Ari's siblings are awake and roaring their fury from the cages. There's a bang as one of them must throw themselves against the metal walls, but I don't look over.

Ari has my entire focus.

Because Ari's head just dropped as his muzzle serrated.

Ava's brow furrows as her eyes remain closed. She pulls in a deep-seated breath and the thread bursts with light again. Tendrils branch out from the source, rivers of energy being born, reaching from Ava to the truck.

She's trying to reach the other's, too?

Like the energy just got divided and the hold on him just loosened, Ari rears up again. He thunders a roar over his shoulder at his brother and sister, then turns back to face us. The roar dies, becoming a menacing growl.

It's then that I feel Ava's concentration fracture, just for a second. This girl owns my heart and soul, and I know without a doubt that she's tiring.

That she's asking too much of herself.

Three wolves who are almost sub-human, probably infected with a violent virus. Against one girl armed with nothing but compassion.

Except, despite the drive for violence thrumming through his muscles, Ari doesn't move.

Ava has him scared or hesitating or torn. It's impossible to know which, only that he hasn't attacked yet.

She's also created a window for us to strike.

But as much as my mind is screaming at me to stop this by ending Ari, my heart sees what Ava's trying to do. I can't be the one to undermine what she's trying so hard to accomplish.

Which means, all I can do is help her.

Stepping closer, I slip my hand into hers, winding our fingers together. As our palms connect, the effect is instantaneous.

The clearing comes into sharp relief. Each body breathing within it in stark contrast.

Between each and every one is a gossamer ribbon, tying us all together in some complicated fabric. I'm literally surrounded by a maze of golden threads.

And the most powerful one connects Ava and me.

I quickly register what Ava's trying to do. She's tapping into the ethereal vein that reaches between her and Ari and is extending it to his siblings. I stifle my gasp. The strength of their bond is apparent in the thickness of the threads connecting the three wolves.

No wonder Akyla and Asta are so wild with anger. They're desperate to protect their brother.

I can feel Ava focusing on the threads, so I do the same, not really sure what to expect. Awe fills me as I watch her channeling her energy into them. No, she's not adding or changing them, she's merging with them!

Ava's energy swirls through the channel so seamlessly that I can't distinguish whose is whose. The blending is so complete that it looks all the same.

It hypnotizes me.

Suddenly, it worries me.

Ava is feeding her energy to these wolves. No wonder she's getting tired.

But what are the triplets going to do with it?

Tightening my grip on her hand, I push my feet into the ground. Ava won't do this alone.

Having no idea what I'm doing, I concentrate on the thread, imagining breathing into it. The threads explode with the most light I've seen so far.

Ari collapses onto all fours, then to the wet ground.

Elation fills me for the briefest of seconds, because so deeply connected to Ava and everything around us, I feel it. Ava's well is running dry.

Wrapping my whole body around her, I concentrate with all that I have, giving Ava everything within me.

Ari's eyes roll back in his head, but I don't get to see if he loses consciousness.

Ava collapses in my arms, and I just have enough time to twist so I hit the ground first as the darkness swallows me, too.

18

SAYEN

"Talk to him."

The words echo through my head, slithering around no matter how much I try to push them out.

"We need to know where and how. We need to make more."

I pause at the end of the hallway as I stare at the door to the basement halfway down.

Heading down to see KJ is a given. Knowing he's joined us is a balm to my aching soul. It's the only piece of evidence that could've convinced me we're doing the right thing after Helix told me what was going to happen next.

After what I saw in that clearing.

If someone as amazing as KJ can see the value in what we're doing, if he believes the sacrifice is worth it, then the time for doubts are over.

Especially now that Helix wants more.

More of whatever surrounded us at Elkhorn Flat. More of whatever stared at me with such malevolence, it's like he knew I was part of what created him.

It must be taking me more to settle my heart rate than I realize, because I almost jump when Mary calls out my name.

"Sayen, I was just looking for you."

I spin around, the pulse I was trying to calm taking off like a rocket. "I was just checking something."

Mary frowns. "I went to clean it yesterday, but there's something wrong with the thing you put the card in."

That's because it's been reprogrammed.

"Don't worry about it, Mary. I've barely been in there the past couple of weeks." I smile even though I want to frown. Lying has become so easy with Mary, but it takes extra focus to make sure I stay relaxed and maintain eye contact.

It's because I'm feeling rattled today.

"I don't mind..." Mary smiles as she puts out the offer. This is what Mary has done my whole life—tried to figure out what she could give me to make it okay.

Never knowing I found a way to do that myself.

"It's fine. I just wanted to check something, but it's not urgent."

Mary nods, peering a little closer at me. "Are you okay after yesterday, honey?"

Something in my chest is squirming, so I hold every muscle stock-still. "It was high drama there for a bit, but I'm fine." When Mary stays there, her gentle eyes assessing, I smile even brighter. "Really, I am."

After Hunter and Ava collapsed, so had the wolf. They'd loaded him up quickly, with much less care for his floppy limbs and head. Getting him contained had been the only priority.

Mary had stayed with Eden as she'd crumpled over her daughter, checking her pulse and smoothing her hair. Hunter had woken to find he'd held his mate to him the whole time, even unconscious. He'd recovered quickly, his worry as he'd touched her tenderly; something I'd had to look away from.

Ava was still unconscious by the time we left.

Mary's gaze softens. "You've always been strong, Sayen."

I want desperately to look away, but I don't. The pride shining from Mary's eyes has always been the hardest to bear.

She smiles a little. "All because of stuff that happened when you were just a baby. Your father strayed so far from what Weres stand for. I know that's something you've always carried."

It was Helix who showed me the burden wasn't because of his choices, it was because others had vilified him for it.

Because others had been too weak and scared.

I stopped being both of those things a long time ago.

John's voice carries from the other end of the house. "Mary, you ready to go?"

Mary calls out that she's coming. then turns back to me. "That's why I came looking for you. We're heading to the center to check up on Ava. Did you want to come?"

Relief roars through me. If John and Mary are going out, I can visit KJ. "Actually, I might join you later. I'll see if I can fix that door and get that file. We're still analyzing whether those wolves have Furious."

Even though I already know the answer.

Mary pats my arm. "Always so dedicated, Sayen."

So was my father.

I smile. "I'll make my way over after that."

The less time I have to spend with Hunter and the Phelans fussing over Ava, the better.

Mary brushes a kiss on my forehead, just like she has since I was a child, and walks away. I let out my breath when she's out of sight.

Seeing KJ will make this all okay.

Seeing KJ will make this all okay.

I swipe my card and push open the door.

KJ is waiting at the bottom of the stairs, lips smiling, eyes warm, red hair its usual crazy mess.

Seeing KJ definitely makes this all okay.

I must glide down the stairs, because I don't remember stepping down. KJ opens his arms and I settle in, pressing my lips against his. Warmth infuses me as I pull him in tight.

Seeing KJ makes everything more than okay.

KJ pulls back, hazel eyes searching my face. "Something's happened."

So much has happened. Even more is going to happen. I open my mouth to say everything is fine, but I can't form the lie. So much mars what I've discovered with KJ. He's still a prisoner in this basement. Helix isn't ready to trust him. No one realizes that the war we've been carefully orchestrating is about to play its song of inevitability.

I'm desperately trying to make sure it doesn't distort the beautiful feelings blossoming between us.

It's the only light of good in my life right now.

So, I go with the only truth I can share. "I wish this was different for us."

KJ inclines his head. "I'll admit, it's not ideal."

I snort. "It's like trying to replicate DNA in hydrochloric acid."

KJ grasps my face, eyes calm and warm. "Which makes what we have all the more amazing."

The band of tension around my heart loosens. "It is pretty impressive."

To have found love.

"It was inevitable." KJ's kiss is slow, giving himself time to let me know he means what he says. "I'm only Were, after all."

He's said that a few times now. Like there's something so special about me that anyone would feel the same.

Like there's something good in me.

KJ grasps my hand, pulling me over to the microscope. "I've almost got it."

My eyes widen. "Really?"

"I'm so close." He looks at me steadily. "I just need some more information."

My muscles lock. "Like what?"

"How did you create Furious?"

My body goes from frozen to liquid, and I grab myself a stool. It was necessary to create it, but I hated being a part of it. "We gene spliced the rabies virus."

"I figured that much. But with what?"

I can't hold his gaze, instead focusing on the microscope— the instrument that can unlock so much power in the most minuscule of parts. "The warrior gene."

KJ flops on the stool beside me. "No way."

I shrug like it's no big deal. "It was the most effective way to dial up the virus. The transmission through the bloodstream was an unexpected bonus."

"You're talking about the anger gene associated with violent criminality, Sayen. No wonder those wolves are so freaking fiery."

I try to look at him, but I can't. "It worked then, didn't it?"

"Holy crap, that's why the infected wolves target humans!"

Which we didn't anticipate, but Helix was very pleased with. "Does that help with the vaccine?"

I've been trying to create one for months. We agreed the only way we could do this is if we had the power to reverse it when necessary.

Except for the pups I saw yesterday. There was something about them...

When I look up, KJ is watching me closely. "You helped create this virus, Sayen. Why is this so important?"

I straighten, jutting out my chin. "We don't like the sacrifices we've had to make. They've been necessary."

KJ arches a brow. "Sometimes, I wonder how much Helix is talking when I ask you these questions."

My jaw tightens. "Have you got what you need?"

His lips tip up in a smile. "Like I said, I'm close."

Which makes KJ my savior in more ways than one. He's salvaged my damaged heart, and now he's creating the redemption for Furious. I nod. "Thank you."

KJ's hazel eyes settle into serious again. "You know I'm doing this for you, don't you?"

My breath vaporizes. This is what Helix wanted all along. For KJ to fall for me, for KJ to join us.

I didn't expect it to be what I wanted more than anything else.

I stand and step closer, slipping in between his legs to clasp his face. "I don't think there's anything I wouldn't do for you, KJ."

I brush the lightest kiss before I step away, suddenly conscious of the words I just uttered. They sounded like a confession.

They sounded like treason.

I turn and sprint up the stairs, not sure what I'm running away from, but knowing I'm acting like a crazy chick.

Outside, I lean against the door, strangely out of breath. I wonder what KJ must be thinking, but I don't have any explanations. Everything is just so mixed up right now.

Helix said it would be chaos when this war started. It's coming, I know it. No wonder I'm so nervous.

As I push away, I realize I forgot to ask how KJ genetically modified the pups. What DNA he used, so we can begin to understand what infecting them with Furious could mean.

So Helix can make more...

But Helix didn't see those rabid animals in the clearing. There's no doubt in my mind they'll wreak the havoc that will finally tip the scales.

Surely, we don't need more.

19

AVA

A lot can happen in three days.

And the media captured it all efficiently and comprehensively.

I was unconscious for two of them. When I regained consciousness this time, it felt like I was coming up from somewhere much deeper. It was a struggle to shake off the darkness, like I was battling through tar, grasping for the surface.

Hunter's face was the first thing I saw, and it was tight with worry. He'd let out a breath, like he'd been holding it the whole time, as he'd closed his eyes. "Thank god."

Being told I was out for two days was a shock.

Being told what's been going on since I blacked out was a blow. I couldn't stop the tears seeping down my face and wetting my pillow. It'd felt like things were moving in the right direction.

Hunter had gathered me in his arms, comforting me, but I could feel he was reassuring himself, too. He needed to know I was okay. I tried to give him what he needed, but the truth is, I wasn't okay. I still felt so tired and weak.

And Alistair had contracted Furious.

I'd sat and watched the news bulletins. The words are still a whirlwind in my head.

"Alistair Davenport, the well-known personality fighting for safety from wolves, was attacked today. He was rushed to Jacksonville General Hospital via ambulance, where he was treated for a cut to his leg. Is it irony that he's been attacked by the very same animals he says are too dangerous to live? Or has Mr. Davenport made a sacrifice to show us what he knew was true?"

Then only an hour later.

"Breaking news. Alistair Davenport, hospitalized only an hour ago, has been filmed in a violent rage. Mr. Davenport attacked doctors and nursing staff at Jacksonville General Hospital, throwing furniture, and promising death to anyone caught protecting wolves."

The footage had been distressing. Filmed on a cell phone, it'd been frantic and unsteady, but Alistair's rage was unmistakable. His wispy hair stood out at crazy angles as he'd stumbled into the waiting area, the remainder of a drip line hanging from his arm. He'd roared and screamed, thrown stationery from the nurses' desk, then wielded furniture like it was a weapon when a doctor tried to approach him. White foam was a circle of doom around his mouth.

Security had grappled him to the ground, the fight violent and messy, as someone roughly injected him with something.

I'd looked away after that, nausea like a twister in my gut.

Now, I sit curled up on my parents' couch, tucked into Hunter's side. Mom and Dad are on their way home from the center, and we need to talk about where to go next. The TV is on mute as the local news channel rehashes everything that's happened, right back from when the family was killed, Alistair's videos online, and now his inexplicable outburst.

One scene shows three rugged men, rifles over their shoulder, heading for the reserve. Wolf culling is about to pick up.

Hunter's hand is rhythmically stroking my hair as he stares at the screen. "How you feeling?"

The dizziness still appears every time I close my eyes longer than a second, but I don't think I'll be sleeping again anytime soon. "Better."

He pauses and I know he's running his own scan through our connection. I make sure I keep my eyes open. Hunter's checking on me because we need to talk.

I nudge him a moment later. "See?"

He harrumphs, pulling me in tighter. I think seeing what this is doing to me is the hardest thing for him to cope with right now.

I pull back, looking at his beautiful, sweet face. His copper eyes are subdued, more like a dusk than a dawn. "It's spread from wolves to humans."

Hunter nods, his eyes darkening even more. "It has."

The only saving grace with Furious was its inability to spread.

The TV flickers, grabbing our attention. A reporter dominates the screen, his face drawn and serious. All their faces have been serious up until now, but something about him has Hunter reaching for the remote.

"Sad news, indeed. After being sedated and restrained in his hospital bed, Alistair Davenport has passed away. The vigilante who wanted us to understand the threat wolves pose to us, died of the injuries he sustained from a vicious wolf attack." He nods sagely. "As many of you know, Alistair's father was also deeply affected when he came across an aggressive wolf. Harold Davenport has been notified. Results are yet to be confirmed, but it's believed Alistair was infected with the rabies virus."

Hunter clicks mute again, but for some reason, there doesn't seem to be any silence. There's a roaring in my ears, and I don't know if it's my or Hunter's heartbeat. There's a scream in my head I know I can't let out, or the fragile hold I have on myself will be shattered.

Alistair is dead.

Furious killed him.

We both jump when the door opens, but we don't move apart from that. Mom and Dad are home.

We have to talk about how to move forward.

I look at Hunter, wondering how we do that. His jaw is square and rigid. His eyes are pools of pain so deep I can see my reflection in them. I frown, for the first time not sure what he's trying to communicate.

Mom and Dad enter the lounge, their faces confirming Dad's words. "We heard about Alistair on the radio."

Mom takes the seat closest to me. "How are you feeling, honey?"

Scared. Ravaged. "A bit tired, still."

Dad comes to stand behind her. They've always needed proximity when bad news has been dealt. I push closer into Hunter. Now I can see why. It's like an affirmation that there's something good shining in all this blackness.

Dad studies me for a second. "You up for a talk?"

I nod, feeling Hunter's strength seep into my soul. "There's a lot that needs to be discussed."

Hunter scratches his brow. "The question is, where do we start?"

Dad crosses his arms as he leans back. "Well, even if Mike pursues the moratorium, it won't stand a chance."

I close my eyes as the knowledge sinks in but quickly open them again when the world starts to spin. "Wolves won't be safe."

Mom's lips thin. "Nor are humans now."

"Because the triplets were infected with Furious." There's a raw anger in Hunter's words that tells me he's been thinking about this.

"It seems to have triggered something in their altered genes."

The fast growth. The unusual human-like behavior.

Dad is rubbing his lower lip. "Furious hasn't been on the radar for a while now."

Mom nods. "It looked like it was on the way out because it wasn't contagious."

"Well, that's no longer the case." Hunter growls. "The question is, how and why did it come back?"

I sit up in shock as something hits me. "The pups were released. The gate to their enclosure had been left open."

Mom's eyes widen. "KJ noticed that infected wolves only seemed to occur around the captive breeding centers."

Hunter's nod is weighted with the knowledge that he's already thought of this. "The pups were released...with Furious."

I gasp as the pieces of this puzzle stab me, one by one. "Mike told us that Helix was responsible for Furious as well as the wolf culling."

Hunter's gaze becomes pained. "Helix is somehow associated with the captive breeding programs."

Mom leans back, her body curving into the chair. "Helix could be Were."

Dad's hands curl into fists. "It looks like we have a traitor."

I can feel Hunter's calmness, such a contrast to the maelstrom that's bruising me from the inside out. As I anchor myself to it, I wonder how he can manage it.

"The questions now," he says, "are who and why?"

Silence circles the room as we all digest this. Someone wants wolves dead. Someone deliberately infected Akyla, Ari, and Asta.

Someone is paying humans to kill wolves.

Someone is getting wolves to hurt humans.

My mind scrabbles as to who would be capable of doing that. Everyone at the center has always fought for wolves, not used them and killed them.

What could twist anyone so deeply that they could even consider that?

Hunter leans forward, clasping his hands. "What do you know of the Tates?"

Mom's intake of breath spears through the room. John and Mary?

I shuffle forward, joining him at the edge of the couch. "John and Mary have worked tirelessly to clear their name after what happened with Kurt."

Dad nods his agreement. "They established a lab at their ranch. They've been instrumental in cataloguing wolf genetics."

Hunter raises a brow. "Which means they had all the necessary equipment to create Furious."

Mom's hand flies to her mouth. "The Tates were there on the day the triplets were released."

I'm shaking my head, but I don't know what I'm denying. The fact that John and Mary could do this, or the fact that John and Mary *have* done this. They seemed like such good people.

But, the fact is, someone *has* done it.

Someone close.

Dad looks like he has to consciously focus to unclench his hands. "It's not common knowledge, but I think it's something we need to take into account. Sayen's father was Daniel Tate."

Hunter let's his breath out on a whistle. "We knew there was something going on with that."

Dad's lips tense. "As suspects go, it's either circumstantial, or very damning."

Hunter clasps my hand as he looks at my dad. "I say we keep

an eye on them. We can't afford anything like this to happen again."

Dad nods in agreement and so does Mom. I swallow down the bile this talk is churning up, then nod, too. Hunter's right. The family at Elkhorn Flats is dead. Alistair is dead.

Too many wolves have died.

Hunter releases my hand and I frown as I notice its absence. I blink, trying to figure out why that small motion was so noticeable. Scanning our connection, my frown deepens. Hunter is cautious, worried, somehow withdrawn.

My spine uncurls, my whole body feeling like I just turned to stone. Hunter hasn't withdrawn from me...since...

He clears his throat. "And the triplets will need to be euthanized."

20

AVA

No. No. No. The denial is a litany in my head that I can't seem to voice. It feels like I'm trying to stop a hurricane. It's too strong. Too inevitable.

But it's going to destroy everything Hunter and I have worked toward.

How can I go ahead without fighting it?

Everyone had looked at me once Hunter had said the words. Mom's entire posture was full of sympathy. Dad looked like he wanted to hug me. Hunter...Hunter had looked like he'd just swallowed glass.

Which is why I didn't say anything.

This is hard enough on my mate as it is. Just like Mom and Dad, Hunter thinks there isn't any other option. That this is the only way the safety of others can be guaranteed.

It just feels...wrong. Counterproductive.

The drive to the center is filled with the absence of sound. Dad drives, Mom holds herself tight. Hunter stares out the window, only a car seat apart, but feeling like he's so far away.

My chest aches as I scan our connection. I find his love, so unending it can never be lost, but I also find pain.

Pain and determination.

Staring out the window, I watch the trees zoom past. So much life is around us, all of it so intricately connected. How do I convince them that death isn't the answer when it could guarantee the loss of so many other lives?

I curl in around myself, lost and hurting. I was so sure seeing the threads was about honoring life...not having to see it end.

When Hunter's hand reaches out and hovers beside me as he continues to stare out the window, I quickly grasp it. It's a small touch, a simple one, so much less than all the touches we've shared. There's no eye contact, no words.

But it's the affirmation I need right now.

That simple gesture says we're in this together.

Our fingers intertwine as we hold on tightly for the rest of the car trip, each lost in our own thoughts, but our hearts connected through our palms. I'm not sure it was Hunter's intention, but as our connection reaffirms our love, so does my belief that the triplets need us.

These wolf pups were born of Hunter's DNA and my power to heal. We can't just put them down.

I just need to figure out how we help them without hurting anyone else.

We pull into the parking lot and I haul in a calming breath, even though it makes my head whirl. I connected with the triplets when we were at Elkhorn Flats. I could feel that I could heal them.

But, all of a sudden, I didn't have enough to give. Like a battery run dry, I'd collapsed...empty.

I just need a little more time, maybe to slow it down or amp it up or something.

Anything but losing them.

When Hunter pulls open my door, I realize I've been sitting in the car, deep in my own thoughts. I climb out, taking his hand as I look up at him. His copper eyes are swirling with anguish. I can feel what he's feeling, but I can't tell what he's thinking.

We follow my parents in and find Dawn waiting for us in the foyer. Her somber gaze matches ours as she greets us. "They're in the isolation pens."

The isolation pens. In the rear of the building, the handful of cages are small and barren with no access to the outdoors. These enclosures were built in case a wolf was really sick or highly contagious.

It seems Akyla, Ari, and Asta are both.

We follow Dawn down the length of the hallway. At the end, past the labs, past the other wolves, we reach a door. Dawn hands each of us a card. "Keep these passes with you, they're the only ones we have."

Hunter nods. "Good. No one else can access them."

Dawn's smile is small and apologetic. "The safety of others is our first priority."

Hunter blinks and I feel the dart of pain at Dawn's words echo my own. These pups were supposed to be beacons of hope, not a threat to those who care for them.

I've been in the isolation pens once or twice before. Back then, I couldn't heal, but I could offer comfort to the confused wolves who were placed here. Being removed from their pack while feeling sick was a frightening experience for them.

But never before have all three pens been occupied. I think Dawn commented when she first saw them that it had to be overkill. She said if that many wolves were that sick all at once, then something serious had to be sweeping through the center.

I grit my teeth, not liking that her words had been prophetic.

The room opens out to three adjacent cages. The walls are

white and bare, the floor grey and smooth. All designed to be anti-bacterial and easily cleaned.

Each cage holds a pup. No, a wolf. Akyla, Ari, and Asta have grown even more and filled out. Their bodies now hold the power and strength of an adult wolf in its prime.

All three are pacing, or trying to pace. The pens are wide enough for them to turn around, no more than that.

Dawn points to a camera up in the corner of the room. "We're keeping an eye on them mostly with this. It means disturbing them less."

I frown. I'm not sure being alone is what they need right now.

Two of the white wolves' growl as they see the bodies fill up the room.

"They're highly agitated and barely sleeping. Results have come back positive—it's Furious."

Dawn's words don't deal the blow I thought they would. I already knew something was seriously wrong with the triplets. Furious explains everything that's happened with them.

Mom scans the three pens. "It's much slower acting with them."

The wolves' eye us with bright gazes, ears erect, tails like thick boas behind them. I step forward, Hunter my shadow at my side, and they freeze. "Maybe if Furious is different with them, it will give us a little more time."

Dawn's voice reaches from behind me. "It would be a shame to see them go…"

It would be more than a shame. Determined to show them these wolves are more than just a virus, I take another step forward.

"Ava…" Hunter's voice is quiet, but full of concern.

I reach out and pat his arm. "These are our wolves, Hunter. They won't hurt me."

A low growl rumbles from Akyla, the wolf in the center cage directly in front of me. He's always been the alpha of these three. If I show he isn't the violent, unpredictable animal they think he is, the others will follow.

I allow my gaze to open, for my sight to see the unseen, and the threads come to life around me. Glorious, golden ribbons surround me, weaving and intersecting amongst us all. The thought that hits me every time I see this, flashes through my mind; *if only everyone could see this...*

Honing into the ethereal fiber stretching between Akyla and me, I find the place we both exist. It takes a little longer than usual, and I can already feel my energy dropping, but I don't stop. Another step and I'm in front of the cage, squares of metal separating us.

Akyla's growling abates, but his alert stance remains. He isn't greeting me, but he's also not telling me to back off.

I slowly sink to the ground, a little relieved it also means a break from holding myself upright. I'm weaker than I thought. But I'm not here to heal Akyla, just say hello.

"Hello, old friend."

Akyla's stance relaxes and from the corner of my eye, I see the other two sit. Hope surges through me and I smile, letting Akyla feel it. This is what my family needs to see.

There's the slightest twitch of his tail, then another. Within the next breath, Akyla has stepped forward and lowered his head, pink tongue peeking out. In that moment, I see the pup I fell in love with.

Reaching forward, I slip my fingers through the wire, putting out the invitation. Behind me I hear my mother's intake of breath, sense her fear, but I never pause. I've never been surer of anything in my life.

Akyla reaches out, carefully sniffing my fingers. I hold still, letting him see they're a peace offering.

When he finally accepts it, stepping forward to lick my hand as his tail begins a gentle wag, my heart soars. Asta lets out a short, high bark on my left, as Ari's tail can be heard banging against the wall.

The three clamber close to their gates, and I juggle scratching each one of them in turn. "See?" I say softly. "They have the potential to be so much more than Furious. Once we find a vaccine, maybe they'll be fine."

There's a shuffle behind me. "Well, I'll be..." It's Dawn, her soft voice full of wonder.

But as she comes to stand behind me, the wolves change. They tense, then step back. Their hackles raise, looking like jagged saws down their spines. I try to reach them again, breathing slowly and calmly, but I feel their rage spiking.

I jerk back when Akyla throws himself at the pen. Hunter's arm wraps around my waist and he halls me back. I watch, horrified, as the triplets fly into a frenzy, saliva flying in arcs, as they snap at the cages containing them.

I retreat, even though I don't want to, ushering Dawn back with me. The wolves don't calm, and I can feel their frustration at the metal between us and them is obvious. The banging and clanging as their massive bodies collide with it over and over is a testament to it.

Dawn opens the door behind me. "This is what they've done every time someone has visited them. We're better off if we leave."

Outside, I see the screen in the corner of the hall I hadn't noticed coming in. It holds a grainy image of the room on the other side of the wall. Akyla, Ari, and Asta are all still in a rage, their teeth bright white flashes in the grey image.

Dawn sighs. "They won't calm down for a while."

I look at the faces around me, wondering if everyone feels as shell-shocked as I do. But no one looks surprised. Instead, they all look grim. Their faces spell inevitability.

I lock onto Hunter, needing an anchor. His mouth is a tight line like everyone else's, but his eyes tell me he knows what I'm looking for.

And that he can't give it to me.

He lifts his hand only to let it drop. "They may not hurt you, Ava, but they'll hurt someone else."

Dad crosses his arms. "He's right, no matter how much we want it to be otherwise."

I look to Mom, not only my mother, but the Queen of the Fae, except her shoulders sag. "We're no closer to a vaccine, Ava. We can't keep caging them like this indefinitely."

Dawn gasps, looking at the faces that tell her the decision has already been made. "You can't do it. These are some of the last remaining arctic wolves. You can't euthanize them."

"Dawn." Dad's voice is gentle, but as hard as the concrete around us. "Lives have been lost. Humans are scared enough to take extreme lengths. There are some Weres saying they won't sit by and let that happen. We can't afford the risk these wolves pose."

Something flashes in Dawn's Fae green eyes, but it's gone too fast for me to decipher it. "You're right, Noah." She looks at my mate. "Hunter. You were always strong enough to make these hard choices. I respect that."

She turns and walks away just as Sayen exits one of the lab doors. She doesn't look surprised to see us, having probably heard everything we just said. "I was just tidying up the lab." She glances at Dawn's retreating back, then back at us. "Sorry to disturb."

No one replies, our words suffocated by the decision that's swelled in the space around us.

She heads down the hall, only turning back as she reaches

the end. "For what it's worth, I think you're making the right decision. These wolves are just too dangerous."

The explosion of anger is so big, I don't know how anyone else doesn't feel it. Hunter storms to the end of the hallway, and Sayen's eyes widen as she watches him approach.

He yanks the pass that was hanging around his neck and the lanyard snaps. He shoves it at her. "Then do it yourself."

When Sayen doesn't take it, her face lax with shock, Hunter grasps her hand and pushes the card into her palm. He doesn't look back as he strides away, the sound of a door slamming a few moments later telling us he's left the building.

21

HELIX

F ools.

All of them.

They think that by removing these wolves from the picture they'll stop the inevitable.

Well, I've worked too hard for that to happen. We're so close.

A quick swipe of the pass and I'm in. The room is black as night, so I let my eyes adjust. The wolves are there, each in their pen, glowing white monsters rising to their feet.

I don't have much time before they'll start making a ruckus, but that's fine. I don't need much.

I didn't bother with the full vet pack. All I need is one gun and three darts. The gun is loaded, the dart full of human growth hormone.

One more dose before they can fulfill their potential.

Peering down the sight at the first one, I expect to feel the usual twinge of guilt.

It was there when I showed Kurt the way so he could have the power he craved.

It was loudest when killing the arctic wolf pups because

Hunter thought he could make do without a captive breeding program.

It tried to gain voice as I was raising Sayen, only silenced when I saw that by teaching her, she could be proud of her heritage rather than filled with shame, that she could sleep without nightmares.

It was just a whisper when I told Alistair where and when to drop that poisoned meat.

Then it grew as I was coordinating the poachers so they could do what they do best.

It was loudest designing a virus that would finally tip the scales.

But now, it's gone. I step in close, resting the muzzle of the gun on the metal wire. There's something exhilarating to be this close to history. As I pull the trigger, there's nothing but the resolve that's always been there, dominating the guilt.

The irony that I called the captive breeding program on Evelyn Island "Resolve" made me smile every time I saw that plaque.

The first wolf yelps, sparking fury in the other two. My chest swells with excitement. Angry wolves. Wolves with the hybrid strength of human and predator.

Humans will be petrified. And history has shown what happens when humans are threatened—they don't stop until the threat is extinguished.

The wolf drops, body rigid as the hormone hits his system. It's what could happen next that has adrenaline flooding through me.

Reloading the dart gun, I line up the second wolf. It glares at me, menacing growls rumbling through its massive body. Happiness has my lips tipping up as I pull the trigger again. The dart impales itself in the canine's neck. It rears back, pain translating to anger.

Stepping back, I watch as it throws itself at the cage, body slamming into the wire, desperately trying to get to me.

I angle my head as I watch it. How wonderful to be free of guilt. To be totally sure that this is right.

The wolf drops to the ground like the first, muscles tight in spasm. No wonder so many Weres are power hungry. Look at the violence that lives in Were bodies. The need to dominate is inevitable.

Which is just what I need. Weres will never sit back and watch their companion animal be wiped from existence.

The last wolf is the female. She's also smarter than the others. She drops her head and growls as she retreats to the back of the cage.

The dark uneasiness nips at the edge of my consciousness, but I've discovered what it's like to be without it. I will not have it returning.

Resting the barrel on the wire, I aim and shoot, savoring the sound of the dart impaling in flesh. She jerks and slams against the wall. The stiffness is instantaneous with her. She drops to the ground, back arched, body frozen.

I let my smile grow. "No one is going to put you down."

Once these wolves have served their purpose, just like everyone else has, the need for peace will be realized. It's essential to stop further lives lost.

Pressing the button to open the door to the hallway is like opening a door to the moment everything changes. It *whooshes* open, holding itself there like it welcomes it. I'll release the wolves; they'll rush at the chance for freedom.

It's all about to begin.

The wolves are beginning to twitch, the hormones rushing through their system, working wonderful, unpredictable cellular changes.

Adrenaline has my heart rate spiking and my hands trembling as I quickly open each of the cages. The gun is tucked back in my pocket, along with the empty vials. Release them, leave, then destroy the evidence. To have done this without being exposed is just another sign this is the right path.

I give into the temptation for a last look from the doorway, maybe I'll even salute them. Failure had been a real possibility until they arrived.

But the wolves aren't twitching anymore. They're trembling, then convulsing. Thrashing on the concrete floor, foam froths along their lips. Breath held, I wait, only to have to release it. The seizures continue, their bodies trying to adapt to the change within.

No! They can't die!

Rushing in, I hold the gate to the first cage.

With the same speed that they began, the convulsions stop. Their bodies still.

Time stretches my nerves taut as I wait to see a breath.

Triumph soars as one wolf sucks in a breath, then two, and finally the third. Their labored breathing becomes a song of victory.

Simultaneously, they struggle to stand.

Yes, you beautiful monsters. You have a destiny to execute.

They stand. They stretch their necks, their backs, their legs.

When they turn, angry canine eyes to me, I know it's time to leave.

Until shock paralyzes me.

One by one, they push up, rising onto their hind legs, aligning their bodies like it's their natural posture. Their chests are deeply muscled, the legs holding them up long and lithe.

When the one in front of me takes a step, my insides tremble.

His muzzle serrates, his growl nothing but feral animal.

But the way he's stalking forward, the way his paws clench as if they were fists.

That is all human.

When the door to the room slams behind me, I spin around. The female takes a few more steps, having just shoved it closed. She angles her head as her hard gaze pins me.

Sweet saints.

What did I create?

22

HUNTER

I hadn't noticed how much I've been sleeping until I stopped again.

Bonding with Ava was like a balm to my insomniac soul. Holding her through the night was what my heart was craving. It was so natural I didn't even notice how essential it had become.

Until now.

Deep into the night, I know that her even breathing, holding her safe in my arms, isn't going to work. There are too many jagged pieces clanging about in my brain.

KJ and I started this. We set these pups on the trajectory they are now. I played a part in Alistair's death.

And with KJ missing, it's my responsibility to fix it.

It's how I get Ava to understand that's the challenge.

Eventually, I get up because I don't want the edginess to be contagious. No point in both of us being a Were with a sore head tomorrow. Plus, Ava needs her rest. It's only been a few days since she tried to heal the pups. She may think she's hidden from me how it's impacted her, but she's wrong. If she closes her eyes for too long, they fly open like she feels she's falling. By the end of the day, she's pale and exhausted.

Creeping out of Ava's room had taken longer than I thought. With three other Weres in the house, I have to make sure I'm quiet, but patience pays off. One stair at a time, each slow step ensuring my silence, I make it to the back door.

Once I'm out, I'm not sure what the whole exercise was for. There's no tundra empty of humans to run my energy off. There are no wolf packs to check up on.

Although there are three wolves I need to say goodbye to.

Before I know it, I'm running, muscles excited at being stretched, not really sure if I'm running toward the triplets or away from the one person I never wanted to let down.

As my feet pound the ground, head tilted to slice through the winter wind, two words become a mantra in my head.

I'm sorry.

I'm sorry.

I'm sorry.

#

STRIDING THROUGH THE PARKING LOT, I'm blinded when a set of headlights flash, impaling me with light. Yanking my arm up to protect myself from the glare, they turn off before a frown has formed.

Who the hell else is out here at this time of night?

The car door opens, and slams shut, my eyes quickly adjusting again to take in who's walking toward me.

Ava's father reaches me and keeps walking past, talking over his shoulder. "At first, I thought it was a herd of rhinos stomping down my stairs. Figured this was where you were heading."

I jog to catch up, too puzzled to be embarrassed. "You followed me?"

Noah arches a brow. "Ah, I got here first."

I stop, breath a white mist in the night, chest still heaving from my frantic run. "What are you doing here, Noah?"

Noah stops, pauses for a moment, then turns back to me. He sighs as he studies me. "Ava told me you tend to be a lone wolf."

"I haven't been alone since the moment I met your daughter. And that's exactly how I want it to be."

"And yet, here you are. Alone."

I frown, looking away. "I needed a bit of air. We're pretty far apart in what we want to happen next."

Noah nods, his eyes grave. "Ava wants to preserve life no matter what. She's always felt death so deeply."

I can't hide the wince. When those wolves die, Ava will feel them bleed in ways we can only imagine. "Do you think what's happening tomorrow," I wave my arm at the building, "is the right thing to do?"

Does he realize what Ava will try to do if we let them live? She'll try to reach them, heal them, fix this somehow. I know he saw how she was when she lost consciousness after the triplets. He knows we had to wait a week to travel after healing me. Healing doesn't make Ava stronger.

It's sucking her life away.

Noah's shoulders sag as he takes in the captive breeding center. His sigh is so deep it bursts out like a plume of smoke. "There's no right decision, Hunter." He looks back at me, eyes so dark they're almost the color of midnight around us. "It's just that it's the only decision."

I nod. He knows.

Inside the building, everything is quiet and dark. Staring down the hallway, I realize I was coming here all along. It was so obvious that Noah beat me getting here.

I'm still not sure why, though. To check up on the triplets? Some secret wish that they've gotten better?

I shake my head. I'm here to say goodbye…

Noah rests his hand on my shoulder. "I'll stay here. You go say what you need to."

I almost smile. It seems the "why" of my run was just as obvious as the "where."

There's a buzzing sound, and Noah's hand drops, and he pulls his phone out of his pocket. "It's Ava. She wants to know if I'm with you."

I almost roll my eyes. This family is tighter knit than mine. "I don't have anything to hide. Tell her—"

Noah glances down again, brows hiking up. "She said she's heading over."

This time, I do roll my eyes.

I couldn't be a lone wolf, even if I wanted to. "I'll head down. Let her know I'm looking forward to seeing her."

With that, I turn and walk down the hallway. I'll have a few minutes with the pups before Ava arrives. That'll give me enough time to tell myself that by default, the only decision becomes the right decision.

I can prepare myself for the only time I won't back Ava up. I can't. Not when her own life is the price.

The movement on the screen at the end of the hall doesn't surprise me. The pups are infected with Furious. They'd be edgier than I am.

But as I move closer, the speed of it has me frowning. Flashes of white are shifting through the grey pixels, streaking faster and further than should be possible in such a small space.

Jogging, not liking the alarm that's ringing through my body, I reach the end within a few seconds.

Those seconds would've been the last moments of Dawn's life.

What the hell is Dawn doing here in the middle of the night?

And how did she end up putting herself in such danger? Surely, she knows better than that.

As I watch the grisly scene in garish black and white, my mouth gapes with horror, not knowing where to look first.

The pups. The triplets.

Are no longer wolves.

They're...they're something else.

Two of them stand as if they've been bipedal their whole life, muscular thighs supporting massive chests, powerful shoulders being held back with pride. Their faces are all Furious wolf—wild, feral, enraged.

The third is crouching on the ground.

Over Dawn's body.

My instinct is to look away from that much blood. It covers the slim body lying face down on the ground, only the flowing white hair making it recognizable as the Fae Elder. The wolf nudges her with his snout and the body jerks but doesn't move. His teeth flash, a growl that looks more like a smile.

My mouth floods with the taste of bile.

Is this what KJ and I created?

The third wolf stands, stretching his shoulders like he's just done a workout, then arching his neck. They glance at each other, then at the door, then at the camera.

Slamming my hands on the screen, I shove myself backward. They know I'm here! It's like their enraged eyes are looking straight at me.

My hands contract just like every fiber in my body does. They can't be. Although these wolves look human, they're still wolves.

And Dawn could still be alive.

Except I gave my pass to Sayen. "Noah!"

Ava's father is by my side in an instant, reading the urgency in my voice. I step back from the screen, letting him see what's happened in the room.

Noah breathes one word. "Lycans."

"What? What are Lycans?"

He stays focused on the screens. "They're nothing but legend. Myth. They were used to tell scary stories when I was a kid—unspeakable animals that were trapped somewhere between Were and human. Everyone knew they could never exist." He turns back to me. "Where's the third one?"

Shoving my face close, I register only two wolves—Lycans—are in the camera shot. Dawn remains lying face down, lifeless. "All three of them were there a second ago. One must be in the back corner."

"We need to get Dawn out."

I nod. "Yes, we do." I move toward the door. "I'll go in first, they know me."

Noah frowns, pauses, but then moves behind me. "We go in, we get her out, we keep them in."

"My thoughts exactly."

I don't bother with a calming breath. There's no time and there's no point. There ain't no way you can prepare yourself for meeting three more-human-than-wolf animals who've probably just killed someone.

Shoving the door open, I shift to wolf and launch myself into the room. As a wolf, I land hard on the concrete, senses already cataloguing where the Lycans are. Two to my right, guarding the body that smells overwhelmingly of blood. The third...I spin around, looking up knowing it's too late.

An avalanche of white falls from the ceiling where the third Lycan had been holding himself, crashing down on Noah. Like me, he was shifting to wolf form, but he crumples beneath the massive weight, his body remaining human and vulnerable.

Noah scrabbles, but the Lycan has the advantage. It's on top and can maneuver like a human rather than a wolf.

And it has the strength of both.

I have a decision to make. The two Lycans guarding Dawn's body snarl as they step forward, so much taller than me on their hind legs. They come in closer, but also closer to the open door...

Noah desperately tries to push his aggressor off, but the Lycan is holding him down. The jaws coming at him are inevitable. They snap close to his shoulder, a string of saliva arcing out as the Lycan raises his head to go again.

Knowing it's a no-brainer—this is Ava's father, the Prime Alpha who started all this—I surge toward him.

The Lycan sees me coming, the other two spring forward.

Everyone moves at once.

I sail through the air, an arrow on a mission, determined that the Lycan's jaws won't connect with Noah's shoulder. The other two come at me, their eyes full of promise.

The Lycan pinning Noah down arcs toward the skin exposed by his torn shirt with a speed that takes my breath away.

The two Lycans hit me first, two battering rams trying to drive me off course. Our bodies collide and I twist, trying to deflect the impact.

I need to get to Noah.

But my trajectory doesn't stand a chance against their fury and size. Their heads crash into my midsection, slamming the air out of me. I feel myself arcing right, now off track, moving away from my target.

At the last moment, I twist again, my legs hitting the wall rather than the back the Lycans were trying to crush. I push off, letting their momentum slam themselves into the concrete as I push back toward Noah.

The roar, all too human, that fills the air tells me I'm too late.

I crash into the Lycan covering Noah, ramming him off. I don't know how Noah doesn't scream in pain again as the jaws holding his shoulder are ripped away. The Lycan tumbles. Not far, but far enough for me to wedge myself between them.

I morph back to human, grabbing Noah under the arms as I scrabble backward. I hear his intake of breath, knowing this must be causing him pain, but I don't stop till I'm flush against the cages behind us.

The Lycan growls, exposing teeth coated in red. His yellow gaze slides between Noah and me as his siblings join him. The three Lycans come together, dropping to all fours, each one a burning ball of menace. Their limbs tremble, their mouths foam, as they size up their prey.

They planted an ambush. Now they're deciding what to do next.

Shifting back to wolf, I step forward, placing myself between them and Noah.

There's a sound down the hall, then two words. "Hunter? Dad?"

Sweet heaven.

It's Ava.

And the Lycans are now between me and the doorway.

One by one, they throw their heads back in a howl. It's a powerful sound, all wild animal, and yet full of the rage I've only ever seen in humans.

They spin around, only one of them looking back, before they disappear out the door.

23

HUNTER

"Go after them."

Noah's words are barely finished before I'm out the door. The scream that echoes through the building a second later has me layering speed on speed.

I don't care how fast these beasts are. Nothing will stop me from protecting Ava.

There's a crash of glass as I burst into the foyer—the doors have been smashed. Wildly, I look around.

I can feel her. I can smell her.

Ava is plastered against the side wall, eyes wide with shock, one hand held against her chest, the night wind gusting through the broken door blowing back her hair.

It takes too long to get to her, but I have her in my arms in the space of three steps. She clings to me, body trembling almost as hard as mine.

I pull back, hand tracing her cheek as I make sure she's okay. There's no future without Ava. When I've made sure the Lycans have done nothing but scare her, I grab her hand. "Your dad."

Ava moves with me and we're running back down the hall,

her heart thumping loudly through our connection. "What were they, Hunter?"

I stop in the doorway, remembering Dawn is in here, too. Please don't let there be two dead bodies...

"Lycans—" My words stop along with my feet. The door is still open, looking straight into the room.

I left Noah lying on the ground, shoulder bleeding. He should be right in front of us.

Except the space is empty.

"Hunter?"

I rush in, mind still reeling with everything that's happened, and not knowing if I can process this, too.

There's blood, smeared blood—

"I'm in here." Noah's voice is faint and hoarse, and I'm able to locate him.

In the shadows of the middle cage, behind the gate, Noah is crumpled on the ground.

"Dad!" Ava rushes forward, falling to her knees. "What are you doing in there?"

Her gasp registers what has filled the air. Noah's shoulder is torn and bleeding, thick red tracking down his chest. Ava scrabbles for the lock, but Noah's good arm shoots out as he winces.

"Don't!"

Ava pauses. "What? What's going on?"

She looks back at me, and for the briefest of seconds I have the bliss of ignorance. Noah is probably going to reassure her that Were healing will take care of the wound in his shoulder.

Then I realize why Noah dragged himself in there and locked the gate.

I rest my hand on Ava's shoulder. "He's been injured. I tried to stop him, but one of the Lycans got to his shoulder."

Ava's hand trembles as it slides down the gate. "No..."

Noah swallows. "I'm infected."

My mate gasps, and I feel the pain ricochet down our connection.

Shit. Shit. Shit.

An alien sound pierces the shocked silence—a cell phone ringing. We all turn toward its origin.

Damn. Dawn.

It's only a few steps to her body. The one that hasn't moved since I looked at the screen.

Surely that wasn't less than an hour ago?

Ava's hand slips into mine, the tremble still there, and I squeeze it. Death is hard for Ava.

How will she feel about someone she's loved her whole life?

"She's not gone..."

Yet.

I kneel beside Dawn, ignoring the sticky puddle that my knees sink into. Grasping her shoulder, I turn her over, then work hard to stifle my gasp.

Dawn's face is twisted and bloodied. Her eyes are wide, her mouth open in a scream...almost as big as the gaping wound at her throat.

Ava kneels beside me. "Dawn, let me help you."

I freeze, the promise of death in front of me, the promise of life alive in the girl I love. Every time Ava has healed someone, she's fallen unconscious. And no one has been as injured, as close to death, as this.

Dawn's green gaze flutters up toward Ava. "The wolves." She swallows, the words slow and painful. "Did they get away?"

Ava nods, her eyes moist. "I know. You worked so hard for this."

A flicker of a frown creases Dawn's blood-streaked brow. "They got away?"

"Yes, they did. I'm so sorry—"

Dawn relaxes as a breath wheezes out. "Good."

I blink in stunned shock. Good? Did she understand what Ava just said?

Before I can find any words, though, Dawn's eyes drift closed. The smallest smile twitches, a smile that speaks of peace and satisfaction, and her body stills.

Gently, I lay her back down again. There's no point checking for a pulse. She no longer has one.

Ava couldn't sew this thread back together, no matter how much she'd want to.

The sob behind me has me collecting my mate into my arms as I hold her. This Fae Elder played such a big part in Ava's life —I can feel the devastation wracking her body.

Except grieving will have to come later. Her father...

Ava pulls away as the thought is born in my mind. She looks up at me, wintergreen eyes wet and aching. "We need to get Mom." She looks around. "Maybe Sayen."

Dammit. We need KJ.

All of a sudden, I'm feeling like I've let everyone down. My closest friend who I've barely looked for. My mate. Her father. Dawn.

There's a clearing of a throat from within the cage. "What was she doing here in the middle of the night?"

I pause, waiting for the answer to arrive. Dawn was committed to the wolves, but always managed to keep herself a little apart. I figured it's how she could raise them and release them without too much heartbreak. Why would she be here...at this time of night?

Ava walks over to her father. "Maybe she was trying to think of a way to keep them alive."

Noah shakes his head. "Or she was saying goodbye."

I frown, not sure why this has caught like a burr in my mind. Why would she say it was good that the Lycans got away?

Looking around, my brain finally slowing down enough to

start figuring out what the hell is going on here, my frown deepens. A tranquilizer gun has been flung on the concrete floor and lies in the corner of the room.

Looking at it, knowing it's out of place, I pause.

Dawn is dead.

Noah is infected.

Surely that's enough for us to deal with right now.

But my feet are walking over, my knees bending as I crouch to pick it up. There's a vial still in the chamber and I carefully pull it out. A small label is on the side, one word typed down the side: Somatotrophin.

Which doesn't sound like any of the supplements we've provided our wolves. Maybe she was... "What's the name of the stuff we use to euthanize?"

Ava frowns. "Pento-something or other. Why?"

I walk over, placing the vial in her hand. She reads the label, her frown deepening as she passes it to Noah. Noah takes it with his good hand, squinting in the darkness. He looks up at us, eyes wide with disbelief. "Somatotrophin is a human growth hormone. We had a problem with kids peddling this stuff at the youth center."

I reel back. What? Why would that be in there?

Ava takes it back, rereading the label. "But why would Dawn have that here?" She goes to glance at the body on the other side of the room but stops herself. "Maybe she found it here? Maybe she stopped someone from doing something?"

Unlike Ava, I do look. I turn and stare at the body lying in a pool of congealed blood.

Dawn worked at both the captive breeding centers that were linked to Furious.

Dawn had the genetic know-how to create the virus.

Dawn, Dawn, Dawn.

But she's a Fae Elder. Why would she want to cause so much

death and destruction when everything they stand for is life and light?

The phone rings again, and I rummage through Dawn's pocket. Pulling out the cell I've seen her use countless times, I frown when the ringtone sounds, but not in my hand—the screen stays black and still. When it rings again, the light of a screen flashing in Dawn's other pocket catches my eye. In a daze, I pull it out.

Two letters light up the front.

S.T.

I press the green button, my thumb slippery with blood, and raise the cell phone to my ear.

"Why haven't you answered me?"

The voice on the other end is high and strident, but I recognize it. It's a voice that's spent a lot of time here at the center.

Sayen Tate.

When I don't answer, she speaks again, her voice lower. I just about guarantee the two Weres in the room hear her anyway. "Hello?"

I stay mute. What is there to say?

The last question is whispered. One word.

A name that confirms it all.

"Helix?"

My hand tightens so much there's the crackle of plastic in my ear. I release my grip, then my breath. I know exactly how to respond to Sayen.

"Helix is dead."

24

KJ

W hen the sound of the door unlocking carries down the stairs, I push away from the microscope in relief. I was about to strangle the bloody thing.

I'm so close to a vaccine for Furious. One that could be potent enough to be used even after infection. With all the information about the virus now at my fingertips, it was a sure thing.

It was going to be my ticket to salvation.

And I can't freaking crack it.

The unexpected visit from Sayen is just what my heart and head need. My brain needs a break from coming up against a brick wall over and over, not to mention I'm slowly going bonkers being trapped in this lab. Stuff is going down out there, I know it.

Which is why this plan has to work.

My heart, on the other hand...it does a highland jig every time that door handle moves. It does some weird barrel turn as it registers these visits are happening more and more often. Daily. Then twice daily. Each time getting longer.

Each time with less talking. More connecting.

Right now, I could use both of those.

Sayen flies down the steps, but not in her usual happy grace. Today, there's an agitated clatter to her, like her feet don't have time for stairs right now.

I wait. I've learned there's some questions Sayen won't answer. They're going to have to wait until Helix gives the green light. It's the last part of Sayen I haven't been able to reach.

The part I'm scared I'll never be able to reach.

But I've hung out with Hunter long enough to learn a thing or two about patience. Man, I wish I could tell him I'm okay.

That there's a way this could all work out.

Sayen stops at the bottom of the stairs, breathing like she just star-jumped the whole way down. "We need the vaccine."

"I'm not sure what else you think I've been doing down here for the past however-many-days?"

Sayen's fingers push back into her hair. "We've run out of time, KJ. We need it." Her eyes finally stop their frantic searching and settle on me. "Now."

I cross my arms, knowing it's symbolic. We've come to a crossroads. "What's happened?"

Sayen swallows, the tension draining from her body. I open my arms and she slides into them, like a key into a lock, and we click into place. I pull in a deep breath, filling my lungs with Sayen, the only thing that can calm me right now.

I don't think she realizes it's her drive to fix this that drew me to her.

I pull back, brushing her waterfall of black hair from her face. "You need to tell me, Sayen."

That last show of trust has to happen for this to move forward. For me to know that the sacrifice has been worth it.

She bites her lip as she slowly, but undeniably nods. "I know."

My breath sucks in like a backdraft. Did she just agree? I

hold myself still, the clock ticking up on the wall the only sound of company I've had the entire time I've been here.

Sayen releases her hold on my waist and flops to the nearest bar stool. "Helix is gone, KJ. Dead."

I grab the nearest thing with legs, too, seeing why Sayen needed a chair. My outbreath just took all my strength with it. "Dawn is dead?"

Sayen's gaze flicks up with surprise, but then quickly slides away. "I should've known you'd figure it out."

"The moment I realized someone switched Achak's samples, everything else became pretty obvious after that."

Sayen looks up at me, eyes pleading. "It's why you connected so well with her. Deep down, you both wanted the same thing."

I close my eyes for long seconds. "She worked with my father, didn't she?"

Sayen nods. "Kurt understood."

Or, in other words, he wanted it enough.

She watches me closely. "Just like you do."

Knowing that Sayen has given me her last gift of trust, I know I have to answer this honestly. I hold her sad, lost gaze. Does she realize that she's looking for validation? "I understand why she started all this."

I know why Dawn did this. I'm just not sure that Sayen does.

Sayen's hands tremble and she clasps them in her lap. "The Lycans killed her."

Now there's a word I haven't heard outside of movies and TV. "Lycans..."

When Sayen looks away, I know this is bad.

Real bad.

"What has she done, Sayen?"

"We needed a way to scare the humans—"

"And make Weres angry." I hold up my hand. "I know the 'whys,' remember?"

Sayen flashes me a look, and I straighten. My girl didn't appreciate being interrupted. "Furious was meant to do that. The poaching was meant to do that."

But it wasn't happening fast enough. Furious wasn't contagious. Wolf numbers were dropping, but slowly.

Sayen glances at the clock—the ticking seems to be getting louder. "When we discovered the pups were genetically modified, Helix got an idea."

The stool screeches back as I bolt upright. "You didn't."

Still avoiding my gaze, she bites her lip. "She did. But she started with human growth hormone first."

My hands jam into my hair, my palms pressing in on my temples. The consequences are trying to blow my mind. Poor Hunter. Poor Ava. "Creating whatever the hell Lycans are."

"I saw the video footage, KJ. They're more Were than wolf."

My stomach feels like I've just chugged a whole beaker of hydrochloric acid. "Tell me."

"The first injections of HGH made them grow—fast and big. Then Furious made them...furious. Dawn released them, but Ava and the others tracked and captured them."

I wait, knowing this is only the bones of the story. It's the flesh that's gonna give it some weight.

"They...ah...injured a human. Alistair Davenport."

Of all the people to attack. "And?"

"He died the following day." Sayen's head drops, her hair falling around her face like a cape. "Of Furious."

I don't say anything, the darned clock counting out the passing seconds. I don't move. I don't breathe.

Furious is not only contagious, Furious can now be passed onto humans.

Sayen pulls in a big breath. "After they were captured, Dawn gave them another shot of HGH. She died releasing them. Noah was injured when they tried to contain them. They were unsuccessful."

"Holy shit."

Dawn was killed by the very animals she created.

Noah is infected.

The Lycans are out there somewhere, a ticking time bomb of Furious virus waiting to be spread.

I swallow, flopping back onto the stool. "Although she's dead, this is just what Dawn wanted."

It's why she created Helix.

Nodding, Sayen comes to stand before me. "The Lycans are going to do just what she wanted. Frighten the humans. Anger the Weres."

"Start a war."

Every cell in my body feels like it has enough kinetic energy amping through it to run up those stairs and bust straight through the door. The handful of people I love are out there, fighting these monsters.

That I helped create.

Except I've made a promise. To Sayen. To myself. To end this, once and for all.

And because of that, I stay seated, knowing energy never dies, but can be stored. For when I really need it.

Sayen is watching me, her beautiful face tense.

I grasp her face. "We need the vaccine."

She nods, her cheeks stroking the palms of my hands. "For when it's finished."

"For when Weres will be the ones to ensure peace and harmony."

Her smile is achingly slow but heart wrenching, nonetheless. "We can't stop it now, KJ. This is everything she worked toward."

Gently, I brush a kiss across her lips, sealing my commitment. "Which means cracking this vaccine."

"Yes. The vaccine will make this all okay."

I stop my hands, knowing she isn't going to like my suggestion. "We need to talk to the others."

An insta-frown yanks at Sayen's smooth skin. "No."

"Listen. I need to talk to Hunter and Ava. It's the only way forward."

"Why?"

I shrug. "Because Ava is the key. Her wolf is the only one to have survived Furious. We just need to figure out how."

It's the ultimate request. A yes would be the ultimate show of trust.

Sayen would have to release me. We'd have to talk to the others.

She shakes her head. "They know I worked with Helix. I called Helix's phone and Hunter answered."

Right. I'm about to grab my hair again when the answer hits me. "We tell them you've realized the error of your ways. That you want to fix this."

"Hunter isn't going to fall for that."

"He will if I tell him." I stare at her hard. "I'd never let anyone hurt you, Sayen."

Sayen nibbles her lip. What will my girl do? Her mentor is gone, the one person who dictated her next move. Helix would never have allowed this.

But then again, things are far more serious than Helix ever promised.

Sayen turns and heads up the stairs, and I follow, quickly quashing any surprise that may have leaked onto my face.

She pulls open the door, then pauses. When she looks up at me, her eyes are wide and vulnerable. "I'm trusting you, KJ."

Reaching forward, I push the door open the remainder of the way. The hallway on the other side is plain, the carpet a dark blue. Who would've thought that's what freedom would look like?

Stepping through, I let the cool air circle around my body. Air I haven't breathed or smelled before. Air that's a little bit closer to my friends.

And family.

Turning back, I smile, my shrug nonchalant. "I love you, Sayen. I couldn't leave you if I wanted."

25

AVA

The dawn brings with it little more than light. It's like the sun isn't even sure what it should do in this situation. It leaves the world in muted grey as it waits to see what's going to happen next.

Mom is a crumbled form beside the gate to Dad's cage. Her lip no longer trembles, but tremors still run through her shoulders periodically. Her hand still clings to the wire.

Dad's dropped when he fell unconscious about an hour ago.

Hunter wrapped me in his arms not long after Mom arrived. I haven't moved from that safe space since I slipped into their strength.

As Dad had slumped, then stopped talking, then started twitching, my heart had ached more and more. Hunter had leaned back a little to text on a regular basis, but he'd never let me go.

Mom had wanted to tend to his wound, but Dad wouldn't let her, insisting that the gate stay closed. Through the wire, she took blood, talking quietly and gently, telling Dad how much she loved him, and rushed off to the lab. She'd returned, lips tight and eyes red rimmed, as she moved back to his side.

Dad had slipped a little further into the darkness of the cage. "You need to be careful, Eden."

She'd shaken her head. "You'd never hurt me, Noah. Virus or no virus."

As the sun creeps above the horizon, we still haven't moved. We've barely breathed.

We're waiting for confirmation Dad has Furious.

Hunter's phone buzzes again, and I feel the now-familiar flex of muscles as he leans over to read the screen. The tension I can feel so tightly wound in his chest seems to do the impossible—it condenses and constricts even further. He brushes a kiss on my head. "We need to talk."

Mom hears him because her shoulders ripple with a tremor again. She knows, just like I do, that he's right.

No matter how much the words refuse to be found.

Grasping his hand, I take him out of the room. One last glance shows Dad asleep on the hard floor, a harsh twitch yanking at his legs.

Outside, the camera captures their still forms. I turn to Hunter, trying to fight the tears that have been waiting to be acknowledged. "This can't be happening."

My father. The Prime Alpha. The man who taught me about love and patience.

He can't have Furious.

Hunter envelops me with his arms, his own brand of forever encasing me, reminding me that this is what we're going to fight this with. "We need to keep moving forward. One step at a time."

I pull back, knowing his words are true, but hearing the strain in them. More importantly, I feel the strain in our connection.

Hunter's holding something back.

"You're right. We need to heal him."

Hunter's lips tense, a narrow line of tension across his

handsome face. "Mitch and some others are on their way now." Which explains the texting. "They'll be here any minute."

I frown. "The others."

Hunter's copper gaze is weighted and dark. "We need to go after the Lycans."

My hand flutters to my throat. "You think we should go with them."

"They could hurt a lot of people if we don't stop them, Ava." His hands reach out, palm up. "You can track them better than anyone."

Because I can see their threads.

"But my father..."

Hunter's jaw tenses. "I know, Ava. It kills me even to suggest it."

He's telling the truth. The tension I sensed in Hunter is the tug of war going on inside of him. He's trying to contain the battle of emotion.

I feel a tear escape as I lose my fight with the desperation building inside of me. "I can't leave him."

Hunter's hands fall to his side, looking unsurprised, but hurt, nonetheless. "We have a responsibility to keep people safe from these...things."

Except Hunter is talking about killing them. Ending their lives. Cutting their threads.

He steps forward. "You only saw the Lycans for a second, Ava. Helix," He swallows, "Dawn created monsters. They're not wolf, not Were, and not human. They can't be allowed to live."

I wince, not knowing if I can accept that as truth. I look up at him, knowing what I'm about to ask is big. "I want to try and heal Dad."

Hunter's eyes widen and his mouth opens, but no words come out.

I jump into the silence, using it to spill the rest of the words. "If I can heal Dad, maybe I can heal the Lycans."

Hunter's fingers spear through his dark hair, the battle to fight the shock playing across his face. "You can't…"

I grasp his hands, bringing them down between us. "This is my gift, Hunter. I have to try."

"Every time you've healed, you've collapsed. It's too risky."

"I know it takes its toll. But this is my father. I don't have a choice."

Hunter's head shakes side to side, a small movement, a tortured movement, a movement that tells me what his heart is screaming. "My job is to protect you, Ava."

"And you're doing a damn fine job, Hunter." I caress the tense lines of his cheek. I wouldn't be suggesting this if I didn't have his strength by my side. "I love you for it all the more."

He swallows, the process looking painful. "You know what you're asking me, don't you?"

I nod. I'm asking him to stand by and watch as I do something that's sapped my life force every time I've done it. I'm asking him to believe that the Lycans can be redeemed.

His head drops, his forehead resting against mine. I breathe in the essence of this Were, feeling my heart swell. How can anything win against this much love?

"Ava…" Hunter's eyes close as he whispers my name like a prayer. "I'll give you this."

I suck in a breath, wondering if I just heard him right.

His eyes open and his copper gaze pierces me. "But if it doesn't work, we do what we have to with the Lycans."

I nod, accepting the compromise, acknowledging the cost this has for both of us.

When I lift my head, I find Hunter is ready to meet me. Our lips brush, the first touch a fragile reconnection. The second taste, though, is an explosion of promise. We collapse into each other, curving in, wrapping around like vines. Lips, mouths, hands. They do all the talking for us.

I press up as I pull down on his shoulders, a hint of desperation creeping into the passion that's recharging me. I need Hunter.

I can't do this without his love, support and strength.

But I keep asking for more and more. I keep tapping into the well that feeds Hunter's love for me. If Hunter doesn't feel he's keeping me safe, then he'll feel he's failed.

And that's a feeling I don't want to be responsible for.

Hunter's body relaxes, his hands coming up to cup my face. His passion cools as his love eclipses everything. He tells me with his lips and heart and soul that what we have is bottomless. Endless.

Infinite.

I smile as another tear breaks the dam. Hunter's telling me that, although there are no answers...

There is the drive to find them.

The sound of glass being crushed beneath boots fractures down the hall. We pull away, realizing that Mitch and the others have arrived. With a last brush of lips, we pull apart. Standing side by side, we clamp our hands together.

Ready to face this together.

They approach us and I take in their numbers. Mitch and Tara are there, along with several of their pack. Everyone's face is somber, many arms are crossed. Mitch nods at us both, his eyes flicking to the screen behind us. "How is he?"

My chest feels hollow. "He's asleep for the moment. Mom is working on the tests."

Tara nods, her hand resting on Mitch's arm. I have a feeling she's both giving and seeking support. "Noah's strong. He'll get through this."

I stand mute, hoping the similar words I've been telling myself don't sound so hollow when spoken aloud.

It's then that I see my cousin Josh. He walks around Tara, his mother, and engulfs me in a hug.

Still holding onto Hunter, I squeeze him back single-armed.

He pulls back. "You're not coming, are you?"

I shake my head, and my throat constricts. "I'm going to heal Dad first. Then we'll join you."

Josh glances at Hunter, who stands stock-still. After a moment, Josh steps back with a short, sharp nod. "I'm half Channon, half Phelan. That means tracking *and* determination are programmed into my DNA. We'll find them."

Mitch and Tara's faces soften behind him and I can feel their gentle pride. The mix of Channons and Phelans stand a little taller behind them.

Josh's gaze narrows. "We need more tranquilizer darts."

I swallow. I noticed that Mitch and Tara are carrying tranquilizer guns. I also register that the Weres behind them are carrying rifles. Biting my lip, I nod. With a quick squeeze of Hunter's hand, I head down the hall to the lab.

Inside the lab, I rush to the metal drawers holding the darts. I need to get back to Dad.

"You sure you can heal him?" Josh's words catch me between the shoulder blades, and I can't help but stiffen.

I turn and pass him the darts, red feathered and preloaded with tranquilizer. "What's the point of seeing the threads, of being able to repair them, if I can't save my own father?"

"It's just that—"

I hold up my hand before he can go any further. I've already been over this with Hunter. "We both know you'd do the same in my situation."

His mouth snaps shut, silenced by the truth. The Lycans can be tracked without me. No one else can help my father.

Josh's hands fist. "If only..."

I wrap my hands around them. He's talking about the two people who may have had an answer for us—KJ, who's missing, and Sayen, who betrayed us all.

"So, we do what we can."

Hoping it will be enough.

All of a sudden, I'm enveloped in a hug. "If this were anyone else, I'd be worried. But it's you, Ava, Miss. Extraordinary, so I'm not. You've got this."

Except Josh has forgotten the whole reason he has faith in me—because I do the extraordinary—I see the threads that connect us all. And it's along the gossamer fiber that connects us that I sense his concern. Despite his words, Josh is worried.

I'm not the only one who can sense that something isn't quite right yet.

I hold him tight for long, precious seconds. "Thanks, Josh."

Josh tucks the darts into the vet pack as we head back. At the end of the hall, Hunter is deep in conversation with Mitch, both their faces heavy with the gravity of the situation.

Mitch's voice reaches my sensitive ears. "Of course, capture is our first priority."

Their first priority...even if the Lycans are brought back alive —what chance is there they'll be allowed to live?

At what stage does a thread need to be severed by choice?

Consciously stopping my train of thought, I look at Hunter. He's the most heartbreaking mix of determination, anguish, hope, and fear I've ever seen. All those feelings mirror my own, both doubling them, but also halving them at the same time.

Feeling like I've found my anchor again, I close my eyes for a moment. The web around me springs to life and I find the threads I'm looking for. They've always been different to the others, but now they're unmistakable. They're rough, coarse, a little jagged. Like damaged nerves.

I look to the Channons and Phelans. "The Lycans. They're heading south."

In the direction of Jacksonville.

Mitch nods as his mouth settles into a grim line. "Look after him—" The blue gaze identical to Dad's pierces me, "and yourself."

Hunter's arm settles around my shoulder, a show of solidarity, but largely a statement—the looking after me part is taken care of.

Mitch nods at him as Tara's lips twitch with a sad smile. Josh salutes us both.

With a scuffle of feet, the soft clanking of the rifles I wish I hadn't seen, they're gone.

Which means it's my turn to do my part. To use my skills.

I feel the movement a second before I see it on the screen from the corner of my eye. Dad's awake and he's slowly lifting himself up in the depths of the cage.

Yanking the door open, we rush in. Dad is staggering as he hauls himself to a standing position, using the cage to support himself. Mom stands, too, face anxious as she studies her mate. "Noah?"

Dad's head drops between his shoulders, his arms outstretched as his fingers lace through the wire. He breathes heavily, his entire body rising with each intake.

Clasping my hands to my chest, I step forward. Hunter is right behind me. "Dad?"

"Stay away." The guttural, rough words are said so quietly, I strain forward, not sure I heard him right.

Mom reaches out to brush the white-knuckled fingers gripping the cage door. "Noah, we're—"

Dad's head snaps up as he yanks himself close to the fence. "Get away from me!"

Mom recoils as Hunter's hands grip my arms and yank me

back. Dad's body slams against the cage, his face a contortion of fury. With the same speed and suddenness, he shoves himself backward into the shadows. "It's not safe! Stay away!" His body twists, muscles fighting themselves beneath his skin as he collapses on the concrete floor.

My heart thunders as my throat tightens. Dad is trying to fight the effects of the virus poisoning his system. Alistair didn't live long once Furious had taken hold.

I look up at Hunter. "I have to help him."

Hunter's eyes close and stay there for a full breath. When he opens them, they're just as tortured and twisted as Dad's body behind us. "Try, Ava, but you need to know if it goes too far, I'm putting a stop to it."

I swallow as I nod, hearing the steel in his words.

Hunter strokes my cheek. "You're too important, Ava. To me. To everyone."

I nod again, drawing strength from his tender caress.

The slamming of flesh on metal is louder this time, the grunt more of a roar. Mom has scuttled back, tears staining her face, as she holds her hand to her mouth.

The foam around Dad's mouth is unmistakable, the rage looking like it wants to erupt from his body. "You need to get out of here!"

Mom is shaking her head, the tears now streaming unchecked. Dad roars again, the frustration evident, the fight for control unmistakable. He grips the gate and shakes it, the rattle loud in a room filled with shock and fear. Then he starts pulling.

When the heavy gauge begins to groan, Hunter steps in front of me and reaches out to Mom. When it starts to bend, he pulls her back to stand beside me.

I know I need to start. Furious is tearing my Dad apart, and it's wanting him to tear us apart, too.

Closing my eyes, I pull in a calm breath. For a moment, all

that dominates is my thundering heartbeat. I can feel it battering my chest, hear it pummeling my eardrums. It's like a drumroll blocking everything else out.

Stemming the panic, I focus on my breathing. It's the breath that is the essence of the threads. It fires it; it feeds it. It's as alive as they are.

It's Hunter's that I see first. So strong, so close, so familiar. Then my mother's, then Dad's...

Dad's thread was my anchor growing up. More of a rope than a thread, it was always there, always dependable. Now, it's different. Tainted by a virus that shouldn't exist.

The golden motes that flowed so freely between us now struggle like they're flowing through a clogged pipe. It's like the thread's been fractured, then hastily glued back together, and the pieces don't fit.

Some don't belong.

Diving in deeper, feeling like I'm sliding through shards of glass, I try to find the place we connect. The place I've always found, no matter whether this was my father, a poacher, or a wolf. When I find it, I gasp.

Usually a glorious well of golden energy, it's now a cauldron of turmoil. Something new has been added, something unwanted, and the energy is trying to reject it.

I just need to help my father's body get rid of it.

I suck in a lungful of air, holding it as I fortify myself, then slowly release it. Maybe it will act like bellows to a flame, gifting the motes the energy they need to rebalance.

The motes flare, their rich light burning bright, and I do it once more. Again, they leap like I just fueled them. They start to race between us, a train of light going faster and faster.

In contrast, I feel Dad's body relax, his own breathing even out.

My head spins—probably all the oxygen—but I stay

focused. I can feel this is working! The fibers are stretching, healing, smoothing. Fragments are falling away, shedding away like wood shavings. As they slough, they fade, pieces of ash dissolving into nothing.

It's working!

The motes slow so I breathe into them again and they flare. We begin a rhythm—breathe, blaze, heal, recede. Breathe, blaze, heal, recede.

Except my head whirls with each cycle. I can feel myself feed the motes what they need, feel myself giving my energy to them. It helps and heals and makes progress, and then I run out of air.

And air is a finite resource.

No! I just need a little longer!

Feeling giddy, my body wavers, beginning to weaken. A hand grasps me, and I lean into Hunter. As I do, energy surges through me again, recharging me. My heart rejoices as our energy blends and continues to feed the healing process.

This is what I needed. I always knew I couldn't do this alone.

In my mind's eye I can see Dad's silhouette. He's now lying down, relaxed. Furious is dissolving, an alien that never belonged in his body being cast out. This is what my gift has been about.

And now Hunter sees it, too.

Then I feel Hunter grow breathless—there's a need to breathe out, without a chance to breathe in.

The motes need more, but we don't have more to give.

I can feel myself falling.

I can feel Hunter coming with me.

He jerks, sensing it, too. This is what happened last time, with the Lycan, and Hunter won't be willing to see history repeat.

No! My dad. We were so close.

But then I feel myself draining, losing the ability to suck in the air that's been taken.

No! Hunter...

A sound pierces my consciousness. A sound that shouldn't fit. A door.

Then, it's a voice. A voice we haven't heard no matter how much we wished for it.

"Oh, crap. I knew there wasn't a good time for this, but seriously?"

26

AVA

I open my eyes and the world blurs, spins, then comes into sharp relief. The moment I've checked that Hunter is okay, only to find him doing exactly the same thing, I spin around, not believing what just shocked me out of my trance.

KJ is standing in the doorway. Beaniless, hands shoved in his pockets, with a rueful smile, not sure whether it should take hold.

"KJ?" It's Hunter's disbelieving voice that echoes my shock. "What the—"

He doesn't finish the sentence because Hunter strides forward and grabs KJ in the mother of all hugs. KJ's grin breaks free as he squeezes him right back, thumping his back. The two cousins hold themselves there for a long time, reconnecting and reaffirming.

Hunter pulls away. "Where have you—"

Then I see what cut Hunter's question off. A girl stands behind KJ. Dark haired and defensive, Sayen angles her chin as her gaze slides to the floor.

Hunter steps beside me. "What's she doing here?"

KJ's hands come up as if to stop whatever's coming. "I know

how it looks. And when I tell you that Helix and Sayen have kept me captive this whole time, it's going to look even worse."

What? Anger detonates through Hunter and I slip my arm around his. I let my own disgust meet his, letting him know he's not alone.

"Helix has killed countless wolves," Hunter growls. "The poaching. Furious. And then she created the Lycans."

KJ nods. "Helix wanted a war."

Sayen steps around KJ. "And she's on her way to getting one."

Hunter glares at her hard and long enough that her defiant gaze drops. My shock mirrors his when we see her hand slide into KJ's.

Hunter's gaze locks onto his cousin's. "You've got to be kidding me."

"Hey, you didn't think you'd cornered the market on impossible love, did you?"

"She works for Helix, KJ!"

I expect KJ to maybe at least rock back on his heels as those words are roared at him, but he holds his ground. "She did. But now Helix is dead, she's here to help us."

Hunter's free hand hits his forehead and slides down. "Of all the..." He looks up again. "You know Dawn had more than one supporter. She's a spy."

KJ frowns. "No, she's not."

"I don't trust her."

KJ shrugs. "But you trust me."

Hunter blinks. He knows he's just been backed into a corner. KJ believes Sayen is good at heart. He's asking Hunter to have faith in his judgment. Hunter frowns, too, but it's far more thunderous.

KJ holds up his palms in appeal. "And all that time I was locked away in a lab, meant I could work on a vaccine." He glances at me, then back at Hunter. "Maybe a cure."

"Ava." It's my mother's voice, quiet, but urgent.

We all turn to find she's folded on the floor again beside Dad's cage. Her green gaze is almost apologetic as she takes in the four of us. "It didn't work."

Dad is twitching again, his head tossing. His throat works, trying to deal with the flow of saliva, but a line of foam is forming around his mouth. A guttural groan seeps from his throat.

I collapse beside her, my chest feeling like a gaping wound. It's only a matter of time before he's awake and angry again, screaming at us to leave as the virus gives him the strength to tear his jail apart.

Hunter spins around, glaring at Sayen. "This is what you created. What you wanted."

She crosses her arms, her eyes focused on Hunter and nowhere else. "It's what Helix wanted."

KJ steps in closer to her. "She's seen that it's gone too far. That it was never right, Hunter."

Hunter looks away, and you don't need to be able to feel him to see his disgust and disbelief.

Dad jerks like a rope has been tied to his midriff, his groan turning into more of a howl. Wherever Sayen's loyalties lie isn't important right now. Dad is dying.

I turn to my mate. "I need to go in again, Hunter."

"No."

The single word is emphatic. Inflexible.

I close my eyes. It's full of love and fear. "We can't let him get worse."

My eyes fly open as my words hang in the air. If I can't heal Dad, if Hunter won't let me, then we face a choice no one should have to make.

A sob chokes in my throat. A Were with Furious is dangerous. The Prime Alpha with Furious is catastrophic.

"We have to try again, Hunter." My voice is pleading, my heart aching as I look up at him. "I got stronger when you connected with me. We can do this."

Hunter's eyes look like they're fracturing with pain as he slowly shakes his head. "I can't be part of that, Ava. It could kill you."

The stalemate arrests the air around us, making it hard to breathe. Hunter and I stare at each other, our heart's deepest desires playing tug-of-war.

"It's a good thing I'm here."

We both turn to KJ, his matter-of-fact tone incongruous with the decisions waiting to be made.

"Like I said, I think I know how we can cure Furious."

Sayen's eyes widen. "It's Ava, isn't it? Ava is the key."

KJ grins with pride. "That's my girl." He turns to us, and I know his chipper manner has got to be annoying Hunter. It's kinda irritating me, to be honest. "Achak is the only wolf to survive Furious." KJ spears me with his hazel gaze. "He hurt you, didn't he?"

My hand flies to cover my forearm. I played down the cut on my arm—it was barely a graze. It never even left a scar.

Those moments flash through my mind. Achak pinning me to the ground, snapping at my face. My hands, sinking into hot fur, trying to hold him back. Denial being quickly replaced by fear, then terror eclipsing everything. The next wild bite grazing my arm, pain rupturing across my skin. A thin graze of red. Achak's mouth, open and snarling, powering down.

I gasp as I look to KJ.

My blood a pale pink smear across his gleaming teeth.

He nods slowly. "Yup."

I glance at Dad, then Hunter. "It was my blood..."

Hunter propels into action. He marches past KJ and Sayen to the door. "We need to get to the lab."

KJ winds his fingers through Sayen's. "Good thing I've got another lab whizz with me. It'll take half the time."

Hunter ignores the comment and the hand holding. "Eden. We'll get a sample of Ava's blood and be back. These two can do what they do. We'll stay with you and Noah."

Mom nods, eyes barely leaving her mate. I want to hug her before we rush out the door, for the first time in my life she looks so fragile, but I don't. The sooner I leave, the sooner I get back.

I watch the first vial fill as Sayen gets her samples. KJ is fiddling with a microscope and a variety of glass dishes over at the bench. There's a sense of urgency in everyone's short, sharp movements.

My pulse trips an excited beat. There's also a sense of purpose.

Of hope.

Hunter is pacing the back wall. "How long?"

KJ doesn't look up from the dropper already full of my blood. "Hopefully, no longer than an hour."

Sayen is just finishing up when the roar of fury booms through the concrete walls. Hunter grabs my hand and we sprint through the building. I hate that I'm just as worried for Mom's safety as I am for Dad's well-being.

In the confinement room, Mom has pushed herself up against the wall beside the door, her face distraught.

Dad is deep in the shadows of his cage, making a sound I've never heard before. His intake of breath is raspy; his exhale of breath a rough, guttural groan.

Mom reaches out and I take her hand. "This is tearing him apart, Ava. I can't calm him."

She's right. Dad will fight the effects of Furious till his last breath. He would never want to hurt anyone. His whole life has been about protecting others.

Just like Hunter.

Which makes it all the more shocking when he launches himself at the cage. With Were speed, it happens in a blink. With Were strength, it's like a sonic boom just slammed through my chest. He roars again, head thrashing, as he rattles the metal holding him captive.

A lone tear tracks down Mom's face. "When he woke. Before...He asked that we don't let this get past the point of no return."

Dad doesn't have an hour.

Assuming KJ is right...

Face taught with strain, chords standing out in stark relief across his neck, Dad struggles to remove his hands from the wire. "Get out, get out, *now!*"

Hunter steps around us, his broad body coming between Dad and us. "Noah. We're working on it. We just need you to hold on a little longer."

A violent howl is the only response. For a flash of a second, Dad morphs to wolf, and then back again.

An invisible clamp slips around my throat. Dad doesn't have an hour...

Hunter turns back to look at Mom. "There aren't any other tranquilizer guns left, are there?"

Mom shakes her head, the movement shaking free another tear. "They took them all with them. For the Lycans."

Hunter looks away before we can register his response, but I feel it. He consciously calms himself. Pulls a cloak of determination around himself.

Oh, no. Hunter is preparing to fight.

My mate against my father. The one who holds my heart against the Prime Alpha...ruled by Furious.

There is no choice.

I need to heal Dad.

My eyes flutter closed only to fly open again to the sound of creaking metal. They open, then stretch, then widen some more.

Dad's face is barely recognizable. Corrupted by fury, full of the promise of violence, he's focused on the gate in his hands. The metal groans again, and slowly, irrevocably, it begins to bend.

Hunter steps back, arms out to usher us toward the door. I grasp him, slamming my eyes closed.

I have to try.

Hunter must sense something, because he grips me. "Ava, no! It's too late!"

The snap of steel echoes in my eardrums, but I keep my eyes shut. I just need to find his thread. I need to undo the damage Furious is wreaking on my father's body and mind.

Mom's hands grasp me, too. "Ava, he's right—" Her words are cut off by a sob.

No! They're signing Dad's death warrant.

Squeezing my eyes tighter, I feel the added energy now that Mom is touching me too. Maybe, with the three of us...

Face scrunched, I inject all my will into sending the power of love through our connection.

Except I'm being lifted, being moved. Hunter hauls me into his arms, cradling me against his chest. I start to struggle, panicked, knowing they don't understand.

The risk is worth it.

When a door slams against a wall, my eyes finally fly open. I'm ready to throw myself to the floor if I have to when I see that Hunter wasn't trying to exit.

People are coming in.

Weres.

Mitch and Tara, Josh and the others.

Mitch already has the tranquilizer gun leveled. He pulls the trigger and there's a pop, passes it to Tara, who gives him a freshly loaded one, aims and shoots again.

Dad jerks as each one impales his chest but doesn't recoil. The fury filling his veins probably masks any pain. He rattles and shakes the gate, another length of square wire popping.

It's only a matter of time before he breaks through.

Two more darts join the red tufts springing from Dad's chest like blood. The sting only angers him even more, and this time, an entire length of steel breaks free.

When I turn back to look at Mitch, I gasp. His face is tortured and pale as he stares down the barrel of a rifle.

He's going to be the last line of defense against his rabid twin.

"No!" I don't realize I scream it out loud until the sound is echoing off the walls. Hunter lets me slide to my feet, only to pull me back against his chest. His strong arm clamps around me, no longer needing to hold me back.

Now, needed to hold me upright.

Dad forcefully throws himself away from the gate. He paces to the back of the cage only to come running back at us, slamming into the wall of mesh separating us from him. Before he can grasp the wire, he throws himself away and runs for the back wall.

Mom gasps. "He's trying to get the sedative through his system faster."

The cycle establishes. The man walking away is the Alpha fighting this virus, the animal running at the gate is Furious battling to win.

Mitch doesn't lower the rifle as he calls out to his brother. "You've got this, Noah."

I look away. Mitch isn't lowering the gun because he's telling his twin he's got his back if Dad loses.

Furious fights it, every breath and every second, it tries to shake off the effects of the sedative. It means when Dad finally drops, it's sudden and hard. He goes from standing and screaming, to slumped and senseless on the cold floor.

And when he does, I finally take a breath beyond the shallow lump of fear lodged in my throat. Mitch slowly lowers the rifle. Mom releases a pent-up sob.

Hunter's arms relax around me but don't let go. I feel him turn, but my eyes are glued to my father. "Thank you," he murmurs.

"Seems it was a good thing we came back early."

That has me turning. Mitch is right. They were supposed to be dealing with the Lycans.

There's a flurry of commotion behind him, and Mitch steps aside as KJ bursts into the room. He holds up a small vial filled with green liquid. "I've got it! A vaccine for Furious!"

27

SAYEN

A lthough most of the Weres have moved to the common area of the center, there's still a lot of people left in the room. Noah unconscious in the cage, Eden as close as she can be considering the metal dividing them. Ava and Hunter. Mitch and Tara and their son, Josh.

All watching.

All hoping.

Eden slowly and carefully injects the green vaccine into her mate through the wire of the cage. Ava hovers behind, her hands tangled tightly together.

Hunter stands back though, a dark frown tight across his face. I'm not sure that Ava's noticed, she's so caught up in her father. But when she does, I get a sense there will be a few things waiting to be discussed.

It's kinda symbolic, really. Helix knew they had to be divided. It's the only way they'd discover they needed to be united.

On the other hand, KJ hasn't left my side.

Or maybe I haven't left KJ's side.

Either way, the experience of being close to him for such an extended period of time is something I want to get used to.

Creating the vaccine was so simple in the end. We knew what we were looking for. Isolating the antibodies in Ava's blood was straightforward. Once isolated, we could duplicate and duplicate again. Blend it into a carrier solution, and bam. My work here was done.

I look over at unconscious Noah. I'm not as sure this vaccine has any ability to be effective after infection. Triggering an immune defense system to fight a virus is quite different to repairing and reversing the damage that Furious does to a body.

After all, there's no cure for rabies.

And Furious is rabies blended with the human warrior gene. It's faster, more accessible to the human body.

But the vaccine is all I wanted. It means we've ensured others won't be able to be infected. Weres.

And Fae.

I slip my hand into KJ's. It's all we wanted.

He squeezes my palm but keeps his eyes on the people around us. How much does KJ belong here? How much does he want to belong here?

I straighten, shoving those thoughts away. It's undeniable in his eyes, his touch, that we belong together. It's what finally convinced him which side to choose.

I wait for someone else to snap out of their emotional stupor to ask the obvious question.

Hunter pushes away from the back wall. "Why are you back so early?"

Mitch's face tightens as he glances at Tara. "We're not the only ones out looking for the Lycans."

My heart rate hikes up a notch, but I still don't speak. Although these people have allowed me to be here, it's only because KJ's asked them to trust him.

I wonder how much Helix knew that KJ would be so instrumental. It's because of him that we've been able to infiltrate these Weres.

Hunter crosses his arms. "What's going on?"

Ava finally turns away from her father. I'm almost glad I haven't had that level of connection with anyone. It looks agonizing. When Helix was killed it knocked my world off kilter, but not enough for me to lose sight of her goal.

Dawn wouldn't have wanted that. She worked for this for too long.

Josh enters the room, pushing a TV on a stand. Mitch claps him on the shoulder. "Thanks, son."

Josh nods, his face grim. We all shuffle around it, me at the back.

KJ by my side.

Mitch grabs the remote. "We were driving down the highway when the news came on the radio."

Tara slips her arm around her mate. "By the time we got to the visitors' center so we could track them, we knew there was no point."

A twisted feeling begins in my gut, and although it feels like uneasiness, I tell myself it's excitement.

The TV screen blinks to life like a light bulb, a serious-looking anchorman dominating it. I can't help the gasp that joins the others as I see the words scrolling across the bottom, a train of letters in a red banner.

WEREWOLVES ARE REAL.

The anchor man's lips are moving but there's no sound, so Mitch quickly turns it up.

"Seven official sightings, plus many dozens more waiting to be verified. People are encouraged to remain indoors while authorities confirm whether this is a hoax, or indeed, whether werewolves are real."

The shot changes to a grainy camera. A group of people are

having a barbecue at the reserve. One young male salutes the camera with a grin and a beer. He's flipping sausages, wearing an apron but no shirt. The camera jiggles lopsidedly as the guy says something, then laughs.

Without warning, the camera topples and lands on the ground. There's a scuffle, as pebbly ground moves in out of focus, then blue sky fills the screen. More frantic jerking and the scene levels out again. Two legs are stretched out in front, desperately fumbling backward as whoever is videoing tries to capture what's happening back at the barbecue.

The Lycans.

Dear god.

Like a panther, it pounces on the shirtless guy, snaps at his shoulder, and leaps off again. On two legs, it surveys the area, sniffing the air. One sharp movement of the head, and it zeroes in on the camera holder. The camera shakes as eyes hot with hatred lock onto him. There's more frantic scrabbling backward, but it's useless.

The Lycan leaps, his wide-open jaws dominating the screen before it goes blank.

"At this stage, there have been no reported deaths, but multiple injuries." The anchor man is grave as he stares squarely down the camera. "All victims are currently being treated in the hospital for bite wounds, largely to the upper torso."

I'm supposed to feel victory, and when it doesn't come straight away, I wait. Helix pointed out over and over again that it took time for that feeling to come to me. She said it was my mother's softness, possibly my father's weakness, that meant I got emotional before I got practical.

KJ squeezes my hand, and I continue staring at the screen as I squeeze it back. He understands. He knows this is hard to watch.

Just like he knows it's necessary.

The anchor man nods at us. "We have this message from local authorities."

A man in a police uniform stands surrounded by reporters. Bulbs flash and a bouquet of microphones are held close to his face. "No, we do not know what these animals are, but yes, we are actively tracking them. It's only a matter of time before they're captured. Do not approach, I repeat, do not approach. These animals are considered dangerous and a threat to life. If sighted, please call the authorities immediately."

Mitch presses "Mute," then turns to us. "When we discovered the Lycans were no longer a secret, and that humans are now deploying, we decided to turn around and come back. We need a more concrete plan." He looks to Ava. "We need to be able to find them quickly."

Humans know about Lycans. And now they're trying to exterminate them.

And now Weres are going to intervene.

Just like Helix said they would.

Hunter finally comes to stand beside his mate. "We need to quickly remove the threat they pose."

Mitch nods as Ava bites her lip.

I can already predict that Ava hates the idea of "removing the threat." It proves Helix right. Even something as evil and dangerous as the Lycans, and she still doesn't want to see them dead.

Dawn hated Ava. More than she hated Eden.

It's like the second generation just grew the emotion exponentially.

She said they were weak. Short-sighted. Too soft to be able to lose a few to save the many. Touch and hope weren't going to save the wolves or anyone else.

Action and sacrifice would.

Tara wraps her arm around Mitch's. "We couldn't afford to

risk an altercation with all this media coverage. So, before we left, we set a trap. If we can capture them before the humans, maybe they can disappear before any more damage is done."

Tara slips a thumb drive into the TV port and a black-and-white image of a small clearing appears.

"We chose the track coming into the visitors' center. The Lycans appear to be targeting areas populated by humans."

Everything is still and silent. A gentle breeze tickles the branches of the pines scattered in the area. Snow has been shoved in uneven mounds in a circular pattern amongst them. In the center lays a stack of raw meat.

Hunter moves in closer, studying the scene. "What traps have you used?"

Tara points to various places. "We've set ten neck snares around the bait."

KJ nods. "Saturation snaring. Good idea."

Tara looks up and freezes. Her gaze stays focused on KJ. He's the first to look away, his lips thin and tight.

There isn't time to process whatever that could mean because something moves on the screen.

It's them!

The three Lycans, white and massive, come running up the trail on all fours. At the edge of the clearing they stop. Rising to their full height, they scan and sniff.

I watch in awe and fear. When Helix first suggested we create Furious, it had seemed a pipe dream. Every now and again, I'd wondered if she had complete hold of her sanity.

But these impossible, ferocious monsters are a product of that virus.

One notices the bait, then the other two.

With another scan, they take a few steps forward. Standing on their hind legs, they look far too...human. As they reach the first mound of snow, they pause and sniff again.

They've smelled the people who were here, which any canine would. They'll wait, check to make sure there's no immediate threat, and then move in on the meat.

Why do I feel relief that these animals will be neutralized? I shake my head and KJ glances at me. His concerned gaze is enough to strengthen my resolve. If KJ, someone who, unlike me, has a heart, can understand the necessity of these beings, then I can certainly remain strong. I've made it this far.

I smile and nod. Helix wanted this.

KJ brushes a strand of hair off my face, his gaze so gentle and loving, telling me he knows how hard this is. I bite my lip, every cell in my body drawn to that look.

The first Lycan, the largest of the three, drops to all four, nose sniffing the air.

"Akyla," Ava whispers.

I don't look her way. Naming them was her first mistake.

Mitch shifts his weight, his body moving slightly closer to the door. "The moment they're trapped, we need to move. No one else can find them."

Everyone in the room holds still.

One of the Lycans steps back, then moves around to one of the trees. Cautiously, it sniffs the trunk.

Tara frowns. "One of the snares are tied off there."

The other two join it. There's more scenting, then the big one, Akyla, paws at it.

Surely not.

A thin line of snow jerks as the motion yanks on the wire.

Hunter sucks in a breath. "They've seen the wires."

The Lycans glance at each other, then around. Akyla's lip curls in disgust. With a look that could only be called contempt, he turns, and the others follow him. With a few loping gaits, they disappear from the screen.

The room fills with shocked silence. The Lycans were clever enough to recognize the trap for what it was.

We're dealing with animals that are not only strong, but far smarter than we realized.

"There's no time to spare. We're going after them."

Eden and Ava's gasps are the loudest. Mitch looks like he's about to have a heart attack.

KJ's two words capture it all beautifully. "Holy crap!"

The words stating, "We need to get going," came from the back of the room.

Behind us.

From the cages.

Noah is standing at the gate, arms crossed, body calm.

Although his face looks tired, a small grin tips up his lips. "If someone could open the gate, that would be appreciated."

28

HUNTER

Ava and Eden have the lock undone and the door open as quickly as they can, considering their fingers are trembling and their eyes are blurred by tears.

The second he's out, Noah grabs his mate and daughter and hugs them like he's never letting go.

I hold back, letting them have their family moment, not sure how I'm feeling. Seeing Ava happy makes my heart warm.

Ava didn't need to cure him by tapping into the threads. That's a good thing.

KJ was right. Ava is the key.

She can cure Furious, and without having to risk her life. The relief is like a tsunami through my chest.

Because risking her life is what she's doing every time she does what she does. I know it with the same certainty that I know my soul is bound to hers. Each time she's connected to the threads, she's gone deeper and deeper, and it's taken more and more from her.

KJ nudges me. "I'm not the type to brag, but..."

I shake my head. "I don't think that's ever stopped you."

"The truly amazing thing was that Sayen was crucial in making this happen."

I glance at the dark-haired girl who only moved so she could blend into the background again. There's something about her that's...out of place. This girl was raised by Dawn. Dawn would've manipulated this orphan in the same way she manipulated all of us.

KJ's watching me and I don't bother to hide my thoughts. We grew up together. He knows exactly what I'm thinking. That KJ's been blinded by his feelings. That Sayen is using him to finish whatever Helix started.

KJ sighs. "Coming from the dude who does nothing but follow his gut, which is just a glorified term for following your heart. If you ask me, that's kinda hypocritical."

I shift back a little, a brow arched in surprise.

KJ shrugs. "Just sayin'. Yes, Sayen was twisted by Helix. The woman was a master manipulator, after all. And Sayen was a lost orphan carrying her father's shame."

I blink. That's exactly what KJ was when he arrived on Evelyn Island.

"An orphan looking for redemption."

I blink again. So was KJ.

KJ is staring at her, and the emotion is powerful enough that Sayen glances up. Her gaze latches onto his and something changes in her. A softening, a straightening.

"And now she's found it," KJ whispers.

I look away, not sure what to make of it. "I hope you're right, KJ."

Because if he's wrong. KJ has brought a traitor into our midst.

Noah extricates himself from his mate and daughter, looking a little wrung out, but pulling himself up like the Prime Alpha he is. "We need to get moving. The authorities will be fanning out from the last place they were sighted."

Oh, yes. Noah is a cop. He'd know how they're going to work.

I nod. "And we know that's not where they think it is."

Noah looks at me. "Exactly. We have an advantage. A small one, but that's all we need."

Eden touches Noah's chest, looking up at him. Subtly, lovingly, she's checking that he's okay. Noah lifts her hand to his mouth, brushing his lips over her fingers.

I look away, the emotion too much for me at the moment. Noah and Eden's love has already stood the test of time and its trials.

Ava is looking at me as she approaches, and my heart constricts.

Why does this have to be so hard?

The room empties; KJ and Sayen off to produce more vaccine, the others off to coordinate equipment and supplies. The plan is to return with three Lycans. Dead or alive.

I can't hold Ava's gaze.

"Do you have a moment?"

Tara is beside me, hazel gaze dark and sober as she regards me.

"Sure."

Tara glances at the door where everyone has filed out. "KJ...my... ah...." She turns back to me. "He knows who Sayen is, doesn't he?"

"Your brother is one smart guy. He knows exactly who Sayen is."

"Right. That worries me."

I pause. It doesn't surprise me that Tara doesn't trust KJ. First of all, she doesn't know him. Second, he's the son who was born and raised to be his father's image.

"KJ left his whole pack so he wouldn't be defined by Kurt."

Tara winces as she glances at the empty doorway again. "And yet he fell for someone who believes in everything Kurt tried to force onto the world." She raises a brow at me. "She kept him hostage, didn't she?" I nod. "That's either Stockholm Syndrome..."

I wait, knowing the second suggestion is going to be worse than the first. Doesn't Tara realize half the problem is we need Sayen right now? Furious will be unchecked without a vaccine.

Furious will have to be cured by Ava alone if there's no vaccine.

"Or he's more of a traitor than she is."

I reel back, stunned. KJ has wanted nothing more than to fix this.

Tara pushes forward. "KJ may have decided Helix was right," she hisses.

I'm already shaking my head. KJ always talked of doing what it takes, but what Tara's suggesting, it's too far. I step back again, deliberately creating space, possibly wanting to get the hell out of here. "You need to spend time with your brother, Tara. Then you'll see what you're suggesting is impossible."

Tara opens her mouth, then shuts it again as she spins on her heel. With a few quick steps, she's gone.

Which leaves the room with only me and the vision walking toward me.

Ava slips her arms around my waist. "I caught the end of that. You okay?"

Looking down at her concerned wintergreen eyes, my chest feels like it's expanding and compressing at the same time. It's a tug-of-war that's as painful as it sounds. There's a lot not okay with things at the moment. The Lycans. KJ and Sayen. Furious.

Us.

The room is empty, and I know this is our last opportunity to talk until this is all over...whatever the hell that's going to look like.

How do I color these last moments of privacy with everything my heart is holding?

Ava's fingers brush my cheek. "I understand why you tried to stop me."

I pull back, knowing that's something I haven't done with Ava for a very long time. Something I thought I'd never do again. "How do I protect you, Ava, when we're not working together?"

Her hands fall to her sides. "I know, Hunter. It's just that..."

My hand wipes across my face, but it doesn't help. This pain is soul deep. "I know, it was your father. But when does it stop, Ava? When do you choose you?"

And us.

And me.

Ava's lip trembles, her eyes wounded pools of pain. Which makes it all worse.

It's a pain I can't take away. In truth, it's a pain I'm responsible for.

Which is where the crux of this issue is. Ava needs me to love her enough to be there for her. To make sure she's not doing this alone.

But Ava needs me to be able to let her follow her gut.

Even though it involves a risk to her life.

I don't know how I can give her both.

And I don't know how to make her see this. "The Lycans—they can't be allowed to live."

She looks away. "I won't stop anyone if it needs to be done."

If? Still, the tension eases a little. Ava's coming to accept it.

Except then I feel the slash of pain those words cause her.

I lift my hand, but when I see how much it's trembling, I let it drop. "Ava. I'm not willing to accept a scenario where we don't win." I swallow. "Together."

There is no future for me without Ava.

She's in my arms as I consider the next breath, whooshing the air straight back out. I grab her, hold her tight.

I hold her like this is precious and fragile and eternal and fierce.

Just like she's holding me.

"Hunter. Your love is what makes me strong. Loving you is what makes me whole. I know I'm asking so much in return." She buries her head in my chest. "I'm scared it's too much."

I lean back a little, lift her head. Lose myself in the glory that is Ava. "What we have is infinite, Ava. There's no such thing as too much." I brush my lips over hers and they tremble. "I just need you to know that we have a thread, too."

She smiles as she pushes up and presses hers soft, sweet mouth to mine. "Our thread is my lifeline."

I kiss her, losing the ability to form anymore words. My heart is too full. My chest is too tight.

Because Ava's right. That thread is my lifeline, too.

The door flies open, and we look up, startled, but we don't let go. I think we're both too conscious that the world is about to come between us.

It's KJ, and he doesn't look surprised to see us wrapped around each other. In fact, he takes us in, then looks like he hates being the bearer of bad news.

His shoulders slump as he holds the door open. "We need to get this vaccine out there. Humans have been infected with Furious."

29

HUNTER

The reporter's words seem stuck on repeat in my head as I march down the hall. "Several injuries and two deaths have been reported. Authorities expect the toll to rise as the werewolves are still at large. Remain indoors, keep your family safe. I repeat, remain indoors."

Humans infected with Furious are becoming violent. The first death occurred in the hospital—a young teen with the faintest of scratches after her mother protected her with her own body.

The second was a male, shot by police as he'd waved a shotgun around a shopping mall, screaming to the people that they'd all pay.

Noah had pointed out what I'd noticed. The Lycans weren't killing anyone. They were infecting them.

Removing the Lycans is now crucial. They're threatening human life along with the exposure of Weres.

Swinging open the door to the lab, I don't bother to hide my irritation. We need to go. Now.

Except for some reason, we're still waiting for the darts.

Sayen is standing beside one of the benches, staring down at the handful of brightly colored darts in her hand. She startles when the door flies open, eyes wide as she sees who's standing in the doorway.

Her hands clutch the darts and my eyes narrow. "I thought KJ was loading those."

Sayen starts to carefully pack the darts in the vet pack. "He's just getting some spares."

Those darts are supposed to be filled with the medication that will dispatch the Lycans. But if Sayen wanted to sabotage this whole thing, then KJ just served it to her on a silver platter...

I stride into the room. "Show me what you filled those up with."

Sayen's lips tighten. "We've run out. That's why KJ is getting the spares."

Dammit. This isn't what we need right now.

Sayen spins around to face me. "It doesn't matter that you don't trust me, Hunter. After everything I've done, you'd be a fool if you did. The truth is, I don't care about letting you down. I care about letting KJ down."

Tara's words filter through, unbidden. *Or he's more of a traitor than she is...* I shake my head, unwilling to entertain that KJ has gone to the dark side.

That he'd align himself with everything his father stood for.

I narrow my eyes at her. "KJ deserves better than falling for a girl who betrays everything he's ever believed in."

Sayen squares her shoulders as she stares directly at me. "Exactly."

Wordless silence fills the room. I have no idea what that one word means. Could Sayen really be what KJ believes she is? A girl, manipulated by Dawn, needing a chance to prove she's not cut from the same evil cloth?

"Besides," she shrugs, almost like it doesn't matter, "if all else fails, Ava can work her healing magic and cure us all."

Red explodes in my head. "Except if Ava heals any more people, maybe even one more person, it could kill her!"

The words were meant to show Sayen, to hurt her, but instead, they plough straight through my solar plexus. It's the first time I've said them out loud, and it feels like I just gave them life.

Like some sort of premonition.

Shit.

Sayen finally opens her mouth, her dark eyes luminous, when KJ appears in the doorway, holding a small glass bottle. "Good news. There was enough for four more in the other lab."

He pauses as he registers the two of us and the tension that probably hit him like a wall.

"Aw, great. You two just had differing opinions on what's best for me, didn't you?"

Shit.

I spin around and shove past him. "Make sure you put your darts on top."

If Sayen has done what KJ believes would never happen—sabotaging the darts—then at least they won't be the ones we'll need to use.

Ava's eyes find me the moment I step outside. She would've felt the emotions I just got pummeled with when I was talking to Sayen. I wonder if I lifted my shirt, whether you could see the bruises.

It's a good thing there's no time to talk.

I don't ever want to have to repeat those words. And I plan on never having to.

KJ and Sayen aren't far behind me, meaning we now have our full complement of troops. We decided to keep it small to avoid detection by humans, plus it's not like we can get physical with the Lycans—they're too strong, too filled with violence.

And Furious.

We can't afford for Weres to be infected with the virus. Humans would never stand a chance.

So, it's Noah and Eden, Mitch and Tara, KJ and Sayen. Ava and me.

Eden looks around. "Everyone had their jab?"

Another reason we're only a small group. KJ and Sayen only had time to make enough vaccine to inoculate us. Anyone else coming would've been left unprotected.

Everyone nods, and I allow myself to relax just a little. One more safeguard in place. "So, the plan is simple. We find them, we inject them." I don't look at Ava as I say this. I can't. She knows we're no longer talking about tranquilizing them. It's too far gone for that. But it doesn't mean I don't feel her sense of defeat, the flash of loss. "Try to maintain a safe distance and let the dart guns do the work for you. Do not engage with them physically. With police and rangers out, we can't shift to fight, and these animals are too dangerous."

Another wave of nods move through the serious faces around me. Everyone knows this isn't going to be safe or straightforward.

Or easy.

I finally look at my mate.

Ava holds my gaze. No lip trembles. No eyes mist over. With her spine and shoulders straight, she turns to the group. "We do this quickly and humanely. These animals were created by the twisted heart of Helix. Today we show that hatred and greed will not win."

Something I didn't expect to feel right now sparks warmth in my chest.

Amongst this dark, dangerous time, Ava has me feeling pride. Love. Hope.

These nods are slower, less grim. Everyone looks expectantly at Ava—they're ready to take the next step.

I hold my breath as Ava closes her eyes.

You can see her center herself, go inward. Her face relaxes, her sweet lines soften. How can something so beautiful, something that is so innately part of her, be so deadly?

She gasps as her eyes fly open and connect with mine. "They've split up. They're going in different directions."

SPLITTING up didn't sit well with anyone, but it wasn't a choice. Eliminating three Lycans from infecting as many humans as they can isn't something we can afford to postpone until we have more trackers. Mitch had passed out the hand-held radios with instructions on how to use them as Ava had worked on refining their locations.

One was heading south-east through the reserve, probably looking to skirt Jacksonville and come in from behind. Noah and Eden would take that one seeing as Noah could move the fastest.

Another was heading west, to the populated tourist area near the reserve. KJ nominated himself and Sayen for that one, and with a flicker of a glance in my direction, Tara had quickly added she'd join him, Mitch and Josh with her. They knew the territory much better than KJ and Sayen, it was only logical. As much as I'd felt like I was betraying my trust in KJ, I'd felt relieved. KJ may believe Sayen had changed, but it seemed others were waiting for her to prove herself.

The last Lycan was like an arrow aimed at the heart of Jacksonville. That was the one I would take out, Ava by my side to see it happen.

The goodbyes were short and grave. Brief hugs. Hard slaps on the shoulder. Eyes telling each other to stay safe.

And they're gone. Noah and Eden melding into the forest around us, getting ready to shift as soon as they can, the others getting into their vehicles. Every moment the Lycans are getting closer and closer to town...with thousands of people to infect.

I chafe against the need to shift. Unlike Ava's parents, we're not heading deep into the reserve, plus Ava needs to keep updating the others on where the Lycans are.

Unsurprisingly, the Lycans stay true to course, obviously focused on their goal. Noah and Eden quickly pick up the scent of the Lycan they're tracking. KJ and the others barrel down the highway. They have a wealth of tracking experience between them which means they'll find the trail once they're on foot.

My heart clenches, knowing they're getting close.

Ava grabs my hand. "We need to be quick. From what I can tell, she's heading straight down the Jacksonville hiking trail. It's easy to navigate, but not the most straightforward way. If we take this trail, we can cut her off."

She? We're closing in on Asta?

My lips flatline. "She's hoping to run into more humans." Please, let them listen to the warnings.

Ava's grip tightens. "Their threads, Hunter. They're so...damaged."

I squeeze Ava's hand as we break into a run. Deep down, I know Ava has the ability to heal the most broken of threads. Her compassion and ability to see beneath the disfigurements, no matter how deep, means she can find the place where Lycans are still part of us. That despite it all, we're part of them. That's the part Helix didn't bank on.

Ava calls them the golden motes. The essence of life.

It's no coincidence that Ava is a golden wolf. It's like she's their ambassador. Their messenger.

Their living, breathing proof.

But just because she can, doesn't mean she should. Or that it won't come at a price.

Injecting a little more speed as we race through the forest,

I'm impressed that Ava keeps up with me. It's when she overtakes me that I'm reminded Ava's compassion has never made her soft or weak.

This is the child of the Prophecy. The daughter of the Prime Alpha and Queen of the Fae.

My mate.

We reach the intersection of our trail and the one Asta will be bearing down in only a few minutes. Although I haven't been long in the area, I recognize we're close to town even though we haven't seen anyone. The vegetation thins and the roads widen. That's good. It means people are taking the threat seriously and staying indoors.

A threat that's growing, but I have no idea how fast. I wish we could tune into the radio for just a few moments. Not knowing what's happening with the humans infected with Furious is unsettling.

I wrap my renewed determination to be the ones who make this right around me like armor. Grabbing her hand, I pull her in close. Ava's agreed the Lycans can't live. She's strong enough to do this, and if it's all too much, our love can heal the wound their deaths will leave.

I'm not sure what she senses, because when she looks up at me, her eyes are weighed with a million words. "Thank you, Hunter," she says simply, before she looks down the trail. "I can face this because of you."

I wish there was time to show the countless unsaid pledges I saw in her eyes, are in my heart too, but there's not. Instead, I brush a kiss across her windswept hair then straighten beside her, noticing that our hearts are beating as one.

Ava pauses, frowning. "She's slowed down."

I look around, trying to figure out why. "Do you think she's scented us?"

Ava frowns deeper. "I'm not sure. I didn't think she was that close."

I doubt Ava's calculations are off, which means the Lycans may have better senses than we realized. The thought makes me nervous. It reminds me we're still not totally sure what we're dealing with.

Feeling like I'm sealing Asta's fate, I pull off the backpack. Inside, the dart gun is already loaded. I made sure everyone got the darts that KJ loaded. Sayen was left to carry the ones she filled. If she's tampered with them, it'll be her life she's risking.

The radio clicks and crackles as Eden's voice comes through. "We've found him. He's not far ahead."

Ava freezes, staring at the black device in her hand. She presses the button on the side as she speaks into it. "That's Ari. He's the youngest of the litter."

She looks at me. "The quiet one."

She's right. The cautious one who always held back, Ari let his siblings go first. Although, once he got comfortable, he was probably the most affectionate of the bunch.

Except that Ari doesn't exist anymore. That Ari never stood a chance. With altered genetics, the addition of human growth hormone and Furious has corrupted the wolf he was.

I'm not sure Ava's accepted he's now a violent monster driven to destroy humans.

Ava closes her eyes, going within. Without opening them, she raises the radio to her mouth. "You're right. You're close. Be careful."

It doesn't surprise me that Ava can not only sense where the Lycans are at a distance, but she can also feel where her parents are. She describes the threads like a web. I imagine right now it's like a map.

"You too, honey," Eden responds. "We'll see you soon."

I grip the gun in my hand, finger flexing on the trigger. Noah and Eden are closing in on Ari. We're waiting as Asta is coming at us. That leaves KJ and the others dealing with Akyla.

"Crapsticks." Tara comes over the radio. "State troopers, looks like they've barricaded the road. This could be a complication."

Ava and I glance at each other. Humans in the area isn't a good thing. Ava speaks into the radio. "Keep it short. Akyla isn't far away."

KJ comes on. "We're only a couple of minutes behind. Might take a detour down Contour Road."

Crap. We're dividing again.

"Good idea," Tara responds. "We'll thank them for their service and protection, turn around and follow you."

I shift my weight, but it doesn't help. Nervousness is bubbling deep in my belly. It's a good thing that Tara and KJ know the area and can sidestep the state troopers, but it still means they won't be together for the next several minutes.

Silence moves around us again and I scent the air. If Asta can smell us, then surely, I can smell her. Except there's nothing but pine and frozen moisture. "You sure she's close?"

Ava's eyes are glued to the trail. "She's not running anymore. But she's coming."

I open my mouth to respond when the radio comes to life.

"Guys." It's Tara again. "The troopers wanted to give us an escort home. It took us a couple of minutes to convince them we can look after ourselves."

Shit. More of a delay.

"We're heading back to Contour Road now."

I grab my own radio. "KJ? Did you hear that?"

"Roger that. There's a barn up ahead. We'll wait there, make sure there are no humans thinking their panic room is going to help during a Lycan apocalypse."

I shake my head. "Good idea. And not funny."

Tucking the radio back into my pocket, I move closer to Ava. Danger is contracting around us.

"Ava." It's Eden, her voice rushed and hurried. "Dad has him in his sights." There's a gasp. "Noah—"

Then radio silence.

We wait, breath held, jumping when the crackle of the speaker sounds again. "Eden?" It's Tara, the crackly line unable to disguise the concern in her voice.

Frantically, Ava presses the button. "Mom. Dad. How are you doing?"

Breathing feels too loud as we wait for something. Anything.

I grab Ava's arm, knowing there's one question that will tell us whether they're okay. "Have they been successful?"

She closes her eyes, a fine frown crinkling her forehead as she concentrates. I watch Ava's face, not liking what I see. She starts to speak, but I already know what she's going to say. The fear and dread are too clearly stamped across her tight skin. "Ari's still alive." She blinks. "Akyla is, too. He's stopped moving."

The crunch of snow heralds that their sibling, the third Lycan, is too. We turn to find Asta standing on the trail. Pushing up from all fours, she owns her full height.

She's glorious and unnatural all in one. White as the snow, she looks like she belongs out in this frozen wild. But standing like a human, gaze unflinching, she straddles a world she doesn't belong in.

"Asta," Ava whispers, her voice hoarse.

Ava's seeing Sakari's daughter. The pup who would lick your fingers long after any trace of food was gone. So much hope was born with this wolf.

Asta's nostrils flare as she draws in a giant breath. Her massive chest inflates, expanding her shoulders and straightening her spine. She angles her head, eyes widening, and I know she recognizes us.

We raised her.

She carries my DNA.

But we also failed to protect her.

With a roar of rage, she launches forward. By the time her front paws hit the ground, Asta already has momentum, and she uses it to her full advantage.

Stepping in front of Ava, I raise the gun and level it, staring down the sight. Watching the massive, moving target coming at me, I know there's not much time. But even knowing the damage she's already caused, the damage she wants to continue meting out, this is the hardest thing I've ever done.

Ending Asta was never something I thought I'd have to do.

When my finger tightens on the trigger, every muscle in my body does the same. I'm bracing myself, not for the recoil of the gun, but for the recoil taking this life is going to have. There's a pop and it jerks in my hands.

I lower it, feeling my heart sink with it. Asta had to die because too many people were scared and angry and desperate and disconnected.

Except the moment the gun fires, Asta lurches left, her reflexes like lightning. She tumbles, only too quickly to right herself. She shakes her head, eyes still wild with anger, her momentum never stopping.

Holy hell.

Asta just dodged the dart! The dart that was supposed to end this.

Sweet gods. Did that happen to Noah, too? And KJ and Sayen could be facing Akyla alone!

There's no time to hope I'm wrong, because a furious beast has our death wish stamped across her canine face as she shrinks the distance between us. I launch forward, hitting the ground as a wolf.

When Asta registers the white wolf coming at her, her eyes

blaze. Her muzzle serrates in a growl, exposing her dagger-like teeth.

Teeth gleaming with saliva. Teeth coated in Furious.

Letting out my own bellow of thunder, I let her know I'm not scared. Only determined.

Asta won't be getting anywhere near Ava.

We run at each other, two trains of war who have set their trajectory. With only a few feet away, Asta launches herself, which is exactly what I was hoping she would do. It's the only opening I'm going to get.

I leap too, but instead of pushing up and meeting her mouthful of death, I spear low and straight. When my body slams into hers, the impact is like hitting steel, but I don't care. I ram her, and I ram her hard.

I slice in just below her jaw, and it clicks shut as we collide. Our bodies crash, crumpling into each other, two opposing forces honoring the power that was injected into their launch. I expect it to separate us, bounce us right off each other, but Asta has the advantage of a humanoid body. She grabs me with forelegs more like arms, twisting her body so she's flush against mine.

We hit the ground, rolling, and my only focus is keeping those jaws away from me. When we stop, all I need is one opening. A vulnerable throat, an open chest.

And Ava will be safe.

I don't bank on the tree. Or on Asta seeing the advantage for what it is. Without warning, she shoves me then peels away. I don't see the collision coming. Or the pain as my body jack-knifes around the trunk, then comes to a halt beside it.

Asta is above me before my caved lungs can pull in a breath. I consider shifting to human, knowing I'm losing my wolf strength, but wanting the protection of arms. What I see has me changing my mind.

A human would never stand a chance against what's bearing down on me.

Asta is a wild ball of fury, snapping and snarling, spittle like ocean foam catching the air. Desperate, I call her name. "Asta! It's me!"

But there's no pause, my words have no impact.

She's too far gone.

Too consumed with rage.

Arms straining to keep her deadly jaws away, I sneak a glance to my right. My heart is hammering a denial I have to face.

If I fail, Ava won't be safe.

Maybe I can tell her to run.

Ava has dropped to her knees, her eyes closed. What sends the greatest bolt of fear straight through me is seeing her face, tense but calm.

Ava's connecting with the threads.

"No!" I scream the word, not at Asta, but at the girl who holds my heart. She can't try and heal the Lycans. They're too strong. They're too far apart.

Doesn't she know? If it comes to me or her, Ava will always come first.

Above me, Asta gets a burst of energy. It's a surge of strength I can't fight.

I lock my arms, but even as the adrenaline surges, I know they're nothing more than twigs trying to hold up a slab of marble. Being crushed is only a matter of time.

Her open jaws spear down, closing in on their target. I turn my face as her teeth slam shut, grazing past the skin of my cheek. Her growls fill my ears, the certainty of my death fills her eyes.

No.

Ava.

Asta pulls back, loading the gun for her final attack. My arms tremble, moving beyond breaking point. They won't have the strength to hold her back this time.

As her trajectory heads down, I shout the last thing I wish Ava would do.

"Ava! Run!"

When Asta collapses on me, I struggle like I've never struggled before. I fight the weight pushing down on me, desperate that these aren't my last moments.

That I haven't failed Ava.

It takes seconds to realize Asta is no longer fighting.

Her body is limp. No life. No pulse.

Dead.

What the—

Shoving the Lycan off me, I scramble to my feet, Ava my only thought.

Only to see Ava crumple into the snow.

30

KJ

We were at a disadvantage from the beginning.

First it was the state troopers. Shutting down all roads in and out of Jacksonville meant something was going down. Hearing about them injected foreboding through me faster than a peristaltic pump.

It also meant Sayen and I had to turn off and go solo. I look over at her, but she's been staring straight ahead. Sayen had been even quieter than usual since we left.

The vet pack sits between us. It was a deliberate choice to let Sayen fill the darts. It was time to follow through on what I'd told her.

I love her.

I trust her.

She'll know what to do and when.

I'm pretty sure the barn was plonked here cause fate knew we would be here one day. Only about a mile out of town, it's all homesteady and white picket fences. Some hobby farmer, from the looks of things. Enjoying the farm life while still living close to town. Whoever lives here probably tells their friends they have the best of both country living and town amenities.

The joke to Hunter had been more of a hope. Please don't let them be stupid enough to still be here.

Leaving the truck, I notice we're downwind, which makes any tracker nervous. Sayen crosses her arms, watching the place intensely.

We both smell it at the same time. Faint but unmistakable.

Blood.

I push down on the radio button. "Ava, can you give us an idea where our friend, aka the killing machine, is?"

Nothing.

I try again, repeating my question without the smart-alec extras.

Silence.

"Hunter? Eden? Noah?"

Anyone?

But there's no response.

I frown. "Probably victory smooching."

Sayen shoulders the vet pack. "We need to check it out."

The scent of blood acts like a trail, bringing us outside the barn.

As we stand there, though, I realize something. "It's not human blood." I sniff the air again. "Sheep, I think."

Then I remember something. The Lycan's haven't been killing humans. Just infecting them.

As we stand there, staring at the door of the barn, something in my chest drops like a concrete weight. I grab Sayen by the arm. "Get the gun loaded."

She scrabbles for the zipper. "You think it's still in there?"

"I'm not sure. It probably stopped off for a snack, but we can't afford to make assumptions."

Keeping Sayen behind me, we enter the barn. My heart is a hammer in my chest as we scan the dim interior. The tang of blood hits us first.

The sight of the carnage is close behind. Several sheep, two cows, and a dog must've been locked in while their owners heeded the warnings and ran. They'd been left behind to be turned into mincemeat.

Being a small barn, it's only a single story. An overgrown shed more than anything. It means a quick scan of the place tells us the Lycan isn't in residence.

I get on the radio. "Lycan has cleaned out the barn, but no sign. I'd say he's moved on."

Tara replies. "Right." There's a pause. "No one else is responding, KJ."

Not good. "You're closest to Hunter and Ava. Check them out first."

"You sure?"

"Our Lycan can wait."

Maybe the state troopers will have some action on their hands. They'd be on shoot-to-kill orders, just like we are.

"I'll keep you posted, little bro."

If there was time to digest that sentence, I'd probably try to figure out how I feel hearing it. But there isn't.

Sayen looks around at the mutilated animals. "I wish we could do something for them while we're waiting."

Grabbing her hand and heading to the sunlight pouring through the door, I almost smile. "I doubt someone like Helix would say something like that."

Sayen pauses, pulling us to a halt. "You believe I'm not like her, don't you?"

Turning around, I let the answer shine from my eyes. "It never crossed my mind that you were."

Her eyes don't widen like I'd expected them to. "You were never going to be part of Dawn's plan."

Swallowing, I shake my head. Lying had sucked.

Showing Sayen who she truly is was my goal.

She doesn't get time to answer. The light behind us is eclipsed. When the Lycan steps into the doorway, it's a surprise it shouldn't have been.

We'd run headlong into a trap.

Alone.

Cornered in a barn.

Bloody corpses scattered around us a testament to what this monster is capable of.

I push Sayen behind me. "Is it loaded?"

She shoves the gun into my hand.

The rest happens in some strange mix of fast-forward and slow-motion. The Lycan jumps, feral and furious, the froth lining its mouth stained pink with blood.

I shoot, for once, thanking my father for forcing me into target practice. It's close range. There's no way I could miss.

Except the Lycan twists midair, like it knew what was coming. The dart impales into the wall behind it.

There's no time to shift. There should've been time to shift. There was definitely enough time to shift.

Except Sayen shoves me hard. I stumble. She jumps.

And meets the Lycan midair, for some reason, not shifting.

The clash of their bodies feels like a sonic boom through my heart. "No! Sayen!"

Snarls and snaps puncture the air, never losing rhythm as they slam onto the ground. I'm about to shift—this Lycan is going to discover it was up against two Weres—when it all suddenly stops.

I rush forward as Sayen stumbles back. Her eyes are wide as she stares at the Lycan lying lifeless only feet away.

I come to a halt beside her. "You killed it?"

Sayen looks down at her hands. "I...thought I'd missed."

I shove the Lycan with my foot, and its white body barely moves. It certainly looks dead. "I think you killed it."

Sayen takes a step back, holding up the dart in her right hand. "I was trying to puncture its throat, but I didn't think..."

I check the pulse only to find nothing. Pushing up, I feel a smile start deep in my chest. My clever girl.

My clever girl who didn't sabotage the darts!

I step forward, still not quite believing we've won.

"Eden! KJ, are you there?" It's Hunter on the radio. "Asta, our Lycan, she's dead. Ava—"

"Ditto." Eden's voice cuts through. "This Lycan is dead, too."

I lift the radio, keen to tell them we have a trifecta, as my eyes rise to meet Sayen's gaze. We did this together. I want to say the words together.

Right in time to see Sayen crumble like a fragile flower in a storm.

I drop the radio, hearing it crack as it slams onto the ground, but not caring. I catch her before she hits the barn floor. "Sayen?"

For a second, I think it's the shock of it all. It's a precious moment of ignorance where I don't realize the gravity of what's happened.

Then I feel the wet, sticky warmth coating my right hand.

Oh, god.

With her head in my lap, I raise my hand, denial coming hard against reality. Thick, red blood is streaked across my palm.

Sayen's been injured.

Which means, Sayen's...

She grabs my hand, pulling it down and out of line of sight. "I don't regret it."

"What have you done, Sayen?" My voice is a hoarse whisper.

Incongruously, she smiles. "Returning the favor."

She's talking about the time I saved her life from a wolf infected with Furious. Except that wasn't some rabid wolf. This was a bloodthirsty Lycan.

I go to lift her head. "I'll get the vaccine."

But Sayen tightens her hold on me. "It doesn't work after infection, KJ. "

I frown. "Of course it does. Noah was cured with this stuff."

She smiles again, the movement a slow and sad one, but doesn't answer. My heart battering my too-tight chest, I grab the syringe and vial from the vet pack. I have to focus to draw the vaccine out because my hands are shaking so hard.

Sayen doesn't even wince when I inject it in her upper chest. Her wound is in the middle of her back, close to her heart. That means the vaccine needs to be injected as close as possible, too.

Yanking off my jumper, I tuck it under her head, brushing back her black hair. "Now we just wait."

Sayen arches suddenly, her body curving up from the ground as her face contorts with pain. I hover, trying to control my panic. "Sayen!"

She collapses, breathing heavily. "It's already starting, KJ."

"What? No! It's the vaccine getting through your system. We just need to give it time to work."

Sayen's hand grips mine tighter. "I'm sorry, KJ. So sorry."

I lean down, bring my face close to hers. "You have nothing to apologize for, Sayen. You didn't know how to do it differently."

She closes her eyes, swallowing. "You did."

"Because I got away. I didn't have someone telling me they loved me as they used and manipulated me."

With a sharp intake of breath, Sayen arches again, this time, a scream wrenching from her throat and echoing through the barn. It feels like it pierces my heart, but all I can do is hold her hand as she grips me like a lifeline.

Her body caves but her face stays twisted with pain. "KJ," she pants. "You need to get a dart."

What? "Like hell I will!" I grip her face, pulling my own in close. "The vaccine is working. We're going to get through this."

Sayen's lip trembles. "I need to show that's not who I am."

My throat feels like razor blades are dancing around it. Sayen has always sought redemption.

Well, this isn't going to be it.

"You already showed that when you loaded those darts. If you'd replaced them, the Lycans would still be alive."

She shakes her head but stops quickly, wincing. "Sabotaging the darts shouldn't be a choice. No one with a heart would consider doing that."

When the next wave hits Sayen, it lifts her torso, and I have to jerk back so we don't collide. Her beautiful face knots and twists, and her eyes flash with something that has my whole body freezing. Violent and angry, they spit venom at me.

Her dark, soulful eyes are full of fury.

No, no, no. The vaccine just needs more time...

As it ebbs, Sayen tries to pull her hand from mine, but I hold tight. Breathing hard, she stares at the ceiling. "You need to get the dart, KJ."

Although I shake my head, I find I can't form the denial. We need more time...

"I don't know how long I've got before I can't control this."

When I finally find my voice, one word shoots out like a bullet. "No!"

Sayen doesn't seem to hear me, because she continues to stare at the wooden roof above us. "You knew all along. You knew I wouldn't be able to see it through."

"It's your beautiful heart that dreamed of justice and fairness that I fell in love with, Sayen. You wanted to use our strength to achieve that."

She turns her head slowly, her waterfall hair sliding over her shoulder. "I like the person I am through your eyes, KJ. That's the person I want to be."

"You are, sweet Sayen. Even Dawn couldn't take that away."

She grimaces, her whole body tensing. "I finally believe you. You have the most amazing mind, and an even more wonderful heart, Kurt Junior. There's no way you could fall for someone who didn't have good in them."

I relax a little. "That's my girl." Suddenly, it hits me. Why the hell didn't I think of it? "Ava! We can get Ava to heal you!"

If Sayen's right, and the vaccine isn't working, then it was Ava who healed Noah.

Ava can save Sayen.

I glance frantically around for the radio, but Sayen's hand tenses on mine. "No, KJ. It's too risky for Ava. Healing drains her every time."

I pretend I didn't hear that. There's no way I'm not asking Ava to heal Sayen. We need her help with the vaccine.

I need her.

I spot the radio a few feet away just as Sayen speaks again, "It's smashed. You won't be able to get a hold of them."

She's right. My heart stops like my lifeline was just severed, but then I realize Ava can find us. "It's only a matter of time before they're here. We just need to keep you safe until Ava arrives. Now that they can't reach us, they'll come."

The next surge of Furious hits with no warning. This time, Sayen shoves me as she sits upright. I grab her as she tries to stand, and she screams. "Let me go!"

Her right hand raises in a fist, and she quickly grabs it with her left. Twisting and turning, she seems to fight herself as she simultaneously fights to break free. I tighten my hold, feeling the heat pulsing from her body, the trapped energy desperate to be let loose. Her shoulder slams into my chest but I just swallow the impact.

Sayen needs to know I'm never letting her go.

The flash of Furious abates and Sayen collapses in my arms, breathing like she's just fought the fight of her life. I stroke her cheek. "See how strong you are? I reckon you could beat this virus all on your own."

Sayen's lips, the ones that fascinated me from the moment I saw her, twitch up in a sorrowful smile. "You make me feel strong. And worthy. It's what finally showed me what Weres need to stand for."

I don't really understand what she's trying to say, but I don't ask. Sayen needs to save her strength. We have to hold it together until Ava and the others get here.

Sayen looks up, and my breath disintegrates. Her face is soft with love, her eyes full of something I'll never find the words to capture. "Thank you, KJ. For believing."

The tear is unavoidable. I hate the sound of goodbye in Sayen's words. I lean down, my heart tearing as I brush my mouth across hers. Her lips tremble and I'm not sure if the moisture is hers or mine. "Sayen, I love you. Everything is going to be okay."

"And I love you, KJ."

When Sayen's body jerks, I pull back, confused.

Sayen's eyes are moist pools of moonlight as she looks up at me. Her hand moves and I see it lift. As she opens it, I gasp as a lightning bolt of pain rips through me.

The dart Sayen was clutching rolls across her palm and tumbles to the floor.

Sayen just injected herself. Using the dart she filled with a lethal dose of life-ending liquid.

"No!" My denial is shouted, roared through the barn, torn from my chest.

And totally futile.

Sayen smiles at me as her hand brushes my cheek. She's silent as the deadly fluid makes its way to her heart. I'm silent as I desperately wish I could stop its trajectory.

Stop time.

Stop this.

Her hand drops to her chest. Her eyes flutter closed.

My heart shatters into a thousand jagged pieces...just as hers stops.

31

AVA

I recover almost instantly.

I smell the snow. Feel Hunter's presence as he scoops me into his arms.

Realize what I've done.

My eyes fly open, taking in Hunter's relieved face, but I'm yanked back into the moments I did the unthinkable.

I'd tapped into the threads, felt the throbbing lifelines of the triplets. Just like the other times, they'd been jagged and uneven and deeply damaged.

A scar needing, no waiting, to be healed.

But as Asta attacked Hunter, voracious in her hunt for death, I'd made a choice. Breathing deeply, unsure that I could even do this, I'd connected with the golden motes. They'd flowed freely between us, seeking and fusing, a glorious bridge between them and me.

Then, with my heart throbbing in my chest, I'd simply, irreversibly, snapped it.

Ruptured the connections.

Severed the threads.

Their life force was instantly extinguished. The motes smothered and suffocated, turning to ash.

This time, I'd welcomed the blackness as it inhaled me.

Now, with consciousness as harsh as reality, the pain slashes at me, shredding me in the same way I shredded the threads. I can't help the wail it yanks from my throat. The tears are instantaneous, but they don't help. They seem to feed the agony, as if they're watering and nurturing the hurt.

"Ava." Hunter's arms are around me, holding me tight.

I cling to him, a broken shard being thrown around in this maelstrom of pain. His hold tightens, pulling us flush against each other, melding me to him. As the wound grows, it tears at me, tries to fracture me, I cling to his strong shoulders. I find the place our hearts beat against each other.

I focus all of me on that one point.

And discover I'm no longer falling apart. I feel myself grow bigger than the pain. I remember I'm part of a whole that is more than just me.

"Hunter." My voice is a jagged whisper, and I have no idea what I'm trying to say.

He maintains his tight hold, one hand splayed across my back, the other a band around my waist. "I know, Ava. I know."

I bury my head in his shoulder, breathing in his scent, taking him in. "I...I killed them."

"No. Dawn signed their death warrant when she infected them. You ended their suffering."

Not sure how much mercy there is in death, I stay wrapped in the cocoon that is Hunter. My mate. Slowly, the ache in my chest lessens, becoming a dull throb. I know without a doubt, the remaining tear to the fabric of my being is something I'll carry for the rest of my life.

Just like I'll have Hunter to soothe it on the days it demands to be acknowledged.

Hunter pulls back, his handsome face full of tenderness, his hand gentle as he brushes a strand of hair from my face. "And you saved countless lives, including mine."

And there was the choice. The chance to heal the Lycans, or the loss of the one who breathes life to my soul. "There is no life without you, Hunter."

This kiss is like no other. Softer and sweeter, deeper and harder. It's the kiss of a love born by choice. It's the kiss made possible by sacrifice and surrender. It's two hurting souls finding healing in each other.

Sounds filter in. My family is talking on the radio—I didn't hear it. Hunter must've ignored it.

Then another sound—a truck.

We're inundated all at once. Dad sounding panicked over the radio, Mitch and Tara rushing out of their vehicle, running toward us. I let Dad know we're okay. Hunter meets Mitch and Tara to tell them what happened.

Everyone hugs. Mom tells us they're on their way.

Tara glances at the dead body of the Lycan, white fur sprawled across white snow. "They're gone. They can't hurt anyone else."

I can't bring myself to look at Ari. I can't celebrate that the Lycans are dead. But as I take in Tara's relieved expression as Mitch pulls her in for a hug, I can be comforted their threat is gone.

Hunter blinks, like it's just starting to sink in. "Helix lost. The Lycans were stopped before they could wreak havoc, and we now have a vaccine for Furious."

We all stand in silence as we absorb that. Tara is the first to move, her face breaking into a grin as she fist-pumps the air. "You did it, guys! We're almost there!"

Just some humans who will need the Furious vaccine.

There were deaths. My aching chest is a testament to the

sacrifices.

But we won.

Dad's voice crackles over the radio. "We're almost there. I can't get a hold of KJ."

Tara frowns, grabbing her own radio. "KJ. Can you hear me?" She releases the button and waits a few moments. "KJ. Little bro, we need a heads up you're okay."

Still nothing.

Hunter is frowning when he looks at me. "Can you check?"

I swallow, uneasy at what I might find. Following a thread only to find it severed would be a hard blow right now.

I find him quickly, a testament to the friendship we've forged, relief making my shoulders sag. KJ's alive. I hear Hunter let out a pent-up breath, and know he's realized it, too. I tense again. KJ's hurting.

"What? What is it?" Hunter's voice echoes my worry.

"I think he's hurt." Oh, god, which means he needs the vaccine! I stop and scan deeper. No, he's not physically hurt.

KJ's in a whole world of emotional pain. I scan wider, then abruptly stop when I find the source. A severed thread, a lifeblood of energy hemorrhaged and gone.

My eyes fly open with shock. "It's Sayen." Tears well and the world blurs. "She's dead."

Hunter stays silent, but I feel it hit him.

Tara gasps. "No!" She grasps Mitch's arm to steady her. "Poor KJ."

The spark of victory that had tried to gain life dies. Hunter's fists clench. "We need to go to him."

Mitch's face is grim as he turns away. "I'll get the Lycan. We need these bodies to disappear."

I don't look, but I hear the truck's suspension compress as the body is loaded. They'll collect the others and destroy the evidence of their existence.

Right now, KJ needs us.

Hunter and I come together, two magnets that are whole when together, as we head to the truck. We're just about to climb in when the radio comes to life again.

"Ava. Hunter." It's Dad, and the tension in his voice is unmistakable. "We can't get to you."

I freeze, alarm spearing through my body. "What's going on, Dad?"

There's a pause, and I almost ask again but then the radio comes to life again. "We can't get past the checkpoint. We're not allowed out of Jacksonville city limits."

Oh, no. Did the state troopers see the dead Lycan they were carrying? But surely, they would've covered it...

Hunter grabs his radio. "What's going on, Noah? The Lycans are all dead."

"But their legacy isn't. I want you to listen to me very carefully, Hunter. You need to get Ava the hell away from here."

Hunter stills, probably bracing himself for what Dad has to say next. I almost want to cover my ears.

"There's a Furious outbreak in Jacksonville."

32

AVA

Tara and Mitch head out, KJ their destination.
My throat aches as I wish we could join them. Sayen's death would've torn KJ apart, and having Hunter there would've meant there would be someone to help hold him together. I only hope that Tara, his estranged sister, can be that person.

Because it's not over.

Dad says Furious is spreading. That Jacksonville is gripped by a state of emergency.

Staying away was never going to be an option, no matter what Dad said.

The highway on the way there is deserted. No one is entering Jacksonville, but more of a concern, no one is leaving. We pass the "Welcome to Jacksonville, your family friendly escape" sign in silence.

"Hunter." We both jump when the radio comes to life. Hunter grabs it, his face tense. It was KJ's voice reaching out to us.

"I'm here, buddy."

"You need to know." There's a pause, like KJ just ran out of breath. Hunter opens his mouth but KJ returns. "The vaccine doesn't work after infection."

I close my eyes as the pain in KJ's voice hits me in the solar plexus. He must've tried that with Sayen.

And it didn't work.

"You've heard about Jacksonville?" Hunter asks.

"Yeah. Tara's here now."

Hunter stares out the windshield, his face grim as we barrel down the highway. "That means we have a situation on our hands."

"Understatement, bro."

"We're on our way to look into it. You okay?"

There's another pause. "No." KJ's statement is matter of fact. "I'm going to head back to the center. We need more vaccines if we're going to stop the spread."

Hunter swallows. "Sayen is a Were we can all be proud of. I'm so sorry it cost her life, KJ."

This pause is longer. "You have no idea."

"Your beanie's in the lab, hanging over your microscope."

I blink at the tears. Hunter put it there when KJ went missing. It was waiting for him to return. Now it's going to be the comfort KJ needs right now.

"Thanks." KJ's voice is choked and raw. "Don't follow in her footsteps, okay?"

It's Hunter's turn to blink. I feel his ache compound mine. "Can't. I'm still waiting for you to make me a decent coffee."

"Looks like you'll be living for a bloody long time then."

Hunter lets the radio drop to the seat, and I grasp his hand. He squeezes it tight, mimicking the band of tension around my chest.

There's no time to talk because the horizon crests and the roadblock appears. It's lined with vehicles, even more bodies in uniform weaving around them. It's a scene you'd expect in a post-apocalyptic movie.

Hunter slows the truck and someone steps forward, waving their arms as they indicate for us to pull over. The truck bumps off the road and onto the dirt, gravel crunching as we come to a stop. We stare out the window, struck dumb by the scene in front of us.

The vehicles—trucks and cars—form a wall, bright yellow barricades lined in front of them. Men and women in blue and grey uniforms stride one way, then the other, looking like tense parents waiting for their wayward teen to come home. Clumps of people have congregated to the right, their frowns highlighted in spurts by the flashing lights of the emergency vehicles.

Beyond that is the outline of Jacksonville. Spotted with the beginning of suburbia, cocooned by the mountains behind it, it sits as motionless and silent as we do. With a sinking heart, I realize it's like us—a still lake hiding deep turmoil and strong currents within.

There's a burst of movement, a body I recognize. "Dad!"

I rush out of the truck, the sound of a second door slamming telling me Hunter's right behind me. But as I move closer to the barricade, it's like I'm a wind to flames. The troopers leap into action, coming up to head me off. The bystanders on the right surge to my side.

They're Weres! Channons and Phelans, even some Tates.

Then I see River and Orin, both Fae Elders, one my uncle.

On the other side of the vehicle, more troopers scramble toward my father. "Sir, we're not asking again."

I stop, not understanding what's happening. "Dad? Where's Mom?"

Dad points at me. "Get out of my way. That's my daughter!"

Finally, I register the final pieces of this scene. Each and every emergency personnel in this scenario is carrying a firearm. The weapons are long and black, and they hold them across their body like a shield.

These people are here to protect, no matter the cost.

One man steps up to Dad. "Out of respect, I'm going to repeat myself one last time, Noah. Step back, please."

Dad focuses on the man in front of him, not as tall or as wide as he is, but full of confidence thanks to the rifle slung across his shoulder. "I was just thinking the same thing, Derek."

Derek shakes his head. "You know I can't do that."

I'm about to call out when my line of sight is obscured by a body. "I'm sorry, ma'am, but you can't get any closer."

Hunter moves in beside me, staring at the guy hard. "An explanation would be appreciated. That's her father, the chief of police around here."

The man grunts. "All you need to know is that you're not getting any further. Jacksonville is in quarantine until further notice."

An entire town is in quarantine?

"Hunter!"

We both swing around at the familiar voice. Mike is striding toward us, his face strained with urgency. "What are you both doing here?"

Mike grasps our shoulders and drags us a few steps back. The guard seems to relax, his hand resting on his rifle.

Hunter grips him back. "What the hell is going on, Mike?"

Mike, the politician who was so determined to end wolf culling, looks tired and old. Defeated. "It started in the hospital, where they brought the infected in for treatment." He glances at the blockade behind us. "After that it was almost exponential. Doctors and nurses injured and infected. People broke out and the virus spread further."

I gasp, my hand flying to my mouth.

"There are dead bodies on the streets, people barricaded in their houses. They're," He jerks his thumb to the state troopers, "Waiting for the National Guard."

Hunter is a vortex of anger and dread beside me. "To do what?"

Mike's lips flatline. "They won't tell me."

There's a scuffle of movement, and we turn around to see Mom come up beside Dad. "We're obviously not infected. I would like to see my daughter."

Hunter and I glance at each other. That's why they're not allowed to pass? Because they could be infected?

Hunter goes to stride forward, only to find the trooper step in front of him. "It isn't a request, champ."

My mate glares at him. "These people are being held against their will when there's obviously nothing wrong with them."

"This isn't a time to be bending the rules. Sorry."

I step in, feeling the tension growing in the narrow space between them. "You don't understand. We need to talk to them."

The guard lifts his hand to his rifle, his face turning to stone. "Now, I'm ordering you. Step back."

The radio on his hip crackles and he steps back as he lifts it to his ear, never breaking the glare directed at us. "Anderson, here."

The crackly voice is faint, and I'm assuming Anderson figures we won't be able to make it out. The average human couldn't...

"Sergeant. We've had two attempted breaches on the southern post. Stay on alert. Shoot to kill."

I have to work hard to contain my gasp. I wasn't supposed to hear those words. They're not supposed to hit me so hard that I want to double over.

"Roger that. And backup?"

"EOI in less than five minutes."

I glance back at the crowd shifting closer and closer. River and Orin put their hands up, either asking what we can do next, or telling me fighting this is useless. The Weres are all cross-armed and scowling.

Spinning back, I single out my father across the barricade. "Mom! Dad! Get out of there, now!"

I don't totally understand what's happening here, but the sense of panic clutching at my throat is undeniable. This is getting dangerous.

Dad looks from me to the man standing in front of him, the Alpha in him knowing he has a choice to make.

The screech that renders the air has me jumping, and Hunter moving in closer to me. It has Dad taking Mom's hand and jerking her to the side.

Behind them, coming from the outskirts of town, the hideous scream sounds again.

It's a woman, and she's running. Fast. Her hair flies out behind her, strands streaming through the air. Her head is down, her arms pumping, as her legs working hard to push her forward with as much speed as possible.

It's her face that captivates me, though.

Her brows are pulled low, her mouth yanked up in a grimace. Her teeth are bared, her lips shiny with foam. Her gaze is black with rage. This is the human face of Furious.

Anderson stalks forward, raising his arm. "Front line, make ready."

The men along the front row raise their firearms.

What? "No!"

I rush forward, only to have Hunter grab me around the middle. Before I can struggle, object, tell him we can't let this happen....

It happens.

"Fire!"

A volley of cracks assault my ears, and the woman jerks back, then drops.

I trap the wail in my throat, the motion making me arch. I want to spin around, bury my head in Hunter's shoulder, but instead I sag as the scream reverberates through my head.

She's dead.

The men stand at attention, lowering their rifles.

Anderson crosses his arms. "Stay vigilant. There will be no breaches."

A lone man marches out and begins dragging the body back to the blockade.

Dad must decide to use the diversion. Grabbing Mom's hand, he runs, head down, shoulders forward like a battering ram. But one Were, Prime Alpha or not, is no match for military trained personnel carrying firearms.

In the blink of an eye his momentum ends. He raises his head to find several barrels aimed at him and his mate. My mother.

Hunter releases me, storming forward angrily. "That is unnecessary! Lower your weapons!"

Another blink, and Hunter is jumped by four troopers. He struggles, managing to get an elbow in, eliciting a grunt from the trooper trying to contain him, before Anderson raises his arm and lands a punch on his cheek. His face slams into the wet ground and the others quickly, efficiently, immobilize him.

"Stop," I cry.

Behind me, the Weres move in, a rumble of dissatisfaction strengthening their ranks.

Please, stop.

They don't understand who we are. Why we're here.

My mate stills, sprawled on the ground as his arms and legs

are locked behind him. My father has frozen, too many rifles still holding him as their target.

Mike steps forward, hands out in a conciliatory gesture. "Let's all take a breath, here. No one wants any trouble."

Anderson dusts himself off. "Then follow orders. I'm pretty sure I didn't stutter when I said stay where you are."

A gust of wind buffets the silence as everyone processes the stalemate we're in. Dad and Hunter move simultaneously. Dad steps back, holding his hands up in surrender.

Hunter yanks at his arms. "Got it, Anderson."

Anderson nods. "You better have." He raises his hand, and with a short, sharp movement, his troops drop their rifles and release Hunter. Dad takes several steps back, eyeing the men around him.

Hunter is by my side in an instant, glaring at Anderson as he rolls his shoulders.

I stand beside my mate as the quiet descends again. What now?

The rumbling of trucks rolls over us, answering my question.

Anderson glances at his troops. "Remain on high alert. Further orders coming."

From the National Guard coming to a stop behind us.

Anderson marches over to where several men, stiff-shouldered and grey, meet him. Their gazes scrape over the scene, taking in the vehicles, the troops, us, then pausing on the dead body of the woman laying off to the side.

They form a circle, Anderson with his back to us, talking in hushed tones.

Hushed tones every Were in the area can hear.

"One infected civilian down when she ran at us," Anderson mutters.

There are a few nods. "The situation in Jacksonville has deteriorated."

I want to grab Hunter's hand, move in closer, but I don't. I stand frozen as ice as the men continue.

Another glances at the houses dotting the too-close horizon. "The virus is spreading at an unprecedented rate. Footage is showing up everywhere on social media. They're either biting each other like animals or killing in cold blood. People aren't safe in their homes; gunshots can be heard as they try to protect themselves."

This time, I do grab Hunter's hand. I can't help it, it's a reflex response to the anguish that's slowly spreading through me like cancer. Innocent lives are being taken. Either by infection, or by the violence Furious is programmed for.

"We've estimated a minimum number of the population has been infected."

Anderson stiffens. "Minimum?"

"Enough for this virus to hit critical mass. It's only a matter of time. This shit is like wildfire."

Hunter's hand tenses around mine, and I can feel every Were collectively holding their breath.

Anderson pauses, taking in the faces around him. Each and every one is grim and hard. "What's our next move?"

One of the men straightens as he throws his shoulders back. "Martial Law has been declared. We've been ordered to extinguish this virus before it can spread beyond the city."

Breathing becomes impossible beyond the fear exploding through my chest. Martial Law. Extinguish. Surely, they can't—

"Our orders are to enter the town. Anyone showing signs of infection will need to be neutralized."

Anderson doesn't move. I wonder if the same horror I'm feeling has stolen his ability to process those words.

Neutralized.

A sanitary term for killed.

Anderson spins on his heel, wooden legs taking him back to

his men. As he passes us, I try to grasp his hand, but my leaden limbs are too slow. "Please, you can't..."

He ignores me, staring straight ahead like his joints have rusted.

He raises his arm to gain his troops attention. "We have our orders."

HUNTER

L ike hell they do.

Orin gasps, stepping forward. "There are innocent people out there!"

Anderson ignores him, striding toward some men looking at him expectantly. They start talking in hushed tones, which is completely wasted. Every Were heard the conversation where they just justified killing indiscriminately.

Ava grasps my arm. "Hunter, we can't let this happen."

"I know. There has to be another way."

The Weres are shifting uneasily behind us, waiting to see what we're going to do. Noah is on the other side of the blockade, watching the men talk. It's only a matter of time before he knows of their plans, too.

"Anderson," I call out, standing where I am. Not only am I not going to risk another unwanted face-plant, but I know without a doubt, that if I move, the Weres will move. A group of angry, strong-looking people closing in on armed personnel is a recipe for all hell breaking loose.

For war.

The man ignores me, so I call out louder, "Anderson. You can't do this."

He stiffens like I just shot him between the shoulder blades. Spinning around, his face looks like a barely contained thunderstorm. "You need to leave. This is now a military zone."

I push my feet into the ground. "We're not going anywhere. This needs to stop."

Anderson's head drops as he shifts forward. The bastard is trying to intimidate me.

But he doesn't realize how important this is.

"Please, Anderson." Ava waves her arm in the direction of Jacksonville. "So many lives are at stake."

"Yes. There are." Suddenly, he storms forward. Subtly, I angle myself in front of Ava. Anderson doesn't miss the movement, zeroing in on me. He stops a foot away, holding himself tall as anger convulses across his face. "People are in that city, dying of a virus we've never seen before. Each moment we wait, more people—men, women, and children—are infected."

My hands harden into fists. "These orders are going to do nothing but raise that death toll."

Something flickers in Anderson's eyes, but it's gone before I can name it. He drops his tone. "If we go in softly, softly, like you bleeding hearts want us to, you risk my men's lives. What's more, you risk this bastard virus getting out. Then what happens, huh?" He jabs his finger into my chest. "We're going to stop more deaths because we have the guts to do what it takes."

Do what it takes.

Words I've heard too many times.

Words I used myself when it came to changing Sakari's pups.

Words that just cemented what will happen next.

I shove my face close to his, not willing to lose hope. "There is always another way."

Anderson's lip curls, his breath hot on my face. "If you don't get your ass," He glances behind me, "and your friends' asses out of here, I'll have no choice but to arrest you."

I step back, breathing in as I create some distance. I turn away but hold his gaze as I snarl my response. "I'm pretty sure I didn't stutter when I said there's always a choice."

I don't look to see what impact my words have. I know they won't change the trajectory these humans are set on. The dread blooming through my veins feels like ice. Where do we go from here?

Grasping Ava's hand, I plan on heading back to the Weres and Fae when a voice stops us.

"Ava!"

It's Noah. He's moved, but instead of coming closer to the blockade, he's taken several steps toward Jacksonville.

Ava stops, and the dread expands and congeals. As I register Noah's face, my body feels like it just became part of the permafrost.

"Ava. You need to get the others out of here. They won't listen to reason."

Ava's shaking her head. "Dad, you need to tell them to let you through."

At Ava's words, the men in the front line stiffen, their hands tensing around their guns.

Eden moves in closer to her mate, and Noah nods imperceptibly. "There's no time."

He knows there's no point.

Noah stares at Ava for long moments. Too long. It's like he's saying...

"We're going back into Jacksonville. To help those we can."

Alarm rings through our connection as Ava registers what her father just said. "No! You can't do that! It's too dangerous!"

Noah's face remains resolute. "It's the choice we're making. We love you, Ava."

Ava runs over to Anderson. The men around him tense, but don't move. The irony that this girl is far more dangerous than I am, and yet they do nothing isn't lost on me. If they want to underestimate my mate, then let them.

"Please, let them pass. Just look at them, they're not infected."

Anderson glares at me, his look full of warning, before indicating to something behind us.

The sound of engines coming to life fills the air, the smell of diesel hits my nose. The troops are moving into position.

There's more movement, and I feel bodies closing in on me. Ava's pack and the other Weres. They're closing around me like a protective cloak.

Ava's hands go to her head, pressing in on her temples. "No, no, no. You can't let this happen."

Helplessness sucker punches me in the solar plexus. Although she was talking to Anderson, it feels like those words were meant for me.

I walk toward her, glaring at any of the men who try to catch my gaze. Guns or no guns, I'm getting to my mate.

I reach Ava and take her hand. The touch is simple, far less than the contact I'd like. But it's enough to tell her she's not alone.

Eden's face is twisted with grief. "Those people need our help. You know we need to go. Always remember that we love you, Ava. More than anything."

Tears are now streaming down Ava's face. She's still shaking her head, unwilling to accept what Noah and Eden already have.

The men around us won't change their course.

Noah and Eden can't move forward.

They're choosing to head back and help those they can as the military descends on Jacksonville with shoot-to-kill orders.

They're heading into a city infected with Furious.

Noah and Eden turn, breaking into a run as they head for Jacksonville. Ava's denial is whispered, wrenched deep from her heart. She knows this could be the last time she sees her parents.

Anderson grabs my arm in a steely grip. "Enough. Get her out of here before you leave me no choice."

My jaw is locked, my free hand fisted like steel. I want to hit Anderson. I want to take every man and his gun out of the equation.

But there is no vaccine for Furious.

No alternative.

I try to tell Ava we need to move back. But the retreat of only a few steps feels like defeat. And defeat right now is synonymous with death for countless lives.

Ava chokes on a sob. "Hunter. So many people are going to die."

Possibly her parents.

An ominous threat comes from one of the Weres behind me. "We're not going to let it happen."

I look back, smell the metallic scent that heralds they're about to change.

The Fae stand back, faces full of distress, as they helplessly watch this unfold.

When all this is done, they'll be the ones left to pick up the pieces. Their compassion and care and drive for peace will be the balm the world needs.

Oh, god.

This was Helix's plan all along.

Cause a war between Were and human.

Then Fae, Dawn's kind, would be the saviors and salvation for a world torn apart by hate.

The sound of boots battering the earth as the army moves forward tells me Dawn manipulated and engineered this like a master craftsman. It's undeniable in the grim expressions on the humans, the determined scowls of the Weres.

The already mourning Fae.

Despite Dawn being killed by the creatures she created...

Helix has won.

34

HUNTER

"You know what?" The painful grip on my arm releases. "If you guys wanna risk yourself? Go ahead. I'm not wasting precious personnel on two idiot teens out to save the world." He points to the crowd behind us. "Anyone thinking they can be a hero will be arrested," He pauses, staring at them with grim determination. "Or shot."

Anderson turns away in disgust. He raises his arm, swinging a fist in the air. "We're moving out, men. You know our orders."

The world around me starts to move forward as Ava and I stay where we are. Men trample past, armored vehicles behind them.

I don't know if it's my heart breaking or Ava's as we watch the slow-moving procession move away from us.

Surely, this isn't how it ends.

Surely, all the pain and sacrifice, the wolves, the Lycans, Sayen, didn't bring us to this.

The Phelans and Channons and Tates assemble around us, edgy and anxious. They're waiting for a sign as to what to do next.

Or they're deciding when the time comes to stop watching and start acting.

"Hunter," Suddenly, Ava's in front of me, wintergreen eyes earnest. "There's another way."

My breath catches. "What do you mean?"

"If the vaccine didn't work on Dad, it means I healed him."

My lungs start to ache, screaming for air, but I ignore it. Something tells me Ava's answer is going to steal it away again anyway.

She swallows, her hand coming up to cup my face. "I'll heal them. The humans with Furious."

"No." The one word is a bullet, aimed at piercing that suggestion and ending it. "Ava, there's too many of them. You know what healing does to you."

And what healing at that extent could mean.

Her eyes squint, narrowing with pain. "I know. Maybe that's what my gifts were all about."

To sacrifice herself?

For her energy to be the lifeblood of others?

No.

No.

No.

Men shout as the distance between us and them grow. Someone growls behind me. "We're running out of time. We can't sit by and let this happen."

My heart is battering inside my chest. Ava can't be suggesting what I think she's suggesting..."

"Ava, my role has always been to protect you. It's why I exist. This isn't an option."

I go to shake my head, but Ava's hand stills me. "I want to choose this."

She wants us to choose this.

My throat clogs and my eyes sting. "How can I sit by and let you do this?

She'll try and heal the countless people infected with Furious. It could be a hundred, it could be a thousand. And there are only two ways this could end.

In the first scenario, she'll be successful. She'll smooth and mend their poisoned threads, and this epidemic will end before it could rage out of control.

In the second, she'll fail. There will be more than we realized. Or Furious will be so deeply entrenched the healing will keep needing more and more. She won't have enough to repair and restore.

But, in both cases, a certainty settles in my soul.

Ava won't be able to survive.

The tears down Ava's face tells me she already knows this. The heartbreak in her eyes tells me she's asking this of me anyway.

Every cell in my body rebels against the idea. She's asking me to do the exact opposite of what the very essence of my spirit was born to do. She's asking me to choose between her and thousands of lives. She's asking me to let her go.

I clasp her hand against my face, turning to place a tender kiss on her palm. "I can't let you do that, Ava. Not alone."

Her lip trembles. "Hunter…"

But I love her enough to never make her choose between love and what she believes is her destiny. "We'll do it together."

35

AVA

Together.
That was never part of the plan.

But as Hunter stares at me, copper eyes so pained and so sure, I know I can't ask this of him without honoring his request. If I'm going to ask him to sacrifice me, then I can't ask him to save himself.

I close my eyes for the briefest of moments as his pain compounds my own. I was so sure that everything the threads stood for would win. Compassion and connection. The two elements that bind us all.

Maybe they still will be.

I just hadn't considered the price.

When I open my eyes, I'm glad all I can see is Hunter. His heart-stopping lines and breathtaking angles fill my vision. This Were who's made so many painful decisions, and yet his beautiful spirit has been my light. My compass. My home.

"I love you, Hunter."

"And I love you, Ava." He brushes his lips against mine, a butterfly of a caress that brushes my soul. "Always."

I kiss him back, cementing the feeling, the taste, the truth that is my mate. "Always."

With that, the decision is made. I step back, taking his hand. "We need to get closer."

Hunter nods, his face bleak but determined. "Then we run." He turns to the Weres behind us, some of them my relatives, all Weres I've known and loved. "We're going in closer. Ava is...is going to see if she can heal the infected humans."

A few of them glance amongst each other, shifting on their feet. "Ah, is that even possible?"

I wish I could smile and look reassuring. The best I can do is not cry. "We're hoping so."

Hunter looks at each one in turn. "You're better off staying here. We can't afford to create trouble with the guard."

There's more shuffling of weight. "We're not leaving."

As much as that makes me nervous, there's no point objecting. Weres are protectors. They would never choose to retreat.

Hunter nods. "Fair enough. But no matter what happens, do not shift."

Hunter's words make me wince. He's thinking ahead, of what happens if we fail. The National Guard will continue to Jacksonville. Humans will be killed.

But Hunter doesn't want these Weres risking themselves for an inevitability we couldn't stop. Against all odds, warmth sparks in my chest. It's pride. Hunter is being a protector and leader till the end.

We don't say anymore, just turn and run. There's no more time. No more options.

The cold wind in my face is a stark contrast to the heat holding my hand. I focus on that. On our connection. I know I'll do whatever I can to heal the immeasurable wound that is now Furious.

I also know that as this drains me, I'll do everything I can not to take Hunter with me.

This road is a direct arterial to Jacksonville. The first few houses are dotted ahead, the rows of vehicles aren't far away, telling me little time has passed. It feels like a lifetime.

I wish it had been. One thing I assumed throughout all this is that there would be more time with Hunter. A lifetime with Hunter.

Not really sure how this is going to work, I pull us to a stop with several yards between us and the convoy. The Weres are about the same distance behind us, which means we're standing in some sort of strange limbo. Not part of the humans. No longer with our kind.

Still too far away from those we're trying to help.

But I'm starting to get scared. This feels too big. Too much to ask for.

Too high a price.

"Sergeant! Sergeant!"

Hunter and I hold still, as up ahead, a trooper runs toward a tall, grey-haired man. Anderson turns, his frown apparent even at this distance. "What?"

"It's the high school, sir. It's under attack. Reports indicate civilians are heading there to protect it."

I gasp, not meaning for the sound to shoot out of my mouth. My parents went to that school. So did Josh. It would be full of terrified teens.

It's the first place my parents will seek to protect.

Anderson spins around. "What the hell!"

As several heads turn and register the two young people standing in the middle of the road, Hunter and I freeze.

Time has run out.

Grasping Hunter's hand, I whisper one word, "Now."

Closing my eyes, I tap into the strongest thread I've ever experienced. The one that connects me to Hunter.

It's glorious and beautiful, like it always has been. It's a beacon of light in this darkest of moments. It lifts me, opens me up, and I feel oxygen fill my lungs.

Then, like a network of veins and arteries, the strand divides and divides again. It works back, to the Weres behind us, showing me what no one else sees—how deeply and irrevocably connected we are.

But those connections aren't the ones that need to be healed.

I focus forward, and the network shoots out again. To Anderson, from Anderson to the men he has promised to serve with; some thicker, some thinner, all honoring our interconnectedness.

From there, it explodes outward in every direction. A golden web shooting out to create a breathtaking woven fabric.

"Hunter, it's so beautiful."

Hunter's hand is like a vice around mine. "I can see it, Ava. It's...amazing."

Elated that someone else is finally able to share this with me, I breathe in deeply, then out, reaching further than I ever have.

"What is it with you two? Have you got some sort of death wish?"

It's Anderson, his thread tightening as he moves toward us. Nervousness dims the energy around me. He can't try to stop us.

This is our only hope.

Although I don't open my eyes, I sense when Anderson is standing in front of us. "I didn't want to have to do this, but—"

Hunter tenses, and my hand moves as he pulls away slightly. No! I know deep in my soul that this isn't something I can do alone. If Hunter deals with Anderson, then we've failed before we began.

"I think you should leave them be. They're not doing anything wrong."

It's Orin! His gentle Fae glow comes to stand beside us. "If you want to go kill sick and innocent people, then go ahead. Leave these two be."

Anderson doesn't reply, so I use the opportunity to focus inward again. Straining, knowing I may not have much time, I follow the threads to Jacksonville.

I barely moved beyond the first few connections, a metaphysical three degrees of separation, when I find it.

Furious.

"Hunter," I whisper.

"I see it, too," he mutters.

"What the hell are these two going on about?" Anderson's agitation is growing. "I don't have time for this shit. You two are under arrest."

"You won't be touching them."

It's Mitch. Tara is with him. Sweet heavens. The Weres are behind them.

The web around me grows brighter and more intense as the numbers around us increase. Anderson and his men are determined to stop us. Weres and Fae are resolute that Hunter and I see this through.

But I've found the virus. The infected threads.

It's time to fulfill my destiny.

Behind my closed eyes, the fabric that is Jacksonville and its inhabitants is a complicated web. I can't see them; I don't know them. But I recognize our universal energy, the part we all carry. It throbs with life. It's laced with infection.

Furious has corroded entire sections, tainting it with darkness, shredding away the humanity. It's angry and violent and hungry for more.

There's so much more than I imagined. It's far more damaged than I anticipated.

There's more pain than I know what to do with.

Doubt starts to crowd in. "Hunter?"

"I'm here." He moves behind me, curling around my body. Our energy fuses, burning even brighter. "We've got this."

"You know what? I'll goddamned arrest you all." Anderson is moving away. "Barnes! Carter! Bring me the van."

I'm so tempted to open my eyes, but I know the connection I've established will be broken. More energy moves as my family and kind become a wall around us. "You're going to need more than a van."

Anger flares through me, and it's not mine. The bodies around me are preparing to fight for what they believe needs to be done.

I only have minutes, maybe not even that.

Finding the closest infected thread, the motes moving sluggishly through their blocked vein, I breathe in and out again. My skin prickles as it feels like I'm trying to glide over gravel, but I keep going.

Another deep breath and I send the motes the energy they need to fight this. They flare with the injection of fuel, moving faster, burning brighter. The sick shards around them begin to disintegrate. Again. Another breath and the cycle repeats itself. My head swims but I stay focused.

It's almost there.

When it happens, it's glorious. The motes flare the brightest I've ever seen them, glowing so brightly and brilliantly, that not a shard of darkness could survive. The light dies as my lungs run out of air, but all that's left behind is the glorious energy of the person we just healed. Their thread pulses gently, the movement of their energy now effortless.

I feel Hunter's awe as my heart celebrates, but it's short-lived. I'm not healing one person. I'm healing many.

The next is close, so I begin again. Air. Light. Energy.

My head spins even faster, my lungs feel like they're giving more than they're recharging. I feel myself start to weaken, even though the second one is barely finished. A new ache begins in my chest.

The fear that I'll fail. That this was always too big a task.

Hunter senses it and tightens his hold around me. I sink into him, drawing on his endless strength and love. Hunter and I begin to breathe as one as we meld with the motes, finding not just what connects us to these people, but what connects them to each other.

The virus is decimated, then extinguished in the second person, but when I fan my consciousness wider, I once again see how much has been corrupted. As I center myself, I see it spreading through the web, sick fingers reaching further and faster than I can catch them.

Despite feeling like a David against this Goliath disease, I move to the next person. They're tightly connected to the two people close by—probably family. Knowing this isn't possible to win by going one person at a time, I connect with them all.

The sap on my energy is instantaneous.

My knees weaken, but Hunter's arms tighten. "I've got you."

His voice is quiet, strong, but full of grief. As breathing becomes difficult, as this starts to take more than I have to give, it's Hunter's strength that inspires me. He's helping me, encouraging me, even as he knows it's taking me away from him.

Swallowing to moisten the dryness in my throat, I suck in deep into aching lungs. Air. Light. Energy.

Suddenly, Hunter's grip slackens. I feel his strength drain. He tries to fight it, tries to dig deeper, but I can feel the inevitability. His hold loosens another notch, his breathing becomes labored. I can feel both of our life forces being drawn out of us.

The energy of the lives we're connected to starts to dim; the darkness starts to grow. Helplessness fills me. It's like we're a chain of buckets trying to put out an inferno.

We can't keep up.

We barely made a difference.

I spin around, grasping Hunter's face, tears already a water-fall down my own. As the knowledge that it was all for nothing guts me, as it eats away at the last of my energy reserves, I want our love to be the last thing I feel. I press my lips to his. I want to tell him we tried. I want to tell him he needs to let me go.

Hunter's hands come up, cupping my head. He deepens the kiss, tightens his hold. He murmurs against my lips, the words breathless and weak. "I'll never let you go."

Our legs start to buckle so I hold on tighter. Hunter will be all that I'll feel when the darkness takes us.

"Oh, no, you don't." It's Tara, and she's swooped in to prop us up. Her arms wrap around us and she jolts in surprise. "Holy crapburgers!"

She sees it, too!

With an extra body connected to us, I feel a surge of strength. Seamlessly, Tara becomes conscious of the threads, her own vitality joining our cause. The motes flare along with my hope.

But then Tara's energy drains, too. She wheezes, like her breath is being sucked out of her body.

No!

"Tara?" Mitch's voice is full of worry. He grabs her, and his energy is added to the pool.

The same thing happens—another surge shooting out through the web. More of the darkness is extinguished. It's a small blast of light in the large fabric that is Furious, but it's something.

It's a beginning.

I look up at Hunter, whispering through my starved lungs. "We need more people."

Hunter opens his mouth, but it's not his voice that speaks.

"More. We need more people!"

It's Mitch, then Tara joining in the call. A hand rests on my shoulder and I instantly recognize Orin. River connects to him, then a Were after that. The same happens on Hunter's side. Hands grip shoulders, arms interlink.

The burst of energy is exhilarating. It arcs out, dividing through the web of life around us, burning the sickness in its way.

When the wave dies though, like they all have, it ebbs and recedes. Beyond it, entire tracts of Furious remain untouched. We've healed many, but so many more are still infected.

"Get your men over here!"

I don't know who calls it, my mind feels like a fog has rolled in. Tiredness sinks into my bones. If it weren't for the people around us, Hunter and I wouldn't be standing. There's so much pain.

Not enough light.

"I don't have time for this shit." Anderson puts his hand on one of the Weres. "Sweet mother of all that is holy."

Another surge, and almost automatically, I push it out.

"Barnes! Carter! Get your asses over here and bring every man and woman with you!"

Now, humans connect into the energy source we've created. I gasp. Many of them. So many of them.

The surge is the biggest so far. In my mind's eye, the threads around me strengthen with the power of touch. The fabric of people we've created is spreading slowly toward Jacksonville. I wish I could open them, see the very same web we're creating right here.

Instead, I become the conduit I was fated to be. I take their gift and send it out through the web of light.

"Make a line into the town!" Anderson's order confuses me for a second, but when the next person joins the web, I realize he's a genius.

He's recruiting more people. He's weaving the human fabric of healing with those who need it the most.

The inflow of energy grows, the outflow of life becomes constant.

Words waft over to me. All voices I've never heard before.

"Take my hand."

"Hold me."

"This is unbelievable."

I feel when my parents join the web, their energy bright and pure.

Happiness infuses my heart. Hope becomes the song of my soul.

All of a sudden, the golden motes are everywhere. They're being fed from the fabric we've created—Were, Fae, human— they draw up from the soil, they tremble in the air around us. They accumulate, becoming a glowing storm around Hunter and me. With the next breath in, they contract, compress. Becoming a sun of light and energy.

When it explodes, it's like a supernova. A cosmic combustion that reaches far beyond Jacksonville. It flows through the earth, explodes through the air. It swallows the entirety of the globe.

Hunter and I arch, our bodies infused, and for the briefest of moments, I see it all.

They all see it.

The intricate web that stretches so far and wide, it connects every soul on this planet.

It's glorious and dazzling and humbling.

Slowly, inevitably, it abates. After the electric, overwhelming sensations, I almost feel bereft.

Silence replaces the radiant light, just as big and just as consuming.

I look up at Hunter, dazed and full of wonder. "What just happened?"

Hunter looks around, copper gaze wide. "I'm pretty sure we...they...just...ah...."

People start to move, looking just as shell-shocked as we are. They release the person they were touching or holding, staring down at their hands. The flower of bodies opens out like a bloom, petals stretching and glorying in the world they see around them. Mitch and Tara stare at each other. Anderson scratches his head.

Everyone has a smile on their face.

I can feel Furious is gone. There's nothing but gentle light around me. Threads that are beautiful and pure.

The roar of celebration is an explosion in its own right. It lifts to the sky like a legion of birds, taking its happiness far and wide.

When Hunter lifts and spins me, my own laughter joins his and everyone else's. I throw my arms out wide and we spin and spin. Joy is dancing through my body, elation has me light and giddy.

Hunter's arms relax, and I slide down the length of his body.

The celebrating, dancing bodies fade into the background.

He looks at me in wonder. "We did it."

This smile feels like it's going to be part of me for the rest of my life. "Damn straight."

He cocks his head, a grin gracing his handsome face. "Right now, saying I love you feels inadequate, Ava Phelan. It doesn't come close to how I feel about you."

Hands on his shoulders, I push up on my toes and lightly, slowly, kiss him. "There is one word, Hunter Rendell, that captures how eternal this is."

His grin dials down to the softest, sweetest smile I've ever seen. He leans in, his lips a whisper away from mine. "Always."

I sigh, knowing that no greater truth has ever been spoken. "Always."

AVA

S ummer in the tundra is short, but stunning. Mother Nature knows she needs to jam the miracle that is the circle of life into a few short months. Flowers bloom quickly and with determination. Animals celebrate by shedding their coat of white and finding a mate.

As the truck bumps over the rutted, marshy terrain, I look over at the driver. "You'll be doing this in a uniform soon."

Hunter's lips twitch. "Eventually. Still got a good year to go before I'll be wearing the ranger badge." He reaches out to grab my hand. "Your uniform is all ready and waiting to be worn tomorrow."

Leaning back into the seat, I smile. "Well, I didn't need to go to college to get that uniform."

Hunter squeezes my hand. "No, you just had to change the world."

I pull in a deep breath. Over a year has passed, and indeed, the world has changed. It was irrevocably altered when we were joined by countless souls to eradicate Furious.

Tomorrow we open Evelyn Island Wolf Education Center. I'm not sure which is more of an indication of how far we've come—the closing of Resolve because captive breeding was no longer necessary, or the opening of a center that will allow others to revel in this new world we live in.

Either way, the glow that burst into my chest on that day hasn't dimmed.

In fact, as I've watched the changes unfold, it's flourished like vegetation around us.

When the terrain starts to get too rough, Hunter pulls the truck over. Climbing out, I draw in a deep breath, loving the compelling scents of the olive greens and russet reds, lingering on the yellow and pink and white sprinkled between.

Hunter meets me at the passenger side, a slight frown on his face. "He's not far."

I shake my head. "Nope. Looks like he wants to say hello this time."

"I've gotta say, it takes a bit of time to adjust to it."

Wrapping my arm around his waist, I tuck myself into his side. A year Bonded and I still get a thrill as my curves merge with his angles. "I know."

Hunter brushes a kiss across my hair. "It's amazing, fascinating, and humbling."

I push up, slipping a quick kiss of my own on his lips. "I know."

There's no more time to discuss it, because there's a howl, a contraction of the golden web around us.

When Achak arrives, he stands proudly atop a stand of rocks only a few yards away. His mate, Luna, is by his side.

It's the rabble of pups milling around their legs that has Hunter and I smiling. Four of them, it's exciting to see them out of the den. They're all white or pale grey, bar one.

This female's name is Nadie. She's taken after her father, all russets and grays that will never camouflage when the snow returns. She's a contrast to her brothers and sisters, a miniature of her father.

I deflate a little. There was a reason her name means hope. "She hasn't lost her color."

"We knew that wouldn't be very likely. She was darker than the others."

I sigh. "I know, it's just that…"

It means she can't stay out here.

Hunter squeezes my shoulders. "You know what he said."

Arctic wolves are white for a reason, and mixing their genetic pool with that of a grey wolf, weakens that evolutionary adaptation. KJ explained it to us, patiently and solemnly. Any pups he has who aren't white are best removed from the population. That way, Achak's presence is far more likely to strengthen the gene pool, not weaken it.

I angle my head, trying to find the silver lining in all of this. "Maybe she'll make him smile for real?"

I feel Hunter sag. We now live in a world defined by connection, and yet KJ is like a loose thread. Although Sayen's sacrifice showed him Weres' capacity for compassion couldn't be corrupted, even by someone like Helix, he discovered his kind were something he could be proud of.

But it came at a cost.

When he lost Sayen, he lost the desire to be part of the fabric around him.

With another brush across my hair, Hunter sighs. "I think he's finally found something that could get him living again."

Which is true. Lately, KJ's found his purpose in the lab again. He's determined to keep the wolf population growing and strong.

The pups, all loose and gangly in their too-big fur, start to play. They roll and bite, their puppy growls and yips full of excitement. Except Nadie holds herself separate. Instead of playing, she stares at us.

She takes a step forward, then pauses. Her bark is high-pitched and curious. A question.

Hunter and I glance at each other. Simultaneously, we walk away from the truck toward her and the others. The pups don't stop playing, having seen enough of us to know we won't crowd them. Luna steps back, wild and cautious. Achak steps closer to his daughter.

Hunter squats down and I join him, my heart lodged in my throat.

Nadie watches us, russet ears erect, furry head angled. When we don't move, she takes another tentative step forward.

"Hunter…"

"I know," he breathes. "She wants to."

Achak leans down, nudging her and surprise bursts through my chest. Nadie takes a few more steps, sniffing the air.

When Nadie makes the decision, it's sudden and sure. She breaks into a lope, launching herself at me with enough enthusiasm to knock me on my backside. We've visited this litter often, but always held back. These wolves are wild, and we respect that. The others were happy with that, although Nadie was always curious. Always watching us.

As we sit amongst the clumps of vegetation, Nadie steadily gains confidence. She clambers all over us, bites at our wrists, uses our fingers as chew toys. She reminds me of Akyla, Ari, and Asta, when they were young.

Before they were mangled and mutilated into monsters designed to start a war.

Before they became Lycans.

A year later, cults have formed to worship them. Vigilante groups still scour Wyoming thanks to isolated reports that they've been sighted. But they're all seen as extremists, those on the fringe. Mainstream society eventually let go of the breath they were holding when the Lycans disappeared.

All thanks to KJ going public, explaining that a genetic mutation, paired with the appearance of a virulent rabies strain, had created what we've only heard of in folk tales—werewolves. With complicated genetic terminology he'd explained how it was possible. The scientific community had been part awed at this young man and his knowledge; part skeptical. But it was all that was needed to allay the fears. Furious was gone. Genetic mutations were one in a million.

Werewolves wouldn't be seen again.

All of a sudden, Nadie stops. Achak, Luna, and the pups have started to move. They're leaving. The pups don't seem to notice that they're one down. Luna whines, watching her daughter across the distance.

It's Achak who makes the decision.

He trots down, coming the closest he has in a long time. As he reaches us, Nadie leaps up at him, licking at his chin. Achak leans down, his tongue gently stroking his daughter. When he looks up, his canine gaze catches mine.

I freeze in shock, not willing to believe what he's communicating.

Is it Achak's acknowledgement of the bond we share? Or maybe it's because of the threads...

It could be all of that, or none of that, but it means I'm not surprised when he picks up Nadie by the scruff of her neck and plonks her in my lap. I instantly wrap my arms around her, looking up at Hunter with wide eyes.

He smiles softly and gently. "He wants you to care for his daughter."

I look down, and Nadie instantly starts licking my face. I smile too, a giggle escaping. Snuggling her in tight, I feel the love for this pup swell in my chest.

Looking back at Achak, my eyes sting with happy moisture. "We'll take good care of her."

Never blinking, never breaking our gaze, Achak leans forward. Gently, sweetly, he brushes his forehead against mine.

It's a bittersweet goodbye. It's an acknowledgement we've just come full circle.

Wrapped in my arms, Nadie whimpers as she watches her family lope away, and my heart aches for her. I can understand how she feels. Leaving my family in Jacksonville hurt, and I still miss them.

But building my new life, fulfilling my purpose, is the balm that makes it bearable. Ultimately, it's the bond I have with Hunter that shows me how we weave new threads, powerful threads, that are strong enough to create a new life you love just the way it is.

I can already sense that Nadie and I will have that. Our thread is already strengthening, thickening, becoming one we will both cherish.

She'll become an ambassador for our new Wolf Center. Visitors will be able to pet her, spend time with her. She'll have Sakari to keep her company, along with any future wolves who can't live out on the tundra.

She'll be living proof of the power of the threads.

The wind buffets the silence for long minutes after they're gone. Soon enough, Nadie starts to wriggle, impatiently licking my hand. Snapping out of the spell that had been spun around us, I glance up to find Hunter looking down at me.

His face is full of an emotion I've seen many times before. It softens his angles, sharpens the copper of his eyes, has me leaning into him.

It's an emotion that sustained me through the crucible we went through, that made this new world possible.

I know its warmth in my soul. I know its song in my heart.

But as I stand there, falling deeper and deeper, it's an emotion I'll never tire of hearing caressed by his lips.

He cups my face, his palm warm against my cheek. "Understatement of the year, but I love you, Ava."

I'm about to lose myself in the heat and passion that's sparking between us when I wince. Nadie just bit my finger. I hold her up between us. "Even now that you're going to become a daddy?"

He chuckles, stroking her as she tries to chew on him too. "I'm thinking we might need a bigger bed."

I don't know whether to laugh or dance or kiss him. That answer tells me he's going to be just as good a father as a mate. Instead, I move in closer, Nadie snuggles between us. "My understatement is that I'm going to love you forever, Hunter."

Our kiss is cut short by the wriggling pup between us, but it doesn't matter. What we have is underscored by a lifetime of love waiting for us. It's a forever love.

It's a love defined by one word.

Always.

As Nadie snuggles down, obviously becoming tired, my watch catches my eye. "Shoot. If we don't hurry up, I'll be going to the Bonding this evening in that uniform we were just talking about. It's the only thing I have ironed right now."

Hunter arches a brow. "You look pretty hot in that uniform."

My heart trips at the heat brewing in his copper eyes. It's also a love so infused with passion and power it takes my breath away.

I can't help it; images of our nights have my skin flushing and my blood quickening. There's a lot to look forward to in this future of ours...

But first we have a Bonding to get ready for.

Grabbing Hunter's hand, we head back to the truck. Excitement buzzes through our connection, just as much Hunter's as it is mine.

It's the little moments in life—meeting strangers, knowing there's something you already have in common; watching family picnics grow to include grandparents, friends, and pets; seeing meat disappear from supermarkets—where you see how much the world has changed. But it's the big moments, the ones where threads are born or celebrated or honored, that it really hits you.

As we watch Gareth bond with the woman he's loved all his life, I won't be the only one who sees the threads connecting him to Lauren and to everyone around them. Riley will probably cry even harder, and Josh will hold her tighter. The Weres and Fae will stand taller and prouder. The humans will smile bigger and laugh harder and love simpler.

Hands will link. Hearts will connect.

Because when we healed Furious, every soul woven into the fabric of this world was touched.

And now every person on the planet sees what I see.

They see the threads that connect us all.

.

BONUS EXTENDED EPILOGUE

Can KJ have a happily ever after??

KJ became such a force in the Legacy books that I couldn't leave him to slowly deal with his grief. I'm a romance author after all, and romance is all about the HEA (Happily Ever After)! It's why I fell in love with the genre way back in adolescence.

So, if you want to spend just a little more time with KJ (it's not essential - Hunter and Ava's story was completed in theses pages), you can download an extended epilogue HERE when you sign up for my newsletter.

Once you're on the list, you'll receive the extended epilogue, and every couple of weeks you'll also get exclusive tasters of upcoming books (in my Tuesday Taster emails), awesome offers and bargain reads (in my Frugal Friday emails), and an opportunity to connect (personally, I reckon that's the best bit).

I'd love to see you over there.

Grab your Extended Epilogue HERE

https://dl.bookfunnel.com/pu0aey3ml9

Enjoyed the book?
You can make a difference!

Reviews are gold for authors; they help with discoverability (one of the great challenges of being an author) and they let other readers know their time isn't likely to be wasted. If you enjoyed Legacy Fulfilled, please consider leaving a review on Amazon (or Goodreads). Even a line or two would be incredibly helpful.

Amazon | Goodreads

I look forward to connecting with you!
Tamar

PARANORMAL ROMANCE AT ITS BEST!

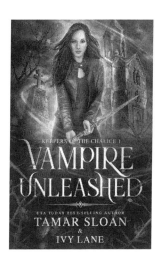

A vampire. A huntress. A cure that could change everything.

Vampires are real. If that's not enough for Maddy to get her head around, then learning she's a descendant of the famous Knights Templar, a secret order of vampire hunters, leaves her reeling. What's more, they want her to join their ranks.

Caleb has a score to settle. Part of it's personal, but the Order is also determined to kill every last one of his kind. When he learns of their new recruit, he knows he has to get close to Maddy, no matter what it takes.

Thrust together, the two discover deeply buried secrets and shocking truths. The Order isn't everything it claims to be. The vampire Master has plans to cultivate humans as a food source. And everyone is searching for an ancient relic that could be the key to it all.

And yet Maddy has questions that desperately need answers. Whose side is Caleb really on? What does she do about the attraction that won't go away? And why does she seem to have abilities no one else does...

Check out Book 1, Vampire Unleashed, HERE.
http://mybook.to/VampireUnleashed

ALSO BY TAMAR SLOAN

KEEPERS OF THE LIGHT

Angels and demons have battled for millennia.

Their inevitable war has begun.

Hidden Angel

Chosen Angel

Marked Angel

Forbidden Angel

Rogue Angel

Cursed Angel

Blood Angel

KEEPERS OF THE CHALICE

A vampire. A huntress.

A cure that will change everything.

Vampire Unleashed

Vampire Unveiled

Vampire Undone

Vampire Undefeated

Vampire United

KEEPERS OF THE GRAIL

Seven Gates of Hell. Seven Deadly Sins.

One impossible choice.

Gates of Demons

Gates of Chaos

Gates of Greed

Gates of Wrath

Gates of Secrets

Gates of Hell

THE SOVEREIGN CODE

Humans saved bees from extinction…and created the deadliest threat we've seen yet.

Harvest Day

Hive Mind

Queen Hunt

Venom Rising

Sting Wars

THE THAW CHRONICLES

Only the chosen shall breed.

Burning

Rising

Breaking

Falling

Extant

Exist

Exile

Expose

Tournaments of Thaw

Conquer the Thaw

The Oasis Trials

The Oasis Deception

The Last Oasis

ZODIAC GUARDIANS

Twelve teens. One task. Save the Universe.

Zodiac Guardians

Libra Ascending

Capricorn Conjured

Leo Rising

Taurus Divided

Virgo Incognito

Aquarius Undone

Sagittarius Charmed

Aries Armed

Pisces Dreaming

Scorpio Sting

Cancer Sight

Gemini United

DESCENDANTS OF THE GODS

Demigods as you've never seen before.

Child of Crossroads

Daughter of Time

Secret of Fate

Son of Poseidon

Blood of Medusa

ABOUT THE AUTHOR

Tamar really struggled writing this bio, in part because it's in third person, but mostly because she hasn't decided whether she's primarily a psychologist who loves writing, or a writer with a lifelong fascination with psychology.

She must have been someone pretty awesome in a previous life (past life regression indicated a Care Bear), because she gets to do both. Beginning her career as a youth worker, then a secondary school teacher, before becoming a school psychologist, Tamar helps children and teens to live and thrive despite life's hurdles like loss, relationship difficulties, mental health issues, and trauma.

As lover of reading, inspired by books that sparked beautiful movies in her head, Tamar loves to write young adult romance. To be honest, it was probably inevitable that her knowledge and love of literature would translate into writing emotion driven stories of finding life and love beyond our comfort zones. You can find out more about Tamar's books at www.tamarsloan.com

A lifetime consumer of knowledge, Tamar holds degrees in Applied Science, Education and Psychology. When not reading, writing or working with teens, Tamar can be found with her husband and two children enjoying country life on their small slice of the Australian bush.

The driving force for all of Tamar's writing is sharing and connecting. In truth, connecting with others is why she writes.

She loves to hear from readers and fellow writers. Find her on all the usual social media channels or her website.

Printed in Great Britain
by Amazon

19513830R00162